Other Books by the Author

Bouquet
Dreams of Gold
The Alpha Project
Siberian Sons

Camp Sage and Sand

RICHARD C. SMITH

WESTBOW PRESS®
A DIVISION OF THOMAS NELSON & ZONDERVAN

This is a work of fiction. With the exception of locations, all of the characters, names, incidents, organizations, and dialogue in this novel are either the products of the author's imagination or are used fictitiously.

WestBow Press books may be ordered through booksellers or by contacting:

WestBow Press
A Division of Thomas Nelson & Zondervan
1663 Liberty Drive
Bloomington, IN 47403
www.westbowpress.com
844-714-3454

ISBN: 978-1-6642-7707-6 (sc)
ISBN: 978-1-6642-7708-3 (hc)
ISBN: 978-1-6642-7709-0 (e)

Library of Congress Control Number: 2022916138

Print information available on the last page.

WestBow Press rev. date: 9/29/2022

When pride comes, then comes shame, but
with humility, there is wisdom.
—Proverbs 11:2

Chapter 1

I WAS TUNING BETWEEN various radio stations, looking for my classical favorite, when I realized that I had somehow strayed off FM and was being assaulted by a heavy dose of AM commercials. The announcer was just saying, "Yes, you can turn in your old car in any condition and take a tax deduction on the vehicle. Your used automobile donation will aid the ongoing work of Camps with Kids summertime programs throughout America."

I thought how I certainly could use a hefty tax deduction on my rusty 1994 Volvo. Besides, I would hardly miss it since I rarely drove around where I lived and worked in Manhattan. I wrote down the 800 number and was about ready to get back to the FM dial when the announcer made one last appeal.

"Not only do we need your old car, but we need you! Camps with Kids has many openings for volunteer workers willing to share their own personal time and talents with eager boys and girls of all ages. This is your opportunity to change even one life for a lifetime! We are looking for craft instructors, riding instructors, gym teachers, personal counselors, and people who just want to be a big brother or sister. The need is so very, very great. Please call us today."

The commercial struck a chord deep within me. Here I was, a single thirty-four-year-old whose life was more than a third of the way over. I was making an OK living as a public relations freelancer, but it seemed a waste not to share some of the tricks of my craft as a writing instructor like the announcer said. If I could change just one little person's life, I would love to do it.

My resolve mushroomed faster than I could contain it. I ran to get a clean pad of paper in front of me and then called the 800 number before I changed my mind. While the phone rang, my heart started to race. I tried to think what I would say. Before I was even mentally ready, a friendly person was saying, "ENDCO. How can I help you?"

I cleared my throat. "I'm looking at the possibility of helping at Camps with Kids this summer. Your radio commercial sort of got to me, and I thought maybe I could be of assistance to some of your young people." I started to say how the announcer had made me think of how my life was a third over, but a new connection was already ringing in my ear.

A very sweet female voice—perfect for soothing any doubt I'd had in making the call—identified herself as Miss Abrams. When I gave my name, Melvin Van Alan, and a quick resume of myself, she sounded very pleased. Her main thrust was to encourage me to come in for an interview as soon as possible. "The summer is already upon us, and we are eager to fill several important positions," she said. So, we made an appointment for the very next day.

The more I thought about it, the more excited I got. I owed it to myself to take some time off. I hadn't bothered to slow the treadmill I'd been on for I don't know how long—three, maybe four years. The last time I could remember was when a cousin was getting married in Stony Brook, out on Long Island. It was quite a trip, so it made sense to stay over. And when I got there, it was so beautiful that I just hung out for three days. I even got to go sailing.

The idea of camping in the woods seemed equally exhilarating. The smell of pine after a brief rain, smoke wafting over from the cookhouse. Maybe even songs by the fire after dark. I definitely felt the need for a break in my relentless schedule, and this assignment could undoubtedly renew me in body and mind.

○◉○

A VERY ATTRACTIVE MISS Abrams met me in her office where the walls were adorned with large photos of children from every race and color obviously enjoying the great outdoors. I didn't see any woodland classrooms, but I expected that showing indoor activities was perhaps less marketable. She explained that Camps with Kids was a division of the ENDCO Corporation. The company's founder and president, General Robert Enders, had originally set it up to give New York children from the ghettos the advantage of a summer away in the Catskills. The program had taken off, and now there were some thirty-five camps scattered across the US.

"Let's get some background on you," she said.

We sat on canvas camp stools at a peeled-log table as she pulled out a questionnaire. "This will help me find just where you will be the most help to us." She took me through several areas in which I identified myself, and as we went on, she seemed a little hesitant.

"Your prep school background and handball activity could be of some use, I suppose, but have you had any one-on-one experience with youngsters about twelve years of age, for instance?"

I couldn't come up with many offhand, until I remembered how I had roughhoused with my friend's two nephews one afternoon up at the lake. "The kids I supervised last summer thought I was pretty terrific," I said. "They still talk about the fun we had and beg me to come again this year."

That helped a little, I think, but it was the very mention of my seven years with the Upper Bronx Saddle Club that perked her up. As a freelancer, I had written many stories about the club. Unfortunately, I was not a member, but I had watched many a blue-ribbon dressage program from the stands.

I began to feel the passion Miss Abrams had in inspiring possible volunteers by her enthusiasm and breathless rush in describing the successes of Camps with Kids. In particular, she told me that their newest camp was situated in southwestern Colorado. Here, among the various native Indians of the region, low-income boys were being given the chance to get away from an environment of poverty and learn basic industrial skills that could give them a chance for a better life. She encouraged me to visualize such a place and think of myself becoming one of their key volunteers.

I have to admit that I am completely awed by the beauty of the Colorado Rocky Mountains. I still keep last year's Gunner's Gin calendar hanging over the phone. Month after month, I get to review again the lovely mountain streams pouring down rock formations and valleys of wildflowers. All year it had made me want to throw caution to the winds and invest in a one-way ticket to pursue writing my first novel from a little cabin in the woods.

I left Miss Abrams's rustic office proud that I might inspire even a few young American Indians with some sound writing techniques. She promised to call immediately following a required background check.

○◉○

Miss Abrams called two days later with the exciting news that I had been accepted into the Camps with Kids volunteer ranks for the full summer. By then, I had built up an eager anticipation about going. I would need to leave for Colorado the following Tuesday, giving me only six days to wind up my client affairs and update my will. I asked her if I would be required to have immunization shots, and she assured me that this wasn't really necessary, although I might want to take some bottled water to start me out until I could buy some locally.

I wasn't much of a traveler, having driven only as far as Lake Erie, and never out of New York state. Considering the extreme distance to Colorado, I worried about my unreliable Volvo, but on the other hand, I couldn't be without my own transportation. I asked Miss Abrams what clothing and gear I should take, and she asked if I had jeans and cowboy boots. It was fortunate that I had purchased both for a recent Western Night at the Saddle Club, but the high-heeled boots tended to give me a headache after walking in them for any length of time.

Still, I was thrilled to feel accepted by such a large corporation through whose connections I might use in helping to pitch future freelance articles on Colorado. I thanked Miss Abrams for being so kind, and she promised to forward everything I would need to know in an overnight packet. What really added to the call was her comment that she hoped to get to know me better and not forget to come by and see her when I returned to New York.

In the meantime, I went through all of my textbooks and notes I had taken at Columbia University School of Journalism and tried to condense the most important portions for a summer's curriculum. I got somewhat bogged down as I enjoyed reviewing the material so much that I wished now I had taken time to reread them since I graduated. I made a note to get back to a more in-depth study when I returned in the fall.

○◉○

Six days later, I was packed and ready for my upcoming summer adventure. I stowed my old reliable computer and printer and plenty of paper in the back seat of the car. I wanted to be able to print out homework assignments as I went. I regretted that I didn't have a laptop, as my seventeen-inch monitor was pretty heavy and took up crucial space. I was going to need a good-sized little cabin with plenty of electric outlets for myself and all my gear.

I packed every piece of underwear from my drawer and all my white shirts just in case I sweat too much while on duty. I did have a couple of poplin blue shirts that I thought would look good with my one pair of jeans. I also had bought some heavy socks for my boots, but most of the time, I would plan to wear my usual calf-length stockings and polished loafers.

I had no family to say goodbye to. Puffy, my twelve-year-old tabby, went permanently to the lady one floor below to add to her own menagerie of three cats. I suddenly felt very strange with the thought of leaving the city, but then I recalled some pretty sage words from my late maiden aunt that made sense now. She said, "Remember, Melvin, if you don't stick your big toe in the water, you'll never learn how to swim."

So, I turned my face to the west with only a bit of hesitance and drove out of town with a full tank of New York gas. "Just think of it," I said to myself. "This is going to be your chance to leave an impression on some young people out there somewhere. Make it count!"

○◉○

I don't recall most of the trip. All interstates look alike. I paused at every third rest stop to stretch. I had a bit of celebration once when I found a croissant to eat with my coffee instead of Danish in cellophane. By and large, the people I met seemed nice, and a few even held the door for me and smiled. I realized that this was actually a pretty nice world, and maybe Americans outside of New York were real people after all.

I never developed an urge to travel. Too much to plan, too many struggles en route, and for what? Being single meant traveling alone, and I had gotten used to not having someone else to share and savor those awesome moments or unexpected sights. I was glad this trip wasn't going to be so much sightseeing as it would be like a job that I was going off to—a kind of volunteer business deal—so I didn't expect there would be much sharing.

I was a loner once again anyway. My girlfriend, Gail, and I had gone together for five years, but I couldn't see myself married to her for the rest of my life. She recently gave up waiting. Other than her, I didn't really have anyone close.

Despite that, I think I am a good catch for all my quirks. Being six feet tall, dark hair, a good build from regular gym visits and health diets, I happily attract women wherever I go. It's just that I'm so particular and much too self-centered for my own good, I find it hard to keep a relationship going for long. I wish things were different in this department, but I was an only child and raised to be perfect in the eyes of my parents and found no reason to change. Both my mother and father have been gone about ten years. My mother's younger sister was my closest relative until she died a year ago. We were quite close, and I saw her weekly if not more. If I seem a bit old-fashioned, it's probably because of that. People have remarked that I say things that are rather dated at times. I guess it's now part of my upbringing. What can I say? I really miss my aunt because she had a terrific sense of humor and offered a lot of good commonsense advice that helped me get through some difficult situations along the way. But she hated to go anywhere far from her little world of a few blocks in each direction that surrounded her in Manhattan, and I guess I picked that up from her. Comfortable, conventional and safe.

It took me three days of conservative driving with all the stops thrown in to get to the one destination I most wanted to see before I began my counseling duties. The March photo on my Gunner's Gin calendar featured the Four Corners National Monument, the only place in these United States where four states meet together at one spot. My atlas had told me that this was also at the very edge of the largest Indian reservation in the United States, the land of the Navajo. I was eagerly anticipating standing on the exact convergence of Colorado, Utah, New Mexico, and Arizona. But when I finally arrived in the late afternoon, I saw a small sign on a barrier across the entrance: "Four Corners Park Closed for Repairs." I humorously pictured a steady stream of tourists taking so many rock souvenirs that the four corners didn't touch anymore. Disappointed, I backtracked to where the camp was supposed to be located—somewhere southwest of Cortez, Colorado.

Miss Abrams had sent along only sparse details about the camp in her overnight packet to me. "Camp Sage" was new to the ENDCO family, but apparently it had been in private hands for many years prior.

I closely followed the small map provided, and just south of Cortez, I spotted the county airport, which was to point me to the next turnoff on the road into McElmo Canyon. The directions then said in a few miles I was to look for a major tower of rock, rising straight up from the banks of the McElmo River.

The landscape along the canyon road proved a marked contrast from the dry desert highway I had just left. The area was bordered by trees and grasses as it followed the river between impressive sandstone formations on both sides. By the time I could see the rock tower in the distance, it was mostly dark. Yet, the way was illuminated by a moon so brilliant with a huge array of stars that I couldn't believe my eyes. I had never been far enough away from city lights to see such a wonderful display of the Milky Way extending from one horizon to the other.

Eventually, after some false starts up one side road after another, I finally came upon a large cluster of tents sheltered by the massive rock wall that rose toward the sky. In the starry light, I could just make out the top high above. And far below, a sizable pond shimmered alongside a short dock and diving board, which was probably fed from the river that I had crossed a moment earlier. A bright security lamp mounted on a high pole over a long adobe building added its glow to the moon shining on the large expanse of gray canvas tent peaks.

By then it was close to nine o'clock, and no one was about. Suddenly, the somber notes of taps sounded forth from an ancient recording over a PA system, blaring loud and shrill and echoing off the rocky cliff.

I guided my car next to the building and got out. After the bugle's last mournful note faded, followed by a few scratchy clicks, the record was audibly taken off the turntable. I headed for a door centered below the blazing light. Above it in fading paint was a sign that spelled out "Camp Sage and Sand" in curved letters.

A large balding man, maybe fifty-five years or so, stuffed into what appeared to be a Boy Scout leader's uniform, turned as I entered. He seemed surprised to have a visitor at this hour dressed in a suit. But with a quick smile, he strode to the counter that separated us.

"What can I do for you?" he said.

I put down my overnight grip. "I'm Melvin Van Alan," I answered. "I guess I'm signed up to be a volunteer for the summer, and I just arrived."

His bushy eyebrows shot up. "Well, Mr. Van Alan, I'm Commander Dougan." He put out a big hand and shook mine. "We were expecting you much earlier. But, hey, I'm glad to meet you. I guess you must think the place is deserted."

"I was wondering …"

"We git the kids down and lights out by nine. No exceptions," he said. "Reveille is at 6:30 a.m., and they all need plenty of sleep. Anyways, you're probably tired too. Why don't I show you to your quarters, and we can talk in the a.m." He grabbed a big battery lantern off the wall and led me out and around the building.

Commander Dougan showed me to a roomy canvas tent that one could stand up in, like all the rest in the camp, affixed to a slightly sagging wooden platform below. It's a good thing I hadn't bothered to bring bed linens, as I could see I wasn't going to need them. It housed two metal army cots with rolled-up sleeping bags. I was at least thankful to see I had no roommate already snoring away.

"You'll be comfortable here. Breakfast is at 7:00 a.m. sharp. The mess is in the building. Showers and latrines too. Have a good night." He turned and left me to figure out where I was in the dark. I wasn't sure about the mess he was referring to. He must have wanted to warn me to avoid it. I was worried it might be from the latrines.

In the muted glow from the camp's nightlight and the big moon filtering through the tent, I pulled my PJs over my underwear. For being so hot during the day, the night air had a decided nip to it, and I was getting frozen. The sleeping bag seemed fairly fresh, but I couldn't help wondering who had used it last.

Luckily, I only had to get up once during the night, and the trip to the latrine was just across the small clearing. Toward morning, it rained very hard, spearheaded by huge thunderclaps and white shards of lightning that I could see even with my eyes closed. I was thankful the tent canvas held up against the heavy downpour. Suffice it to say, I got very little sleep after it started.

Chapter 2

THE BUGLE FOR REVEILLE came all too soon, but the sun was already up. I dragged out of my warm sleeping bag and tucked my washcloth, towel, and shaving kit under my arm. Then I stuck my head out of the tent to see what was going on.

Kids of various young ages were silently trudging, carrying white towels, rubbing their eyes, and dragging along in their bare feet through an inch or so of mud toward the big adobe building. The morning rain had turned the powdered dirt into thick cocoa. I recoiled and pulled my head in to think things through. I was going to start my morning with caked mud on either my slippers or bare feet. But wait! Thanks to Miss Abrams, I'd brought a pair of cowboy boots. The only problem was they were in my car.

So I dressed in yesterday's clothes and, rolling up my pants, stepped gingerly in my bare feet through the muck around the building to my car. There I retrieved one suitcase and got back to my tent. With a bottle of Evian pure water, I washed my feet, put on my new white socks and new jeans, pulled on my boots, and joined the line at the latrine.

Despite my early-morning problems, I was awestruck by the breathtaking location of this little camp. As described on the map, an utterly gigantic solitary cliff served as a backdrop that rose perhaps 350 feet above me. The dawning sun produced dancing shades of pink and light cream on the red sandstone face, revealing brown vertical streaks where the runoff water had carved lines from its flat top, almost like a great monument. Various indentations and caves marked the surface, and a few hardy junipers had taken hold and were growing against all impossible odds of life on the sheer wall.

Commander Dougan spied me and came over as I stood in line to wash up. "You don't have to go in there with the kids." He pointed to another door, "Counselors Only," and gave me a friendly shove.

Inside, two other men were shaving at the double sinks. I gave a quick hi, and they watched me find a place for my things. They were both either of Spanish American or Indian descent. I couldn't tell.

"You the new instructor?" one of them, a rugged muscular fellow, said.

"That's right. The name's Mel."

"Nice to know you." He turned to me with shaving lather on his face and gave me a wet handshake.

The other man just stared.

"This here's Jesus Joe," he said. He pronounced his first name with an "H" on the first letter, but a "J" on Joe. Hesus Joe. "You can call me Steve," he said.

They finished, and I was left alone to wash the best I could. I looked longingly at the showers and made a plan to get back in here as early as possible.

Breakfast was an eye-opener. When I saw a sign for the mess hall, I realized what the Commander had been talking about the night before. From a quiet, sullen, droopy start, the young campers had come alive and were calling loudly to each other, wrestling for biscuits that were piled on big platters on the long tables or waiting impatiently in line for scrambled eggs and bacon strips to be put on their plates by two Indian ladies, sweating over their steam tables.

I figured there were about fifty or so youngsters, ranging in age from maybe eight to fourteen. These kids were mostly black-haired, dark-skinned Indian stock, and all were boys. I was briefly panicked to wonder how I was going to draw out their writing skills, if any. Not one of them seemed the kind to sit quietly and write a piece on "How I Plan to Spend My Summer."

Commander Dougan was holding court with a bunch of men at one of several tables in the corner reserved for the counselors. He waved his hand in the air to catch my eye before I got stuck in another line. "Come on over and join us," he called.

He introduced me to those at his table while a woman from the kitchen set a big plate of eggs and bacon in front of me. "Steve is Recreation Director, Jesus Joe is his assistant and also a silversmith, Howard is Equipment and Maintenance, and Don is Industrial Arts." Each man nodded or gave thumbs-up as his name was mentioned. I got a bunch of nods of welcome from the men at the other table as they watched our introductions.

"Melvin here is our new riding instructor." He patted my back with fatherly enthusiasm. "Even though these kids know a lot about what they're doing, this year I wanted to have someone who could hone those skills a little better. Maybe even produce some real performers." I smiled at everyone at the table and was pleased to hear that perhaps these children had some talents that I could work with after all.

"After breakfast, I expect you'll want to git down and meet our wranglers. They've been watching for you every day," the Commander said.

I didn't follow him. "What's a wrangler?" I asked.

Everyone at the table laughed, and I found myself laughing with them for no particular reason.

"Maybe you call them something else back East." He chuckled. "They handle all the horses and see to everything in the corral."

I was still mystified and wanted more clarification. "Wait a minute," I said. "What do horses have to do with writing?"

Everyone went into side splits again, as if this was the best joke they ever heard, but this time I got the feeling it was at my expense. "Tracy! Good, good morning!" The Commander suddenly shoved back his chair and stood up.

Hurrying across the room to our table was a shapely young blonde in a white smock. Her bright face showed a look of real pleasure upon seeing all of us. Until now, I had noticed the Commander and I seemed to be the only fair-skinned adults in the camp.

"Come give me a big hug and sit." The Commander gestured broadly for her to join us at the table. He obviously was a big fan of hers.

She appeared to be in her late twenties. Her blonde hair shimmered as her head moved. "I'm in kind of a rush. I have an emergency patient in my office."

The Commander confided behind his hand, "She's the best nurse you ever saw." Then he turned back to her. "Now, what's the problem?"

"Stomach pains, possible appendix. Can you get me some transportation to Cortez, stat?"

"No sweat, little lady. Van Alan here will take you."

I was stunned to be suddenly offered up as some kind of chauffeur or something, and I hesitated with my thoughts still tumbling. "Yes, I guess so," I finally said, somewhat under pressure. "Is this a real emergency?"

"It looks like it," she said with a wistful smile, holding her hand out. "My name's Tracy Palmer. Would you mind awfully?"

I shook with one hand and wiped egg off my mouth with the other. "No, I want to be of help, of course. My car's still out front."

"That's good of you, old boy," the Commander said.

Leaving my breakfast unfinished, I scurried around the table behind the departing Tracy. I couldn't help noticing her tight jeans under the flap of her white smock.

She held the door while I ran to catch up, and then we were on the other side of the building at my car. She peered in the windows. "Can you clear the back seat for Little Joey while I go get something to cover it?" I looked into her gray-green eyes and saw she wasn't asking—she was telling me.

While she dashed off, I stood there scratching my head. Where in the world was I going to put my computer, keyboard, printer, and seventeen-inch monitor? With no time to think, I started unloading them into a corner of the main office next to a set of shelves displaying an assortment of broken Indian pottery. In the process, I about yanked my back out in the rush to pull everything out of the car. Just as I struggled with the last armful, Tracy was there to spread sheets on the seat. The next minute, she was pushing the boy toward me in an old wooden wheelchair.

Little Joey was Navajo or something, I guessed, perhaps eight years old. He moaned as she helped him gently through the car door and had him lie down. She covered him with a lightweight blanket, placed a delicate hand on his little forehead, and said some sweet things to him in his ear. Then, hopping into the front seat and donning a wide-brimmed sun hat, she said, "Let's go."

It took a couple of tries to start the car, and Tracy gave me a questioning look. When the engine finally roared to life, I breathed a sigh, and we took off with a lurch.

"Careful," she said. "Every movement causes him pain."

I eased out of the camp through the thick mud, and for the first time, I was able to look around at my environment. Where were the lofty mountains with streams gushing through the verdant pines?

All around were flat-topped mesas and low scrub with clusters of pinion pines here and there. The old dirt road was covered with stray tumbleweeds from the early-morning storm, and there were deep mud puddles that I had to steer around.

When we got to the main road, Tracy pointed the way, and we enjoyed its smooth pavement compared to the bouncing and shuddering we had just come through.

"So you came in last night?" Tracy asked, breaking the silence between us.

"I guess I was a bit late for the start of camp."

"Well, the kids have only been here for two days, but the counselors arrived a week ago. There's a lot to get ready."

"That makes me feel guilty that I wasn't here to help," I said. "But considering I heard about the Camp with Kids program just two weeks ago, I came about as fast as I was able."

"Well, of course we're grateful to you, volunteering and all. Just your being here is wonderful. I know the kids are looking forward to getting organized into teams and competing for prizes."

"I never heard of such enthusiasm for writing," I said. "Are these kids that hungry to be verbal and communicative?"

She looked at me with a blank stare. "What are you talking about? Every one of these boys has been riding for years, and all they want is someone to teach them how to perform."

Things somehow weren't adding up, and I began to smell a rat. A big, fat rat. The Commander had confused me at breakfast, and now the nurse was doing it. I wanted to just pull over to the side of the road and say, "Now what is going on?" But, of course, we were racing to the hospital, and my questions were having to take a back seat.

As if to underscore that location, Little Joey made one huge groan and threw up all over the floor.

"Oh my goodness! I didn't put a sheet down there. I am so sorry," Tracy said. She turned in her seat and reached over the back to mop Joey's face with a towel. "Just hang on, sweetheart," she said soothingly. "We're almost there. You'll be fine in just a little while."

Little Joey was crying now, and I felt bad for him, as well as my back seat floor, but thankfully, I could see the town coming up in the distance. I said, "We're getting there now."

Tracy guided us through the streets to an impressive community hospital, and within minutes, we were pulling into the emergency entrance. I parked and ran around to the passenger side. No one came out to help, so I gave Tracy a hand at easing the boy through the car door. It was awkward, and I finally said, "Here, let me carry him. You go ahead and find someone."

Little Joey was thin and lightweight and very easy to lift. As I cuddled him in my arms, a huge feeling of compassion came over me, despite the sour odor from his clothes. A mop of black hair covered his eyes, and I wanted to smooth it back and dry his tears. I had never been called upon before to take care of someone as young as this.

Inside the hospital, an orderly brought a gurney, and I gently laid Little Joey down and stepped back. He curled up into a tight fetal position. They wheeled him into an examining room, and Tracy and I followed.

A physician's assistant was on duty. "Got some tummy pains?" she asked.

Little Joey's head nodded up and down.

"OK, we'll take care of that. Don't you worry." The PA tenderly stretched Joey onto his back and probed his stomach in various places.

Joey jumped when she hit a sore spot.

"Looks like his appendix, all right. Probably needs some surgery. We'll do a couple more tests first and then take him down the hall to see the doctor. Why don't you folks go sign him in and have a seat in the waiting room?"

Tracy bent down and gave Little Joey a kiss as he was wheeled off. I managed to wave, and we went to sit down. The lounge had a nice coffee machine, and I got us both a cup as we sat in a sunny corner.

For the first time, I was able to have a good look at her. That golden hair was not overly long, but it flowed nicely behind her shoulders. Her eyes were startlingly green in this light, set in a slight almond shape. Her skin was well tanned, and I expected she was a swimmer by the good muscle tone around her shoulders. She had taken off her white smock at the camp and wore a simple tan T-shirt with jeans that were rolled up at the cuff.

"Have you been nursing long?" I asked, to break the ice. Then I realized what I'd said, and I know I turned bright red.

"I graduated as a nurse two years ago and set up a free clinic with my parents at the mission—until they were killed in a car accident last year."

"Oh no," I said. "That must have been terrible for you."

"It was. I'm still getting over it." Her eyes teared up, but she cleared her throat and went on. "They were missionaries to the people right here for thirty years, and I grew up assisting them in hundreds of ways. So, you might say I've been helping nurse people for as long as I can remember."

"And is this your first year at the camp?"

"Definitely not! Mom and Dad founded Camp Sage and Sand, but this is my first year as the official nurse."

"Sage and Sand?" I had a big question on my face.

"Well, that's what it was called until some company bailed us out when they bought it last year. I think they shortened it to Camp Sage to make it sound more inviting."

I began to see why Miss Abrams had so few details to put into her overnight packet.

"OK, now. Tell me something," I said. "I'm a writer, and I've come all the way across the country to teach a bunch of kids how to use the English language, and everybody's laughing at me. I want to know why. Isn't that the job of a writing instructor?"

Tracy turned and looked at me with her eyes still full of tears and totally shocked me when she burst out in laughter.

Here we go again, I thought.

And once she got started, she couldn't stop. She tried to talk through it but got caught up again and couldn't utter a word.

I just sat there, taking the abuse, trying to smile, and hoping no one else heard her carrying on so in the hospital.

Finally, she slowed down enough to get some control and pulled a tissue out of her jeans to dab her eyes. "I'm sorry. I'm really sorry," she said, and then she started to laugh again. "That was terrible of me," she went on through her chuckles.

"Well," I said, trying to be patient. "What so wrong with what I said?"

"Oh, Melvin. You weren't hired as a writing instructor. They needed a riding instructor!"

"A what?" I couldn't see why she repeated herself. It all goes back to being a poor listener, I guess.

"R-I-D-I-N-G," she said. "You know, with horses?"

It hit me then. No wonder the Commander talked so glibly about wranglers and horses and all that. Suddenly, I was so embarrassed. I was mortified. I put my hands over my face and groaned. "Oh no! How could I have been so wrong? I just can't do anything right." I went on like this for several minutes.

Tracy took my arm and whispered, "It's OK. You didn't know. It's an honest mistake. Don't beat yourself up so."

I had gone all this time believing I had something to give. I excitedly pictured producing a swarm of little storytellers and novelists. Who knows what could have happened? And now I was alone again, this time a couple thousand miles from home, a misfit. I stood up and started to pace.

Tracy patiently watched me while I had it out with myself.

Finally, I stopped and turned to her. "I can't go back to the camp. What would I tell them?"

"Just tell the Commander you made a mistake. I'm sure he'll understand. But more importantly, we need you to stay. We don't get any volunteers here, and we need you."

"Yeah, but what could I do?" I asked, trying to keep the whine out of my voice.

"I don't really know, but there are so many things that come up with these kids that I'm sure you'll fit in someplace. They all need so much love and attention. Many of them, like Little Joey, are orphans from the tribal area. And, who knows, the Commander might be thrilled to have someone help them learn about writing and all that."

I hadn't been around children since I was their age myself, and now I wasn't sure I wanted to be, all of a sudden. But then I thought about Little Joey and how vulnerable he was, and I wondered for a moment if I might learn.

The PA stepped into the waiting room and said, "We've taken the boy up to surgery. He's pretty sick, but I think we'll get his appendix in time."

"How long?" I asked.

"Maybe a couple of days. It depends. Are you the parents?"

Tracy shook her head. "No, I'm the camp nurse at Sage and Sand, and he's a counselor." She pointed at me.

"Can you be in touch with them? We need permission to go ahead."

"He's an orphan," Tracy said. "I'll call the home and get them to give you the go-ahead." She turned and walked into the hall to use the phone.

"And what do you do out there at Sage and Sand?" The PA was being friendly while she waited for Tracy.

"To tell you the truth, I haven't a clue," I replied.

chapter 3

WE DIDN'T TALK MUCH on the way back. Joey was being taken care of, and my thoughts now were how I would handle the expected ribbing from the other counselors.

As we pulled up to the main building, Tracy turned with a smile and said, "Thanks so much." She gave my arm a squeeze and then went in to report to the Commander as I sat and pondered my next move.

Presently, she came out and stuck her head in the window. "He wants to see you." With another sweet smile, she walked toward her clinic.

I slowly pulled myself out of the car. The morning mud had already dried to a hard crust, and my cowboy boots went this way and that as I walked in the uneven car ruts.

"Come on in, my boy, and sit," the Commander said as I entered. He was hunkered in a big chair behind his desk with a cup of coffee and a doughnut. "That your stuff piled in the corner? Didn't they tell you we don't have electricity and running water in none our tents yet?" He followed this with a deep belly laugh.

I thought, *Here it comes now.*

I started to explain, but he halted me with his palm up to shush me. "Tracy filled me in to save you the trouble." He took a big bite of doughnut. "I knew this morning you wasn't what you was advertised to be. Too smarty-pants. I'll wager you never sat a western saddle in your life. Am I right?"

"Right." I sat with my forearms forward on my knees and my

head down, looking at the floor. I was once again in the principal's office, wishing I were dead.

"You got to admit that the mix-up was a real hoot, but listen, boy, what hits me is that you stopped what you was doing back East and drove all the way to some unknown place in southern Colorado to do something unselfish. What made you do it, I don't know. But I want you to know we appreciate it, and we appreciate you. And we're not about to let you go back, neither. We need you bad."

Surprised, I raised my head and looked up into his eyes to see if he was fooling. His face had changed from the usual solid granite to a soft, gentle smile. I no longer saw him as the great dictator in a military uniform and immediately knew that he had a tender side to him that was hidden from view by his job. I never remembered hearing anyone say they needed me.

"Will you stay?" he said.

Without hesitation, I answered, "If you still can use me somewhere."

"Now what did I just say, boy? We need you bad."

"But what can I do?"

"Who knows? The Good Lord's given you more than one gift, I'll wager. Why don't we just coax it out?"

All I'd ever done was write. That's all I'd studied. All I had planned on. I didn't think I had any other so-called gifts.

The Commander sat forward, his stomach pushed up against the edge of the desk, and said, "Tracy has asked for you. She says she wants you to work with her. What do you think of that, boy?" He clicked his tongue and winked an eye.

If Tracy really knew me, she would know that I don't have much patience. I need things done just right, and most of all, I had zero experience working alongside good-looking girls like her. I was pleased, however, that she might need my help.

Still, I didn't want to be shuttled off doing menial work. I had come here specifically to be in charge of their writing program. Instead, I heard myself saying, "I suppose that would be all right. She seems to be very competent."

"You bet your sweet bippy she is. Why, I've known her since she was just a little thing, and I can tell you she could run this camp all by herself if she had to. She's an anvil iron coated in velvet. Now, take your computer and plug it in over there and make yourself at home. That'll be your desk." He pointed to a rickety old table across the room. "After that, report to Tracy. And from time to time, I'll have some projects to make sure you keep busy. Are you OK with that?"

"Yes, I think so," I said, hesitating again. It wasn't easy being thrown a new challenge that I hadn't planned carefully in advance. "Thank you."

"Don't mention it, boy," the Commander said as he stood up and swaggered around the counter and out the door. "And get a hat, you're going to need it," he added just as the door slammed behind him.

Chapter 4

I BUSIED MYSELF WITH setting up my equipment and unpacking the rest of my car and then found a bucket to clean up the floor of the back seat. I surveyed my tent and tried to make it seem a little more like home with my underwear and shirts in the dusty chest of drawers. Finally, I wandered down to the clinic to see Tracy.

She was taping the ankle of an older boy who was propped against the edge of an examining table. When she saw me, she nodded her head toward a low stool and said, "Be with you in a minute."

From the look on the boy's eyes, he was relishing the touch of her hands as she skillfully applied the tape. Snipping the last piece, she brought it around the back and pressed it in place. "Now take it easy for a while, but you need to walk on it a little to keep it limber." Then she said a couple of words in a dialect that I had never heard and sent him on his way.

She rolled over toward me on her stool, and we sat almost knee to knee. "What do you think of my idea?"

"Working for you?"

"No, silly. Working *with* me."

"I like it. But what can I do?"

"I saw how you carried Little Joey. I want you to be a father to my orphans—and a big brother to the others."

I was doubtful. "I don't know the first thing about kids," I said. "They always seem to be disruptive and running around, and most of all, I don't know what to say to them."

"They probably don't know what to say to you either. You have to start by just being yourself, maybe take their hand, squat down to their level, listen to their ramblings, smile and joke with them, and love them no matter what they do."

"I wouldn't know how to start."

"Well, since this is a camp for children, the only other suggestion I have for you is to pack up and go back to New York and write something." It was obvious she was getting a little frustrated with me.

"No, no. I want to try. But I need your help. Tell me what to do."

Tracy got up and started to put her things away. "OK. We'll try going slow 'til you get the hang of it. It's really not all that hard, you know?"

"I'm glad to hear you say it. Anyway, what do you want me to do first?"

"Go out and find a group that's playing—and look for the boy who's sitting all alone and watching them. Sit down and get to know him. That's all."

That didn't seem so bad, but it was eleven thirty, and I was hungry without getting a chance to finish my breakfast. I figured I could start my assignment right after lunch, but on the way, the first thing I saw was a kid sitting alone on the side of an organized softball game. I kept on track to the mess hall anyway, but then, feeling guilty, I went back and stood next to him. Somehow, I needed to start learning how to connect with the kids. "Aren't you playing today?" I asked.

He looked up at me, and without saying anything, he showed me the cast on his right wrist.

"Oh, I see." But as I started to walk away, I heard Tracy speaking in my mind: "Get to know him."

I turned back. "So, you from around here?" *That was dumb.*

He nodded yes.

"Whereabouts?"

He pointed off toward one of the higher mountain ridges in the distance.

Now what do I say? "You been having fun?"

He shook his head no.

"Why not?"

He shrugged both shoulders.

At least he understands English. I think. "What's your name?"

"Roland."

"That's a nice name, Roland. What's your last name?"

"Roland."

"Roland Roland?" *Who would ever name a kid with the same first and last names?*

"No, Bobby Roland." He sounded a little irritated.

Whew, now we're getting somewhere.

"Oh, OK, kid. Sorry. My name is Mr. Van Alan."

Hmm, sounds a bit high and mighty.

"You can call me Mr. Van if you want."

He nodded and looked back to the game.

I squatted down. "Why aren't you having fun?"

He stuck out his wrist again. "Oh, you'd like to be playing?"

He nodded yes.

"Well, all you need is one good hand. Is that right?"

He shrugged again.

"Here, let me see," I said, picking up an extra softball from a pile. "Give me a toss."

He gave me quite a look, but he took the ball and backed up. I was suddenly left with the horrible thought of having to catch it, not being too athletic.

He took up his position, and the ball sailed straight for me. To my amazement, I caught it squarely. I was personally elated. "That's the way. Nice going," I shouted. I lobbed the ball back to him, nice and easy underhanded.

He caught it easily with his left hand and started smiling. Then he wound up, and I could see he was going to send it harder this time.

I hunkered down and squared both legs. It came straight through again, this time with more power. Wham! It hit my palms with a smack, and they both stung. Once again, I caught it, but I wasn't sure how long I could keep up the good work.

This time, he backed up even farther after I returned it. I had to give him credit for doing everything with one hand, but now I was really getting nervous about my part in this. The whole thing was escalating.

He let it sail, and I did my best to snag it, but it zipped through my hands and into my chest. I made an "oof" as the breath got knocked out of me, and my sternum suddenly was on fire.

"Ha ha." I pretended to laugh. "You are about the best pitcher I've ever seen," I said, but it came out more as a groan. I was hurting bad. "There's no reason you can't play."

"But I can't bat," he yelled back.

The inning was changing, and some of the guys called out, "Get in here, Bobby."

He looked at me a moment and took off for the center of the field. Now I saw that he was probably their star lefty pitcher. He had seemed so lonesome sitting on the sidelines. I had a lot to learn about what kids were thinking. Would I ever get anything right?

○◉○

Lunch was held in different shifts so that various camp activities could continue without interruption. The staff would eat whenever they could get away. The young boys in the hall were strangely silent when I arrived a bit late, and as I stepped in, the screen door closed behind me with a loud bang. It was only then that I realized everyone was standing for a prayer being led by the Commander. And of course, every kid turned his eyes toward me at that moment to see who had disturbed the quiet.

I stood there, embarrassed in the stillness, hoping the Commander had not noticed. Finally, the blessing of the food came to an end, and there was a loud commotion as the assembly started talking and pulling out their benches. Quickly I made my way to the counselor's table, but not quick enough. The boys who had seen me first began tapping their spoons against their water glasses as I passed. In a second, the sound increased with every glass being clinked as the audience watched me cross the room.

"What are they doing?" I asked Steve when I reached my table. I know my face was bright red by this time. "Is this about me?"

"It's their little way of hazing a newcomer to the staff," he said with a laugh. "They want to get a reaction."

I knew that the noise was bound to continue until I did something, so I stood in my place, took a couple of deep bows with my hands in the air, doing a "praise Allah," and sat down. Luckily, this was enough to bring their little game to an end.

Commander Dougan leaned over as he reached for the plate of hamburgers and said, "Well did you find something to do?"

"I guess so," I said, rubbing my aching chest. "Tracy wants me to encourage the lost kids around here. Is that going to make a difference?"

"It will to those who are lost, now, won't it?"

"I suppose so. I don't have much experience along these lines."

"Don't worry. We won't be keeping score." He turned his attention to his food and left me to wallow alone in my low self-esteem.

Tracy walked in then, and the glasses began to ring out once again. Instead of taking refuge at the counselor's corner, however, she went from table to table, speaking to various boys, tousling their hair, and sneaking a french fry here and there. When she finally arrived at our table, she was full of smiles and imparting waves of sunshine around her. "You boys are going to get fat eating all that grease," she said. "Pass the salad please." She took some lettuce and a supply of carrots and cold beans, and that seemed to satisfy her.

"How's Little Joey?" the Commander asked her.

"Haven't heard yet. I'll call this afternoon. The orphanage was going to send over one of their people to be there when he woke up."

It was then that a fight broke out at a table midway across the room. Two boys stood up, overturning a bench, and then the whole table came alive, as each kid seemed to take a side in the battle. The rest of those in the room froze, watching to see what would happen next.

"Go take care of it," the Commander suddenly ordered me in a low voice.

Here I was, the new guy on the block, being ordered into battle! I sat a moment, trying to collect my thoughts.

"Git going," he said with increased authority.

I jumped up and ran across the room, wondering what I was going to do. I got there just in time to take some of the cascade of sticky lemonade that one kid threw all over his opponent. It hit me square in the face, and I was momentarily blinded.

Laughter erupted from the rest of the kids, but it broke the tension of the moment.

"Hold it, you guys," I managed to shout. Luckily none of the other tables were getting involved. "Just stop it now!"

I was able to separate the two who had started the fight, and the others at the table moved back to watch. "OK, what's the problem?" I demanded in my best military voice.

"He called me a chicken." This kid was pointing at a much older boy, and his eyes were beginning to fill with tears.

"Well, you are," the older boy said.

"OK, just sit down," I ordered, as I grabbed a paper napkin to mop my face. "Let's quiet down and work this out."

They sat but glared at each other. I was afraid they might start hitting again at any time. I found enough room to sit too, but it was in a pool of lemonade. "What started all this?" I said in a more soothing voice. I was hoping things would stay calm.

By now, the younger boy had tears streaming down his face, and he wiped them away with a quick swipe of his hand. "He wants me to go with him, and I want to stay here."

"Where do you want to go?" I asked the older boy.

"Forget it, man," he said. "It's none of your business."

"It certainly is if you're going to fight about it." Then I turned to the younger one. "Now, where does he want you to go?"

"He wants to get out of here and live with some guys, and I'm not going."

I looked at them. They had similar features. I guessed the younger boy was about twelve, and the older one probably sixteen. He had an unruly mop of long dark hair that kept getting in his eyes, and he was clearly older than most of the young boys in the room.

"Are you two brothers?"

The younger one was now getting under some control. "Yes," he said.

"Look, this can certainly be resolved if you two will talk about it, but now's not a good time. Why don't we get together once you've cooled off? How about meeting me here at two o'clock, and we can figure things out?" It seemed a good idea to set an appointment when things were calmed down. Besides I was anxious to clean up and get my clothes changed.

The twelve-year-old was quick to agree, but his brother was not interested. "What good will that do? I'm going to take off. This place is for the birds," he said.

"At least give us a chance to talk about it," I said. "I'll be here at two. Please hang on 'til then. OK? Now what are your names?"

"Johnny," the younger boy said. "He's Marcus," pointing to his brother.

With that, Marcus got up and strode off. Johnny watched him go and then followed him.

I went back to my table. At least my cold, half-eaten hamburger was there. My hands and face were sticky from the lemonade, and I imagined my hair was probably matted. I was embarrassed in front of the other counselors.

"What was it all about?" the Commander asked. "They're two brothers with a disagreement."

"Yes, I know," he said. "Marcus wants to be out of here."

"Can't he just go?" I asked.

"Not unless he wants to go home. We're trying to help him. His father is an alcoholic, and we have a much safer environment here. He'll just get beaten up if he leaves and goes back home."

"He wants to go live with some guys."

"We can't release him without his parents' approval. He agreed to come here, and I'm not going to let him go without their OK."

"The boys are meeting me at two o'clock, so I'll see what they say," I reported. "Can you join us?"

"I expect you'll handle it fine," he said. "That's what a counselor does here."

○◉○

AT TWO O'CLOCK, Johnny and I sat alone in the mess hall, waiting for Marcus. I tried to get some talk out of him, but he was stubborn. I could tell he was struggling with something. Finally, after I looked at my watch again, he spoke up and said, "He's not coming."

"How do you know?"

"He took his bag and left camp right after lunch. He's going to hitchhike."

I was getting irritated. "Why didn't you say something earlier?"

"He said he would beat me up if I told."

"Listen," I counseled Johnny. "Perhaps this is the best thing. You brother is probably not going to come under our authority here no matter what we do. He's bound to continue fighting the system. Unfortunately, he's going to have to learn about life through some of the hard knocks."

"No, no," Johnny protested. "He needs to be here. He's going to get into bad things with those guys. I know them. Drugs and everything. They're going to mess him up."

I figured with Marcus gone, there would be that much less to deal with at camp. Let the troublemakers find their own way. We certainly had enough to handle without babysitting the ones who didn't want to be here. I got up and took Johnny by the arm. "We're going to have to tell Commander Dougan."

We walked out of the mess and around to the office. The Commander was asleep at his desk with his head back. We woke him in the middle of one loud snore.

"I'm sorry to bother you," I said rather timidly, "but Marcus has left camp and is headed off to hitchhike somewhere."

The Commander struggled to waken and leaned forward, extensively clearing his throat. I expected him to spit out a large hairball.

"Well, git yourself out the door and go after him. And you'd better find him and bring him back."

His attitude angered me since I had never in the world signed up for talk like this. It was one thing counseling some needy kids and talking to them nicely, but now I was being forced to be a policeman and find a young tough who didn't want to be around us and somehow change his mind. I knew nothing about such things.

I started to say that I wasn't the guy for this job when the Commander yelled, "Well, git going!"

My heart jumped into my throat, and I scooted for the door, leaving Johnny standing alone. *Nobody talks to me like that,* I thought as I stood outside. *I don't need to be here. Good grief, I'm not getting paid to be treated this way.* As a matter of fact, I wasn't being paid at all! I decided I could just pack up and leave camp right now and go back to where I was appreciated. The only problem was that all my computer equipment was on the desk in the office next to the Commander, and I was afraid to go back in.

I hurried to the clinic to ask Tracy what to do. Maybe she would go with me. There was a sign on the door saying that she would be back at 4:00 p.m. If I waited for her, Marcus would surely be gone for good. He had almost a two-hour start, and right now, I was the only person who apparently might do anything to help him. *Let him go,* I said to myself. *He's not going to be happy if I do find him. Forget it.*

Still, the Commander had given me a straight order, and I was actually worried what he might do to me if I didn't obey.

Once again, I had to struggle to start my car, and I sat there mumbling under my breath and hitting the steering wheel in frustration. Inwardly, I hoped that it would refuse to run, and I could go back and say that it wouldn't work. But suddenly it roared to life, and against my will, I was moving out of the camp along the long dirt road, leading to the main highway.

I turned toward Cortez, taking a chance that this would have been the direction Marcus would have gone. And if I didn't see him, I could at least go by the hospital and visit Little Joey to make the trip worthwhile.

As the miles went by, I became very pleased that I hadn't spotted him. But closer to town, I saw Marcus sitting on his bag alongside the highway. What a disappointment, because now I was going to be forced to deal with him. I pulled up and rolled down the window, trying to be nonchalant. "Hey, Marcus, fancy meeting you here. Where you headed?"

He sat on his bag and stared back down the road, ignoring me.

"You want to jump in and keep me company? I'll take you to town. I'm on my way to the hospital." I could see he was considering it. He must have walked the full distance without getting a ride. "Jump in," I repeated.

Finally, he laboriously pulled himself up and opened the car door. "Don't try anything fancy and take me back to camp," he said. "I've got other plans."

I didn't answer, but he reluctantly swung his bag over the seat and got in. We rode for a couple of minutes in silence, and I said, "Where are you headed?"

"Denver."

"Wow, Denver's a long way off. You have any money to get there?"

"Nope," he replied.

"Well, look. Things couldn't have been that bad back at the camp. What was your problem? People not like you?"

"They was OK," he said. He folded his arms in front of him and hunched his shoulders. I saw his maturing biceps stand out around his thin T-shirt, as he pulled his arms tightly together.

"Well, then why leave when you're getting three squares a day and plenty of outdoor activities.

"I was getting bored, man."

"After just a week?"

"They was playing kid's games and treating me like my little brother."

"You know, I'll bet there's a lot to do if you'd ask. Aren't there maintenance jobs or some work around the horses? I'm sure a place like that needs someone like you."

"I need to make some money. They don't hire kids my age."

"Well, they don't hire men my age either. I'm just a volunteer."

"Well, that's your problem, not mine."

"Why don't you come back, and I'll put in a good word for you—and maybe they'll pay you to work."

"Forget it. The Commander's not about ready to spend any money on me."

"We should at least ask him, don't you think?"

"I'll get a job, and it won't be for the stinking Commander. You can let me off in town, and I'll get a ride from there."

It didn't look like I was going to convince him of anything. He was stubborn and not about ready to listen to reason.

I was straining to think about how to handle him. I could take him to the police in Cortez, but I didn't know if they would do anything about this runaway, even though he was underage. How would the storyline deal with this on the Hallmark Channel anyway? Did I have to call one of his parents to get someone to act? All this was going on in my mind when I suddenly saw a car dead ahead cut out from the oncoming lane to pass a slowpoke and barrel straight for us. I swerved the wheel sharply to avoid the crash, and we plowed into the soft shoulder along the right side of the highway. Like a vise, the gravel gripped my front tire, and our momentum lifted us up, and we spun over and over into the sagebrush. It was like a bad dream as we rolled and collided inside, being flung from the roof and then the dash. When I slammed against the side window, I must have been knocked unconscious because everything mercifully went black.

Chapter 5

COMING UP FROM THE black depths to some kind of awareness was like swimming to the surface of a very thick pond—or like being one of those old radio tubes that took their good time to warm up. And then when I did wake, I hurt in every part of my body.

It occurred to me that I was in a hospital. I could hear someone calling out for a nurse across the hall. A face swam over mine and said, "Are you waking up now?"

It was Tracy. She had a big smile and looked so sweet.

It was good to have her there because I was suddenly scared. "How am I?" I moaned.

"You're remarkable," she said. "You have a single leg fracture, and your face is bruised with a big black eye, but that's all! The doctors don't expect internal injuries as there appears to be no indication on the x-rays. I saw your car, and I have to give praise to the Lord that you're even alive. You wouldn't recognize it."

I thought of the old Volvo. I wouldn't miss it. "What about the boy? What's his name?"

"Marcus? He's in intensive care."

"Oh no," I said. "Is he going to pull through?"

"We're praying for him. He's in pretty bad condition. He wasn't wearing a seat belt and was thrown out. His mother and father are here, and I brought Johnny from camp."

"I feel so terrible," I said. "They're going to kill me."

"Don't go blaming yourself. A witness said you almost had a head-on."

A nurse came up alongside. "Mr. Van Alan, I'm glad to see you're awake. How do you feel?"

"Terrible," I said. "Have you got something for the pain?"

"Of course. I'll get it," she said. "Just stay right there." Her humor was lost on me.

I told Tracy I was thirsty.

"Oh, sorry," she said. "Not until the doctors give your insides the final OK." But then she went out and came back with some ice, and it felt good on my dry lips and parched throat as the cool water trickled down.

○◉○

Later, after I had come out of a drug-induced sleep, I learned from the nurse who was taking my blood pressure that a scan had confirmed my body was whole, and I was on my way to recovery. The halls were quiet. In the dark, I began to visualize my little world in New York City so far away from here, where I had managed to build a life for myself—where I felt safe. Maybe it was dull, and I had only a few friends, but it was mine, and I was comfortable there. Foolishly, I had left it only days ago to come here in a vain attempt to give something of myself to help others. And what had it gotten me? A lonely bed in a remote hospital at the end of the very first day at camp! So far, I had earned a big fat zero in my quest to make a difference. And now with a broken leg and no car, I was going to be at the mercy of others for who knew how long—at least until I could somehow get back home to resume what little life I was living before.

Because the truth was there really wasn't much to go back to either. Now into my midthirties, I had nothing but a bunch of press clippings to show for all the time I had invested in my pitifully small list of clients. Every article had seemed to be such a triumph at the time, and I celebrated a little bit of success with each one, but the exuberance never lasted. Clients expected me to come up with something even better the next time, and the question on their lips was inevitably, "What have you done lately?" My heart began to hurt worse than my throbbing head, and I had to take a deep breath to keep from saying, "Woe is me."

Then it came to me. This was my chance. Could this accident have been a wake-up call? Maybe it was time I got off my little treadmill and began the novel that was constantly rewriting itself in my mind. I'd put it off for so long that I knew I'd never do it if I didn't start soon. My biggest hurdle would be the lack of a regular income, but this might be the time to tap the little eighteen-thousand-dollar nest egg my aunt had left me. In her will, she had said, "Save this. You'll never know when you can use it."

I would leave this hospital and find the nearest airport. I would pull my broken body onto the first plane heading east and get out of here. My car was headed for the junkyard. I'd leave all my computer stuff for the camp and claim a deduction. I was going to need a laptop now anyway. Nobody would miss me, and I certainly wouldn't miss them. I just wanted to be home.

This got me excited. I had a new and workable plan. It's good that the nurse had just checked my blood pressure as my heart was now pumping with new excitement, and she would have been alarmed at the way my blood was pounding through my veins.

○◉○

THE NEXT DAY, I found myself filled with renewed energy and happy to be alive. I was expecting to be discharged. Before I left the area though, I wanted to visit the two boys who were confined somewhere in the little hospital. I had no idea what I would say to either of them, but if they were as lonely as I had felt last night, they might enjoy a visitor. The cast on my leg was clumsy, and since I had never walked with crutches, I was totally unstable. A therapist walked me up and down the hall a bit and then left me on my own. Everyone was telling me how lucky I had been after the local paper had published a picture of my old Volvo upside down on the side of the road.

With the assistance from a volunteer worker, I was wheeled down the hall in a chair, with my leg sticking out in front on a metal extension, to where Little Joey was being housed in a ward of four.

I was surprised and very pleased to find Tracy leaning over him. She was looking fresh and cool. "I was just coming to see you," she said.

"Beat you to it," I answered with a smile.

"They're releasing Joey this morning, and I'm taking him to the orphanage for a few days until he's ready to come back to camp."

"How are you feeling, Joey?" I said.

Tracy moved to let me wheel up close to the bed.

He was shy, but his big eyes were alert and friendly. "I hurt down here." He pointed to his stomach.

"Of course you do," I said, "but that's going to go away."

"I know," he said.

I took his little brown hand and looked into his face, which was surrounded by a big mop of black hair. He seemed fragile, but there was a toughness to his look. "If you could have anything you wanted, what would you wish for?" I asked.

He thought a minute and then with a sly smile said, "A red fire truck."

Not really aware of the simple desires of little kids, I didn't realize how much he meant it. A truck was definitely something I could get him without strain. Maybe not a fire truck, but something similar, before I left for New York.

I nodded and told him, "You just let me get out of the hospital, and I'll see what I can do." I let go his hand and turned to Tracy. "How is Marcus?"

"Still in a coma, I'm afraid. But his vitals are good."

"Can I see him?"

"Only one or two of the family is allowed in ICU. The rest are in the waiting room."

"I'd like to see them then. Are they here?" I asked. I needed to tell them how sorry I was.

Tracy nodded as she pushed a small juice box in front of Little Joey and adjusted the straw for his mouth. "Drink this, and I'll be back in a few minutes to get you dressed." She stroked his black hair with a loving caress and gave him a big smile.

My volunteer worker had left, so Tracy handled the wheelchair duty. We took the elevator up one floor and entered a waiting room decorated in various greens. Several soda machines crowded one wall facing an assortment of chairs and couches. Only one family sat huddled together in the corner, and I could see Marcus's little brother, Johnny, sitting between two adults.

Tracy pushed me close to them and then took a seat next to a somber woman in a plain dress sitting quietly with a big shopping bag alongside her chair. Like her boys, she had the face of the Navajo, and looking at her wrinkled and weather-beaten face, it was hard for me to tell whether she was Marcus's mother or grandmother.

Tracy spoke in their native tongue and pointed to me. Then she turned to the man and told him something, probably about me.

Both adults sat without expression.

At the same time, I felt this overwhelming sense of compassion for them, knowing that their boy was lying comatose in a nearby room, and I had caused it to happen. I wheeled up slowly and extended my hand to the father. "I'm so sorry for Marcus." There was a catch in my throat. "It was truly an accident. I wish I could do something to help him."

The man remained still, not responding or taking my hand. His sad eyes bore through me without judgment.

"They speak very little English," Tracy said. "I've told them who you are and that you are very sorry for their son. Johnny has already told them how you tried to go after Marcus and bring him home."

Marcus's mother nodded her head up and down several times and then spoke, showing one tooth missing. "Thank you," she said.

I was greatly relieved to know that she apparently didn't blame me for the accident, but I wasn't so sure about Marcus's father. I still felt heavily responsible.

Johnny got up and came over to see me. He pointed to my leg. "Does it hurt?"

"Just a bad ache." I was pleased that he cared.

Tracy said something more to them and took their hands and squeezed them, and then she wheeled me away. I gave them a slight wave, but they sat without movement.

Chapter 6

IT APPEARED THAT I was to be released at the same time as Joey. As I waited on the bed in my room with my arm around my crutches, there was a rap at the door.

A police officer stuck his head in. "Mr. Van Alan?" he said.

I nodded. "Yes, come in."

He walked about halfway to me and took a stance. "Sir, my name is Sergeant Peterson with the Colorado State Patrol. I'm doing a routine report on your accident last night, and I'd like to ask you a few questions.

"Of course." I pointed to the chair.

He didn't move from his position, but he opened a metal clipboard and took a pen out of his shirt pocket. "Were you the driver of the Volvo in which you and one other male were injured south of Cortez?"

I said yes.

"Do you own this automobile."

I nodded.

"Were either you or the other male drinking, on drugs, or in any other way impaired?"

I told him I wasn't, but that I had no way of knowing about Marcus.

"What was your destination?"

"This hospital, to see a boy from the camp where I'm working."

"And the same for your passenger?"

"No. He was from the camp but had run away. I saw him sitting alongside the road, so I picked him up in hopes of bringing him back. He said he was on his way to Denver."

The policeman continued on with a series of basic questions that weren't hard to answer, but then he hit me with the real reason he had come. "We found a plastic bag containing over one ounce of marijuana in your wrecked vehicle. Does it belong to you?"

"Absolutely not!" I stammered. "I've never smoked pot in my life."

He watched my reaction without saying anything.

"Where did you find this stuff?" I demanded.

"The duffel in the back seat."

"That wasn't mine," I said. "That belonged to the boy."

"Well, for now, until we get this thing sorted out, I need to ask you to stay where we can get hold of you. Are you going back to this Camp Whatsitsname?"

"Sage and Sand," I said. "No. I'm planning to fly back to New York ASAP. I have no more business around here."

"I'm sorry. As I say, we may need you to come by the station and answer some more questions about this substance we found. We've had a marked increase in drugs within the past month. We'll notify you when you can leave the area." He closed his clipboard and touched his cap. "Have a nice day," he said as he left the room.

Boy! That really bugged me. How am I ever going to escape the bad karma that has attached to me since I got here? Now I was confined to the area for who knew how long. With my bad leg, the Commander wouldn't need me, so I was probably going to have to stay in a motel until the police could be satisfied.

Tracy popped in. "What was that all about?" she asked.

"It's ridiculous! The State Patrol found marijuana in Marcus's backpack, and they're trying to involve me too."

"It's illegal for anyone under twenty-one."

"And they want me to stay around here so they can question me whenever they feel like it, I guess. To tell you the truth, I've about had it."

She looked at her watch. "Joey's waiting for us in the lobby. We've got to go. Let's figure things out as we go. OK?" With that, she helped me get situated in the wheelchair while holding my new crutches at my side, and we slowly made our way to the main door. Outside, she packed us both into her small Honda. It took some doing to get me into the back of the two-door Civic, but it was the only space that would take my leg cast and crutches.

First, we dropped Joey off at a ranch with a rambling farmhouse situated comfortably in a nice grove of trees just outside of town. Joey pointed out his cabin to me among a cluster of little buildings near a set of swings and a circular slide. Tracy got out of the car and gave Joey a big hug goodbye. He seemed happy enough to be home, but he made Tracy promise to come get him in a couple of days.

Mrs. Mason, the director of the orphanage, came out of the house and met me and then pulled the boy up against her plump body. "You're so good to Little Joey, and he talks about you all the time," she said to Tracy. "The camp is a godsend to us, you know. You can't imagine how much the boys look forward to going out there all summer. It's wonderful how you care for these kids so much."

Tracy rumpled Joey's hair. "Every one of them is special to us—just like this little guy," she said. "If we can help them grow up with lots of good memories, it'll make me very happy."

Joey waved as we pulled out of the drive. I had a sudden memory of seeing myself waving goodbye to my father years ago when he left on a business trip. My mother had her arm around me just like Mrs. Mason did.

As we drove into camp, Commander Dougan saw us coming and walked up to the car.

I twisted in my seat to speak with him through the back window.

"So, the road warrior has returned," he said, putting his big hand against the door frame.

"I guess," was all I could think of to say.

He pointed to my eye. "You got a nice shiner there, boy. Looks like you've been in a fight. I don't know whether I want to keep a counselor who's been brawling." Then he laughed with a big roar.

"I don't think I can be of much help now," I said. "I'm pretty slow on my feet."

"Hey, boy, you were injured in the line of duty, and we don't abandon our troops. You can still help Tracy. She'll keep you busy, won't you, honey?"

"Absolutely," she said from her seat behind the wheel.

"Well, git to it then." He gave the metal roof a good pop, making us both jump inside the car.

Tracy drove around to the clinic and helped me out of the back seat. "I can't leave you in your tent to fend for yourself," she said. "There's a little room with a bed in here that I can make up and a handy bathroom. I think it will do nicely."

I gratefully accepted her offer and found that living here was quality compared to the tent city where everyone else was housed. There was even a table and chair where I could put my computer stuff if I wanted to start my novel.

I sat on my new bed and propped my heavy leg up. "Sit down, Tracy," I said. "Tell me about yourself."

She looked around the room as if she wasn't used to sitting and relaxing. I figured she liked to be on the go, keeping herself busy, and this talking personally was foreign to her.

"What do you want to know?" she said as she looked at the little chair for a moment and then reluctantly pulled it out and sat down.

"So, tell me. Why are you here, taking care of a bunch of wild Indians, no pun intended," I said.

She frowned at my little joke, but sat back in her chair, and crossed her legs. "This is my home. I've never been anywhere else. This is where I want to be."

Until recently, I had never been out of my little world either, but this was certainly not where I wanted to be. "Were you born here?"

"Almost. My father was a Methodist minister, and he and Mother moved from Wisconsin to set up a mission to the Southwest Indians when I was just two—so it's the only home I've ever known. I love these people. They're gentle and good and live simple lives. At the mission, we provide food and clothing for those in need. They don't ask for much, but we help them get along from day to day. Many live unhappy lives fighting alcoholism, fetal alcohol syndrome, drugs, criminal offenses, and suicide. What we offer them is not only material things but salvation with the hope of eternity and new life that comes as a result of a belief in Jesus Christ."

"But are they open to your kind of evangelism? I mean, don't they have some pretty deep religious beliefs of their own?"

"Oh, yes. They look to the land, the sky, the wind, and a Great Spirit that guides and protects them. But for our part, we point them to God as that unseen spirit, and then we tell them about the Son of God. Many have become Christians, even though they like to hang onto some of their old beliefs and maintain the traditional lifestyle.

"What kind of lifestyle?"

"Well, there's quite a diversity of cultures. Here in Montezuma County, most are Ute, but there's also the Pueblo, Navajo—who call themselves 'Dine'—and the Apache tribes. Their family structure is generally much better than other low-income people because most households have mothers and fathers with extended relatives close by. Unfortunately, the opportunity for meaningful careers as we know them are not readily available since the area is just not industrialized and is too arid for farming, except for livestock. So they are forced to depend on their own resources such as weaving, jewelry, and other artistic skills. Happily, many Indians are very good at this.

"This beautiful parcel of land was given to us years ago by Josiah Hobbs, a rancher with no family of his own who wanted to see a few boys saved from the poverty mentality of their families and introduced into some kind of productive activity. My parents were overjoyed to receive his gift and worked endless hours to build on it. But when they died last year, I'm afraid we lost their combined intensity and had to get help from your New York company to keep it going.

"It's an important outreach from the mission for the children of the Ute and the Navajo," she went on. "You may not have seen it yet, but not only do the kids play a lot here, they work all summer to create some very nice things. We teach them important skills that can pull them out of the cycle of being given a handout all their lives. We've had some remarkable things happen to some of our boys, and they've come back later to tell us how they've progressed. It's worth everything I've given up to see that happen."

Her eyes sparkled as she spoke. The blood flushed in her cheeks, and her hands were expressive. I was captivated as I listened to her. I forgot about myself and my own needs for a moment and simply concentrated on someone else for a change.

She became aware of my fascinated attention and realized she was talking too much. Her hand went up to her face, and she covered it, blushing and laughing. "How did I get to carrying on so?"

"I think it's wonderful to share what's so important to you," I said. "There's no reason to be embarrassed. You're doing a beautiful thing here, and it makes me appreciate what I see."

She stood up. "There are things that need to be done."

"Wait a minute," I said, not anxious to have her leave me. "I'd be interested to know who operates the camp now. And what about the mission building? Where is it?"

She stopped and leaned on the door. "The mission is farther down the road on reservation land toward the Four Corners. My parents set it up to be run entirely by the local Indians themselves, so the impact of their sudden passing has not stopped the work being done. Until a couple of weeks ago, I continued to live there and be their nurse, but now I'm here for the summer. Until we had to get help from New York, the camp was a self-sufficient nonprofit with the Commander heading it up. He's a retired navy officer who saw his last duty during Operation Desert Storm a few years ago. So, does that answer your questions?"

I said yes. She was clearly ready to get back to business, so I sat back on the bed while she went in and busied herself in the clinic. I could see her through the door. She was a beautiful person. While I tended to be self-centered, she was all giving. In my world of the big city, most of the people I knew were like me—trying to compete for position, working to make the big bucks so they could live a better life than their neighbor, and generous, but mostly when they thought it would help themselves. Even though this was probably not true of the majority of New Yorkers, I had somehow surrounded myself with some pretty narrow-minded people, and it was starting to become rather obvious to me.

○◉○

I made it to lunch, getting a better hang with my new crutches. The campers got quiet as they watched me struggle down the middle aisle. When I got to my table, I acknowledged their stares with a raised crutch like a triumphant athlete. The noise level returned to its peak when I sat down, wondering if I would get to finish this meal without interruption.

Steve was very concerned about my accident and how I was feeling. My face was red and slightly lacerated, but while my black eye was quite a sight, it didn't hurt anymore.

"You are some lucky dude," he said. He seemed to know what happened.

"I was lucky, and I only hope that Marcus comes out of this with no lasting complications. Do you know him at all?"

"Oh, sure," he said. "Marcus and Johnny are well known to everybody."

"What kind of kid is he?"

"Not a bad one, no." Steve thought about it. "He's mixed up like so many his age, and his father demands strict adherence to the tribal ways. For some, it's too confining, and they rebel. That's Marcus's main problem."

"You know, the police found some marijuana in his bag." I told him about the policeman's questions. "They think it might belong to me. What should I do? Tell the Commander?"

"I wouldn't bother him with it. If the police follow it up, they'll call him. The Commander has enough against that boy already."

I wasn't so sure about his advice. "Are drugs a big problem in the area?" I wanted to know.

"Probably no more than anywhere else. As far as you're concerned, you might find that you're under more suspicion because you're from New York. They don't know you. The locals can be wary of outsiders."

That bothered me. I was being detained until further notice, and I didn't want to get brought up for dealing, especially at a camp for boys. The Commander wasn't at lunch, so I decided to see him immediately following.

He wasn't around as I entered the main office, but several boys were at my computer, pounding away at the keys and staring closely at the monitor. "Hey, hey, guys," I said. "Get your hands off that equipment. It's valuable, and you could mess it up. I don't think you should be in here either."

The boys stepped away and stood watching me as if I was going to beat them up on the spot. I was really disturbed that they had just come in and started using my stuff. I came around the desk, whacking my crutch against the chair by mistake, stopping to look at what damage it had inflicted.

They had turned on the screen, and a colorful computer game was blinking at me.

"How did you get into this program?" I asked, astonished that not only were they smart enough to find my password but also to bring up a game that I didn't even know I had in this system.

"We didn't mean to hurt anything," the youngest boy of about eleven said.

I sat down in the chair and pushed it away from the desk to give them more standing room. "Go ahead. Show me how it works."

They immediately jumped forward and went back to punching a certain set of keys that moved a young knight around the castle and away from fiery dragons and other monsters. I wondered how in the world these kids knew so much about computers when I never got past word processing. And while they were excited about the game, they actually showed a decent amount of care with the equipment that I soon lost my concern they would beat it to a pulp.

The phone rang. We were the only ones there, so I got up and hopped over on one foot.

"Speak to Commander Dougan?" the male caller asked.

"He's not here," I said. "May I take a message?"

"Tell him Lieutenant Don Parish, State Police called. Have him call me back as soon as possible. Thanks." He hung up.

I figured I knew what that call was about. So, now it was even more important to get to the Commander right away to tell my side of things.

"OK, guys," I said, turning to the boys. "I've got to shut this thing down, but you can come back again when I'm here and play some more. That be all right?"

They were disappointed but went about cleanly shutting the system down and filed out the door without a word. I sat there, very impressed with their computer skills. Perhaps this might be a way to get to know some of them better if I was going to be forced to stay at the camp for a while. I was going to need something to help me pass the time with the other inmates.

Chapter 7

I FOUND THE COMMANDER having a late lunch alone in the mess hall.

He watched me as I made my way around the tables and signaled for me to have a seat across from him. "We're in trouble, son," he said with a sigh. He looked tired.

My heart skipped a beat as I wondered how he could have already found out about the police and the bag of marijuana. Still, the police could have called him at any time that morning.

"I know," I confessed, "but you've got to believe me, I didn't have anything to do with it."

"Of course you didn't. It's my own doings," he said.

I couldn't believe my ears. The Commander was actually taking the blame.

"I really appreciate this," I said. "I didn't know what to do next."

"Hold it, boy," he said and put his hand up. "You and me have a history of talking along two paths that'll never cross. Let's get on the same page, OK?"

He brought out a letter and took out a pair of reading glasses. Even upside down, I recognized the arrowhead logo of the National Park Service imprinted at the top. He went ahead to read out loud:

> Dear Commander Dougan,
>
> This is to inform you that Camp Sage and Sand is being cited for the improper extraction and handling of important and historic artifacts relating to the

> archeological culture of the Pueblo (Anasazi) Indians in and around the area of your camp property. You are immediately directed to cease all operations that would compromise any objects of antiquity and hold in place under lock and key those items that have already been removed from their original place of rest.
>
> It is unlawful to injure, destroy, excavate, or remove any historic or prehistoric artifact or object of antiquity from public lands or lands adjacent to United States National Parks, as they have great scientific and historic value.
>
> A team headed by Dr. Riga Armor, Director of the Southwestern Historic and Cultural Studies Institute, will be calling upon you in the next few days to review any violations you might have made in accordance with the American Antiquities Act of 1906, a copy of which is enclosed.

There appeared to be more, but the Commander folded the page and took off his glasses. "It's the worst kind of news," he said. "The camp may not survive this."

For the moment, I was distracted from my own problems. "What caused this to happen anyway?"

"My guess is that someone saw my little collection of pottery in the office and told the people at Mesa Verde. Are you familiar with the Indian cliff dwellings down the road?"

"Mesa Verde National Park? Yes, I have a great picture of the ancient cliff dwellings on a calendar back home. I plan to visit the site sometime before I leave."

"Well, now and then, I've picked up a few shards and some nice pieces of pottery in a spot back along our cliff," he said. "After a while, I got quite a pretty little display, and I use it from time to time to explain the history of the area to some of the boys. I never dug for anything."

"That shouldn't bother those scientists, should it?"

"Negative. This is just what they've been looking for. They are, in fact, accusing me of theft—with the intent of possibly selling this stuff. They've been after our place here for years, and now this is their chance to make a big deal of it and pick up some extra research property. I can just see them rubbing their hands together. That Dr. Armor has been mad ever since this little piece of land was deeded over to the mission."

He brought out an attachment to the letter and put his glasses back on.

"They enclosed a copy of the American Antiquities Act. Now this old Act of Congress goes through a discussion of how public lands must be protected against looters and those who would destroy historic areas, and it also states you have to have the proper permits to examine and excavate such sites. It imposes fines and imprisonment on those who don't comply. That could be a problem for me right there, but here's the kicker that scares me:".

> Provided that when such objects are situated upon a tract covered by a bona fide unperfected claim or held in private ownership, the tract, or so much thereof as may be necessary for the proper care and management of the object, may be relinquished to the proper authorities, and the Secretary of the Interior is hereby authorized to accept the relinquishment of such tracts on behalf of the Government of the United States.

The Commander put the paper down, took off his glasses again, and stared right through me. His thoughts had drifted off, and I hated to interrupt them. Finally, his eyes cleared. "I'm telling you, we're in a pile of deep doo-doo."

I wished with all my heart I had a ready answer to help him out. He was confiding in me, and I wanted so much to be of some value. All I could do was be there for him to talk to. "Have you told Tracy about this?" I asked.

"No. I got the letter this morning after you two returned. I've been out walking, trying to figure out my next move. They're going to want an explanation for how and where I picked up the pieces of pottery, and even more, they're probably going to dig up half the campground out back. Once they get in here, they'll shove us into a little roped-off compound and then pull it tight. We could even be forced out by the end of the summer, I expect."

"Can you bring in a lawyer?" I asked.

"Oh sure, but we don't have the funds for that. ENDCO in New York isn't going to want to spend any money on us either since they kind of took us on as a favor last year. They've already picked up our regular operating expenses, but this will be way over and above what they bargained for." He sighed. "Anyways, what were you wanting when you came in?"

My problem had shrunk to nothing against the Commander's situation. I could wait to explain it at a better time. "Just that I took a call from a Lieutenant Parish of the Colorado State Police when I was in the office a few minutes ago. He wanted you to call back."

"Now, what do you suppose he wants? I don't need any more bad news. Must have something to do with your accident."

"It's possible," I said. "They were asking me questions this morning at the hospital."

"Like what?"

"About finding some marijuana in the wreck. They wouldn't believe that it wasn't mine. I hate to blame Marcus, but that's the only possible explanation."

"I wouldn't put it past the boy," the Commander said. "He's gotten in with some rough characters around here, and that's why his parents asked me to take him for the summer. Kids get in trouble when they're out of school. It didn't surprise me when he wanted to chuck it all and run."

"Can you get the police off my back?" I asked.

"Probably. I know Parish. He's fair. You should be cleared as soon as Marcus comes to."

So, at this point, I figured I'd better start hoping the best for the boy, so I could at least get out of here as soon as possible.

Back at the clinic, Tracy was as equally upset as the Commander when I told her about the letter from the Park Service. "That Dr. Armor is a private consultant, and this would give her a huge feather in her cap. She isn't going to give up the attempt to obtain this property. Years ago, she was working for the National Park Service and informed my parents then they should never have been allowed to acquire this place because it had historical significance. I know there are isolated little sites all over this area where the Anasazi lived, but when is this threat of a wildcat takeover ever going to end?"

I knew nothing about this Armor gal, but it seemed reasonable to me that the government would be within their rights in protecting our ancient history. There should be some easy way to come to terms by letting a few archeologists poke around on the grounds and see if they come up with any buried treasures. What were a few pots and pans anyway? If they did find something valuable, wouldn't there be some good compensation for the land—and the camp could just move down the road? I'd make sure that I'd stick the government for a bundle if they forced me out after all these years. Somehow, I couldn't bring myself to worry about these concerns for the future because I wasn't going to be involved here for long anyway. Of course, I didn't want Tracy to know I was basically disinterested, so I asked, "What do you think you're going to do about this?"

"Well, we'll want to give your New York company the heads-up that the government is sniffing around. Other than that, I don't know what we can do. We'll just have to wait to see what happens next."

The phone intercom buzzed. When she hung up, she said, "The hospital called, and Marcus is more alert. The Commander suggests I be there when he wakes up. Do you want to go?"

"I sure do," I said, gathering my crutches from the floor. I had hopes that this new turn of events would get my own situation cleared up.

○◉○

MARCUS HAD ALREADY COME to and been moved out of intensive care by the time we got there. This time, we were allowed to enter his private room where both parents sat in stoic silence beside his bed. I saw the name, "M. Dry Cloud," written on the door tag. His head was encased in bandages, and the nurse told us that was where he primarily landed. I felt really bad for him and wished I'd let him continue to hitchhike.

His eyes were open, but he didn't appear to focus on anyone or anything. He had a breathing tube taped to his open mouth, and he appeared to have a broken arm.

We waited at the foot of the bed for quite a while without talking. There wasn't much to say, and until he could speak, I didn't think I should try to ask him about the marijuana.

The curtain suddenly slid aside, and Sergeant Peterson stepped in. He briefly looked at Marcus's parents and then moved in front of them to stand over Marcus. "Can you hear me, boy?" he said in a sharp voice. His words startled us in the quiet atmosphere that we had created.

Marcus's eyes cleared, and he looked at the man.

"Can you hear me?" Sergeant Peterson repeated.

Marcus gave a slight nod.

"We found a bag of marijuana in your wreck. Does it belong to you?"

Marcus stared at the patrolman for a moment and then turned to look at me. He shook his head no.

"What?" I said. "Marcus, you know it's yours."

The nurse came in and said, "You're all going to have to leave. That's enough for the boy right now."

"Wait just a minute." I had to get this thing cleared up. "Marcus, that stuff is yours."

His eyes moved from me to his father, who stood next to the nurse, and I could see he wasn't going to confess in front of him. He slowly shook his head no.

Sergeant Peterson turned to me. "He's indicating it's not his."

"So I saw, but are you going to believe him?"

"For now. In the meantime, you hang close until this thing's resolved," the sergeant said. "Keeping a handle on drugs is a priority here. We'll be talking more to the boy as soon as we can."

There was nothing I could do. Tracy and I left the hospital and started back to the camp. I was in a foul mood.

The only good part of staying around was Tracy. She had a way about her. This time, I was seated next to her up front in her little car. She had pushed the passenger seat way back to make it comfortable. I watched her as she drove, and I liked her take-charge manner. Although she was quick on the accelerator, I could see she was a polite driver, giving the right-of-way to people whom I thought didn't deserve it. Yet, on the whole, drivers here were so much more laid back that I finally relaxed enough to watch the various locals going about their business.

Suddenly, Tracy stiffened. "Look over there. Can you believe it? That's Dr. Armor crossing the street," Tracy said. She nodded toward a cluster of tourists, following like chickens behind a big hen who was gesturing this way and that at the hills around the town. A white van obediently followed behind, on the ready to pick them up.

Dr. Armor was exactly the way I had pictured her. She was stout with gray hair pulled up in a bun under a pith helmet. She wore a long brown dress with a white ruffled blouse and walked in sensible brown shoes. She carried a clipboard under her arm and referred to it from time to time. Her charges numbered about ten people. Most of them were in their fifties and sixties and appeared in rapt attention to what the good doctor seemed to be saying.

"I could run her down right here," Tracy said somewhat under her breath, "before she starts real trouble."

"Wow, you're really serious," I said. "Is she all that bad?"

"You bet your life she is. You give her an inch, and she'll take a mile."

The doctor and her group passed immediately in front of us and on down the street.

Tracy sat and steamed behind the stop sign until we got the horn from behind. It woke her from her thoughts and we moved on. "She's going to come after us with the government on her side. I'm afraid we're going to have to fight it this time."

"What can you do if you don't have the money to battle the feds?" I asked.

"It's going to take something that stirs people to see our side," she said. "It's a shame because we've been helping kids make a better life for themselves at the camp for years, and most people have never heard of us. If they knew more, maybe the community would rally to help us keep what we have."

"How about a feature in the paper? Have you ever had anything like that?"

"Never."

"Well, you know that's what I do for a living," I said. "If I could put it all together for you, do you think you could get the local paper to cooperate?" I was thinking that this just might be the thing that would get my mind off having to hang around the camp until Marcus decided to come clean.

"The editor was a good friend of my parents. I'm sure he'd be glad to cooperate. Let's go find out." She turned the car around, and in a minute, we pulled up to a storefront on Main Street.

Bill Bradford came out of his small back office to greet us the minute he saw us come in. "Tracy, I was wondering what had become of you. Have you been hiding at the mission?" He gave her a hug. "It's great to see you."

"Not hiding, Bill. We're underway again at Sage and Sand. Hey, it's good to see you too. How have you been?"

"Never better," he said.

Tracy turned and introduced me to the editor, and in the conversation, I had a minute to give him a bit of my background.

"What brings you both to town?" he finally asked.

"We came to get your opinion," she said. "What do you think of government threats to take over Sage and Sand?"

"Take over? What for?"

"Commander Dougan received a threatening letter from the Park Service that they are about to sic Riga Armor on us. This time, it sounds like it's for real. I don't know what persuaded them to come after us all of a sudden, but it shows they haven't given up their plan to take over."

"Yeah, I remember your folks went through this some time ago. Actually, I have an idea why this is coming about. The government has finally loosened up some of the purse under the 'Save America's Treasures' Historic Preservation Fund, and I'd expect your property has been on their list for some time. They'd be expected to give this job to Dr. Armor. She's a tough cookie."

"What's her purpose in all this?" I asked.

"Here's the story as I know it," Bill said. "Dr. Armor used to work for the National Park Service in the Department of Antiquities. About five years ago, she ruffled enough feathers within the agency that they quietly moved her out after about twenty years of service. To keep her quiet, they helped her set up her own consulting organization and continued her on as their expert in expanding new archeological programs. The rumor is that the rock wall near your place is sacred and an undeveloped treasure trove of Anasazi Indian artifacts and who knows what. She's been trying to get her hands on this piece of property for the Park Service ever since Tracy's parents inherited it. The newly allocated grant money might be just what they needed to do just that."

Tracy said, "Melvin and I think that public exposure might be a way to save our piece of property out there—at least to let people know that we have an important community summer program going on. We want to know if you'd support a feature story on the camp and what we do to benefit the kids of this area."

"Sounds interesting," Bill said. "I'd have to take a look at what you come up with, but if it has merit, I'd be willing to have our photographer take some pictures and assign a reporter to work with you. Go ahead and pull something together, and I'll be thinking about it in the meantime. As you might guess, I'm a big booster of the Park Service and their role in the economy of this area, so I don't want this to become a 'you versus them' sort of thing. But, if it means that the giant is coming in to squash the little guy, I can help people realize that things need to be worked out rather than seeing a big takeover. Does that make sense?"

This was exactly my position too. I found it easy to agree with him and promised to promote the merits of the camp rather than get into a squabble that might occur, especially if this Dr. Armor was a hothead. For all I knew, the property might reveal some new and very exciting discoveries that needed to be found. On the other hand, I had come to respect Tracy's part in this ongoing melodrama in the Southwest desert, so I had to be open-minded about the whole thing.

Bill gave me some journalistic guidelines that the paper used, and we tentatively set our sights on a Sunday edition within the next two weeks. I would normally have charged quite a nice fee for this type of article, but as a volunteer, I was going to have to get used to giving my time away.

Chapter 8

BACK AT THE CAMP, Tracy and I met with the Commander to outline our idea for this proactive attack on the enemy. As expected, he was highly enthusiastic and started laying out a plan of action for me to take.

I interrupted him. "Commander Dougan, why don't you give me charge of this operation since I've got some experience in this area. You'll get a chance to look at the finished product, but I need you to give this project your blessing and then stand back."

He sputtered for a moment and then said, "Quite right, my boy. I've gotten out of the habit of delegation. You'll have my complete cooperation. Just tell me what we need to do."

"The first thing I want to have is an in-depth interview with you to establish your background and credentials. People need to know that you are very capable of leading this camp and have a heart for it—how you work to develop a successful attitude in everyone here. Then I'm going to want to uncover some stories from those who have graduated out of this program. I also want to be made aware of what plans are afoot for the future of the camp and how ENDCO is involved. There are lots of details I'm going to need to make a credible appeal to the readers, so I'll appreciate your opening your files to me as we go along."

"Perfectly fine, my boy," he said. "Just ask."

"And, Tracy, I'm going to ask you to be a central part of this story. How your parents established the mission and then the camp. Their dreams for the future. And how you have taken up their ministry to the people of this area. It seems to me that this is the perfect example of the selflessness that underlies what is being accomplished in the lives of the boys who come. Can I get you to be the key person in all of this?"

Tracy's head was down as I had proposed my ideas, and now she raised her eyes to look at me. "It's the last thing I want," she said. "I have no desire to be the poster child here, but I know that Daddy would have asked me to go along with you if you think this is what needs to be done. Just don't make me out to be some kind of Mother Teresa, please."

"I can do that," I assured her. "But they've got to see that a woman who's in her midtwenties is something of an angel who could be married and starting a family of her own but has given that up for several hundred or so needy families. A beautiful person like you deserves to have a life of your own. I'm sure that the people here will be awed by what you are doing—if they don't already know you. I hope you'll give me the opportunity to tell the honest story about you."

"Hear! Hear!" the Commander added.

I didn't get an immediate answer. She was thinking about it and the process was probably difficult for her. Finally she said, "Do what you have to. This camp has got to survive."

Now that I had established my own set of marching orders, I suddenly had my doubts that I might not be able to pull off the promotional effect like I knew it should be done. It would be a tall order to reveal the inner spirit of the camp and its leaders, but I hoped I could do it justice. And I didn't have the luxury of time to plan it carefully. I was just going to have to go for it and rely on my years of experience.

○◉○

I spent a long time talking to the man around whom the camp revolved. He was a dedicated military man whose last operation was captain of a naval supply ship. When he retired, Lieutenant Commander Elliot Dougan envisioned spending the rest of his days operating a motel with his wife in Durango, Colorado, but cancer snatched away her life and his dream. After spending a year drifting around the area, he walked into the little Indian Mission in Cortez, presided over by Arthur and Edith Palmer. The love emanating from these faithful missionaries was exactly what the Commander needed to heal his heart, and he stayed close to the Palmers, serving in whatever capacity he was called. The following summer, Reverend Palmer handed his role as head of Camp Sage and Sand over to the Commander, whose skill in turning boys into men had been honed to a fine edge through years of military service. He had been its guiding light ever since.

Commander Dougan told of the night the Palmers were killed out on the highway not far from town. Their truck was loaded with food and clothes from generous church people in a nearby community.

"Art apparently had a heart attack at the wheel, and Edith was unable to keep the truck from going over the edge of the road into the canyon below," the Commander said with tears in his eyes. "The police called me, and I had to go break the news to Tracy back at the mission. I was in such dread of having to tell her the awful news that I was a total wreck, even before I got there. Never in my war days had I come apart so bad. The Palmers had become my best friends, and Tracy was practically my daughter. But do you know what she did? She took my hand and ministered to me! She calmed me down and had me throw some water on my face, and then she put her arm around me—and we prayed together. I'll never forget her angelic touch and the calm with which she took the news. She told me that she knew where her mother and father were, and she was at total peace with that. And she was the same loving and comforting person who spoke to each and every person who came to the mission carrying armloads of flowers and plates of food. She turned grief into triumph, and I was so proud to be a part of something so spiritual."

After that interview, I came away more thoughtful and with a resounding respect for both the Commander and Tracy. These dedicated people were going to make my story something special, and I was becoming personally affected by it.

Walking back around the building to my little room at the clinic, I was congratulating myself on finally getting the hang of the rhythm of the crutches, even though much of the dirt roadway still harbored ruts from the previous rain. With all my concentrated attention, I about ran over Johnny Dry Cloud who was standing directly in my path.

"Hey, Johnny," I said, pulling to a halt in front of him. "What's the latest on Marcus?"

"Nothing. He can't talk 'cause he's got that tube in his throat."

"I'm really sorry about that," I said. I knew that until they took it out, they couldn't make him confess anything, and maybe not even then with his father standing close by.

I bent down. "You get around the camp a lot. Do you know any older boys who could tell me some interesting stories about what's going on here?" I had in mind the possibility of interviewing a kid who had recently turned his life around or discovered a new skill that would make a difference.

Johnny stood with his eyebrows in a frown for a minute as if he was making some kind of decision, and then he turned toward the cluster of tents and said, "Come on."

When he started to run ahead, I had to tell him to slow down. We wound around the various tents, some newer than others. They were set up like a little town in blocks with street names on signposts that said "Straight Arrow" and "Wild Pony." A few blocks in, he stopped and pointed to one. "This was where Marcus stayed," he said.

I didn't think I was going to get any quick interviews with no one around, but Johnny was already untying the tent flap.

I said, "Hey, Johnny, better we wait until somebody comes?"

"No, no," he said. "You wanted to know what's going on around here. Right?"

"Yeah, sure, but ..."

Johnny pulled me close to the entrance. He had a weird look on his face. "This here's what's going on."

I glanced inside, and in the muted light, I only saw a bunch of clothing strewn around and an old vinyl suitcase. I didn't understand Johnny's insistence.

"Over there," he said.

I looked again with more focus but didn't see what he was referring to. Then he went past me and moved to the far side. Leaning over, he pulled at the edge of the wooden platform and removed a big board. "See? This is what I mean." He was waving his hand to get me to come in and see for myself.

I thought about it a minute and then put one crutch down and stepped up into the tent with the other. I hobbled my way across the platform for a closer look.

"Down here." He pulled me nearer.

I leaned over and saw many rolled joints in a plastic bag and a good-sized packet of something. "What's this?"

"It's pot, man!" Johnny said with a certain breathy awe of a twelve-year-old who's known all about some secret things but never told anybody.

This was bad news, and I could see I was in real trouble here. I no longer felt the wonderful innocence of being a volunteer camp counselor. I was now in the middle of something I was probably going to regret by sharing the same secret that Johnny had been keeping. I was scared because I had already been semi-accused of possessing an illegal substance, and now I knew the whereabouts of a stash many times larger.

He started to reach down and get the bag.

"Whoa, don't do that," I whispered harshly. "You'll get your fingerprints all over them. Put the board back down—and let's get out of here." I didn't want to get caught anywhere near this stuff.

He complied, but he had some trouble getting the board to fit.

I leaned down to help give it a push, and my crutch fell with a clatter. Immediately I stopped everything to listen if anyone had heard us. No one came running. I nervously took out my handkerchief and tried to wipe the floorboards of any prints we had left. If the authorities ever dusted for them, I didn't want mine showing up. Then we bolted from the tent and tied it just in time to face a mob of campers coming back from class.

A cluster of four older boys immediately formed around us.

"It's Tony and his gang," Johnny whispered to me.

"What are you looking for?" Tony had an aggressive attitude, and apparently this was his tent.

I tried not to let my voice break. "I asked Johnny to show me some guys who've gotten something positive out of being at the camp. I'm writing an article and need to talk with some of you."

"Forget it," he said. Clearly, he was anxious to get me out of his way and check for signs of a search.

"Was Marcus your tentmate?" I asked.

"What of it?" he said as he untied the flap.

"Nothing, except that he was with me in an accident, and I care about him."

"Oh, so you're the dude who almost got him killed." He turned and put his face in mine.

I stepped back.

One of the gang kicked my crutch, and I almost fell.

"It wasn't my fault," I objected. "We almost got front-ended. Marcus didn't have his seat belt on and was thrown out."

The little group crowded even tighter around us. Tony spoke for all of them. "We don't like it here, and you can put that in your article. There's nothing here but a bunch of do-gooders who think they can change us."

I was trying my best to hold my own and not let these kids intimidate me. "Wouldn't it help to develop some kind of skills before you graduate? Can't you learn a little something here?"

"Don't make me laugh," he said with a smirk. "There are better ways to make plenty of dough, and it's not in shop class."

The other three guys laughed and nodded.

If he's running drugs, he's probably right, I thought. I could see that I was getting nowhere and in deep trouble if he found that we had been inside his tent.

"Let's go, Johnny," I said. "I guess I'll have to find myself a happy camper somewhere else around here." I had to literally push my way out of the group and then went crashing wildly away on my crutches, this time with Johnny running behind until he went off somewhere. I was just glad to be alive at this point.

Chapter 9

ALL MY LIFE, I had gone out of my way to avoid the gangs in New York City, and here I was in the middle of one in Colorado! There was some serious underage drug running going on right under our noses, but I was afraid that if I told the Commander, because I was now closely involved, it might just stir things up with Lieutenant Parish enough to get me into even more trouble. I didn't want to take that chance.

I needed some privacy to think things out. Tracy was busy with paperwork in the clinic, so I quietly passed by on my way to my room. I shut the door and lay down to consider my options. My head was pounding around my sore eye, and I was having trouble calming down.

There was a tap on the door.

"Are you all right?" Tracy asked.

"I'm fine."

"You were too quiet and didn't look so good when you came in," she said through the door.

"My head hurts, and I just need to lie down." I hoped this would satisfy her.

"I'll get you something for it," she said. She wasn't going to be put off, and I could hear her opening a cabinet, and then she was back. "Can I come in?"

"I kind of wanted to sleep."

She opened the door a crack. "Take these, and I'll leave you alone."

"OK, come on in."

"It's just that I think you could use a little cheering up," she said as she brought a paper cup of water and a couple of pills to the nightstand. "I've never seen anyone develop so many problems in such a short time. Is this the story of your life?"

"Not in the least," I lied, trying not to think of the thousand and one other times I had messed up. "But things seem to have snowballed on me. First, I thought I was going to teach a writing class, then a car accident, the bag of marijuana, and now this."

"What do you mean by this?" She put her hands on her hips while she waited for me to down the two pills.

"You're not going to believe it, but I've found a stash of pot right here in one of the tents, and I don't know what to do about it."

Her eyes widened, and her mouth fell open. "There's marijuana in this camp? How much?"

"You'd never believe how much," I said.

"Well, how in the world did you ever find it when I know the Commander has all his counselors keeping a hawk eye out for it?"

"Don't ask me. I didn't want to find it. Marcus's brother, Johnny, showed me a bunch of it hidden under the tent platform where Marcus and this other guy, Tony, stayed. I came close to getting caught in their tent. I'm sure there's some kind of gang dealing in it, and believe me, I don't want to get involved."

Tracy sat down at the foot of the bed. "You've got to tell the Commander at least. Let him take it from here."

"Yeah, well, I thought of that, but you know what he'll do. Probably start a big investigation. Right now I'm being looked at as a possible druggie myself, and so what are the police going to think? I'm a new guy in from New York, and the timing is just too perfect. I can't take the chance of getting involved with them any more than I am now."

"So, do you have any better ideas?" she asked.

"I've been thinking if there was some way to get these guys to expose themselves—show that they've had the stuff all along—it might not implicate me. I'd like to get Marcus to tell the police that his pot is part of a bigger stash and that it came from here. I've got to find a way to get him to talk."

"But what about the camp?" Tracy said. "You're supposed to be helping us write a positive story about how we develop future leaders, and then this thing comes out? What about that? It'll give the Park Service all the ammunition they need to shut us down."

"I know. I've got to think."

"Well, we can't wait very long. This whole thing could blow up, and we could lose the camp overnight. And we can't just go on letting a gang of kids keep supplying drugs without calling the police. The Commander needs to be informed sooner than later."

I lay back down and closed my eyes. "I couldn't agree with you more," I said. "Just give me a chance to think."

I knew that I was being selfish to worry about myself when it came to what was at stake at the camp and the welfare of the good boys who might be drawn in by the gang, but I couldn't help trying to work out a plan of my own that might save my skin and get me out of here. If I could somehow persuade the gang to move their stash, I could continue my article and try to get it to the paper by the deadline. This was a tall order.

I began to think that the key was with Marcus. I was sure he knew what was going on. If I scribbled some kind of a note that looked like he wrote it and got it to Tony, I might get this hood to react. It didn't matter where they took the stuff—just as long as they removed it from the camp.

Tracy had gone back to her work, and then I heard her leave. The Tylenol had done its job, and I felt much better when I got up and went to find some paper in her office. I found a pad imprinted with a pharmaceutical house logo and decided it would be perfect. It would look like Marcus used a hospital note to write on.

From an assortment of ballpoints, I found a beat-up pencil with teeth marks. Its blunt lead had just the poor quality that looked real good. I wrote the words slowly so it was messy but could still be read: "Get all the stuff out. The police are coming." I underlined the word "all," hoping that if there was more marijuana in any other tents, they would get rid of it too.

Now all I had to do was to get the note to the gang. Johnny was the only person who could provide the connection with Marcus and Tony, their leader.

Tracy walked back in, and I stuffed the note in my pants.

"Feeling better already?" she asked.

"Yeah, the pills did the trick. I was just on my way out again to do some more writing."

"What did you decide to do? Are you going to tell the Commander?"

"I probably should, but not right now," I said.

She looked at me with a little frown as I opened the door. "Well, don't wait too long," she cautioned.

○◉○

THE NEXT DAY, I went looking for Johnny. I had no idea where to find him. Steve came along and I stopped to ask him. "You know where I can find Johnny Dry Cloud?" I asked.

"He should be on the lower playing field. Is there a problem? And how's Marcus doing? Do you know?"

"He's out of the coma, and I hope they took the breathing tube out so he can talk. I haven't heard the latest."

"OK. And you? You don't look too steady on those crutches. How long are you going to need them?"

"The doctor said a couple of weeks, and then I can get a walking cast."

"That's good, man," he said. "Let me know if I can do anything to help."

"Thanks." I smiled, and we shook hands. It was nice to know people who cared. I turned and started down toward the ball field, hoping I could make the distance.

I found Johnny Dry Cloud playing center field with a bunch of kids his age. The coach told me they had just started, but he could spare Johnny for a bit as soon as the side was retired, so I sat down to wait.

I wondered if he would go along with my plan to pass the note to Tony. It implicated his own brother about the marijuana and might lead to Marcus getting arrested for drug dealing if the police became aware of it. I consoled myself with the fact that it was Johnny who showed me the stash in the first place. I just wanted to get the stuff out of the camp without telling anyone.

When he came off the field, Johnny sauntered over. I briefly described my idea and showed him the note. He was a smart little guy, and I could see him thinking about if he wanted to do it or not. Finally, he nodded and put the note in his pocket. He told me that he'd take it after the game. It didn't seem to matter to him whether or not there was marijuana, but he seemed willing to do as I asked.

I sat and continued to watch the game. At the same age as these kids, I was reading books instead of playing with other kids. For some reason, I never seemed to fit in. As I watched, I felt a bit of regret over missing out on this kind of fun when I was growing up. It looked like every kid here was having a great time. This was the very heart of the story I wanted to write. A story about kids who might not have the advantages of a family or were roaming the streets. Even if there were only a hundred or so boys at this camp, they were being given a healthy opportunity to interact. Forget a few gang-related misfits—I expected the majority would have some positive life experiences.

Just before the game was over, I worked my way back to the clinic to lie down. All the stress and walking had really tired me, but hopefully this thing would be over soon. I was expecting the gang to get the message and react swiftly to get rid of the drugs. Then, with the first part of the plan accomplished, I wanted to visit Marcus to get him to tell the truth about his own little bag of marijuana. As soon as I could offer some kind of proof that I was no drug dealer, I was on my way out of here.

○◉○

About an hour later, I was wakened from a very nice nap by a commotion in the clinic. Tracy was trying to quiet somebody and not disturb me, but she wasn't doing a very good job.

Suddenly, the door of my room burst open, and Johnny came piling in. It looked like he had been in a fight. Tracy was struggling to restrain him and wipe his wounds with a cloth at the same time.

"They didn't believe the note, and they made me tell who gave it to me," Johnny cried out through his tears. "They're gunna come after you now! That's what they said."

My heart skipped a beat, and I saw stars as I sat up. "What happened?" I croaked. "Why didn't they go for it?"

"They said that Marcus is a blood brother, and he would never tell. They knew I told you about them and guessed you wrote the note."

Tracy was checking to see if Johnny's nose was broken. "So, this is the way you decided to handle it?" she said. "Now they're going to move the marijuana and come looking for you at the same time. Don't you think it would have been better to have nabbed these guys with it right there in their own tent?"

"We couldn't afford the publicity," I said.

"So, now don't you think you'd better go to the Commander? We can't hide the fact that we have a major problem—even if the future of the camp is at stake."

I couldn't believe how things had turned sour. I'd thought it was such a good way to get the drugs out. Now I had to go lay it all out to the Commander. This was going to be tough.

I stood up and went over to Johnny. "I hope you'll forgive me for the way those bullies laid into you. I'm going to tell the Commander what happened right now so he can deal with them. Would you be willing to give him their names?"

He hesitated. "I guess." He was not eager to take any more of my ideas.

"How about now?"

Tracy said, "Just let me get him cleaned up a little more, and we'll all go."

I was quite relieved. Her presence would be more than welcome when we went before the man himself.

○◉○

I was shaking inside when we all crowded through the door to the Commander's office. He was on the phone so we had to wait behind the counter. I wandered over to get a better look at the infamous display of pottery that set off the sirens at the Park Service. From a distance, the pieces were a jumble, but as I looked closer, I could see some very unique designs painted on sandy-colored clay in various hues and tones. I could even make out some indentations and curves made by human fingers. At least one piece was totally complete with only a small crack along the side. I wanted to pick it up for a better look, but with my recent track record, I didn't dare touch it.

Finally the Commander hung up and turned to us. Then seeing Johnny's face, he got up and came over. "What happened, boy? Did you get in a fight?"

"Not exactly," Tracy spoke for him. "Some of the bigger boys beat up on him because he was over in their tent."

"What were you doing? Sneaking around?"

Johnny shook his head. He was clearly scared in front of the Commander.

"I guess it's sort of my fault," I admitted. Now I was the one who was scared. "Can we come in and sit down?"

We moved around the counter and took seats next to the big desk. "OK," I said, taking a deep breath. "Here's the deal. I was starting to do the story on the camp, and I met Johnny outside the office here. I asked him if he knew any interesting stories about what's going on. Well, in his innocence, he took me to one of the tents and showed me a secret stash of marijuana."

The Commander sat straight up in his chair and said, "What?"

"I about flipped when I saw it," I said. "We almost got caught by a group of older boys who kind of ganged up on us, but I talked our way out of it."

"Who are these guys—and where is this stuff?" The Commander's voice was loud enough to make me jump inside.

"Johnny's promised to tell us, but there's a little more to the story."

"Well, git on with it."

"Ah … well, I thought that with the camp wanting to demonstrate its good standing in the community, that having as much marijuana as I saw in that one tent would blow us out of the water. So I concocted a note for Johnny to take to the guys that was supposed to look like it came from Marcus, saying that the police were on to them and to get rid of it. I thought that would be the end to it and—"

"You what?" the Commander exploded. "How dumb can you git, Van Alan? Don't you know that there've been strong rumors about this stuff going around? It was after Marcus showed up with a bag of the stuff in the accident that we figured out where to look. That phone call just now was Lieutenant Parish, from downtown, telling me his men and dogs would be here within the hour."

My one consolation was that the police probably guessed all along that I wasn't a druggie from New York. They pinpointed Marcus, once they found the marijuana in my car, and all they wanted for me was to stay around as a witness in the investigation. But our reputation for having a clean camp was pretty much down the toilet.

Bill Bradford from the newspaper showed up with Lieutenant Parish. When he saw Tracy and me, he shook his head. "I gotta follow this story up and not whitewash the facts. Perhaps there's just a small group of misfits who are dealing drugs. If that's the case, the rest of the camp may come out OK. We'll have to see."

The dogs jumped all over the place as soon as they got a whiff of the wooden platform in Marcus's old tent, but no packets of the marijuana turned up.

The Commander looked at me as if I was dirt, but he didn't say anything to the lieutenant about my note to the boys.

"Looks like this was a fresh hiding place for the stuff," Lieutenant Parish said. "We'll want to question the kids who are normally in and out of here to find out where they're getting it."

Commander Dougan pulled aside several older boys from the little crowd who had gathered to watch the proceedings. He told them to go to the office and wait. As they were singled out, a couple looked at me with narrowed eyes in a way that gave me a chill.

"We never have problems with the young ones; it's the older kids that we need to watch," the Commander said. "When they get to be sixteen, the reason they're in camp is that they can't get jobs, and their parents want them under supervision. At this age, they get bored and are liable to get into mischief. I'll split them up and reassign them new tentmates. The counselors need to be on alert."

Every one of the boys pleaded innocent of having marijuana in his tent, so there was nothing the Commander could do but to let each of them go back to their activities.

Out of self-preservation, I didn't volunteer the fact that Johnny had shown me the large stash. I felt personally responsible for the failure of the drug bust, but I thought the dogs had proven that drugs had been there. I was just hoping they would find them in another location before they left. Until then, Camp Sage and Sand was not going to be above suspicion. It made me doubly anxious to get out of everybody's hair and leave the troubles of the boy's camp behind.

Luckily, Bill Bradford agreed not to report the raid so that the police could continue their investigation without raising concern among the parents and the community at large. He agreed to wait a few days to get all the facts before he let loose with a story.

Tracy came into my room after I went back to lie down. "Don't be too hard on yourself. You were only trying to be of help. You've got to realize that with so many boys to look after, there's going to be all sorts of mischief. Harboring drugs in the camp is very bad, and we've got to put a stop to it immediately. Whoever is responsible is going to be caught. I don't think you have to worry about the reputation we have. Too many boys have gone back into the community all the better for being here. It's time to feature a story about our good side. And if they do find drugs, you can still show how we do our best to look out for the majority of the children who have been put in our care."

I thanked her for the encouragement, but I wasn't so sure that I could be of help any longer—not with the look the Commander had given me.

Chapter 10

LATER, AS I WAS sitting in the sun on a bench in front of the clinic, with my leg up on an old crate, an aging black Buick convertible with its top down drove slowly into the compound. I recognized Dr. Riga Armor sitting tall and stiff in the passenger seat. She looked neither right nor left, but her eyes watched me closely as they passed by.

Her driver, a huge American Indian, hung with silver and turquoise around his neck, wrists, and waist, got out and went into the office. He returned momentarily with Commander Dougan. I couldn't hear their exchange of words, but the Commander abruptly ushered Dr. Armor out of the car and into the building. The big Indian stood at the door as sort of a sentry.

I put my leg down and gathered my crutches to walk the short distance over to the man. "Howdy," I said, coming pretty close to saying "How."

The Indian looked me up and down and returned his stare to the distance. I recognized his profile from a cigar store statue I had seen as a kid.

"Very impressive," I said as I took a close look at his jewelry. It must have weighed several pounds in total. "It's beautiful."

He looked at me with serious eye-to-eye contact and said, "Move on."

Surprised, I straightened up from the close look I had been giving his silver ensemble and said lamely, "OK." The tone of his voice sounded like he might kick the crutches from under me if I didn't comply immediately. I went back to my bench to wait for what might be coming down, following Dr. Armor's visit.

A few minutes later, she came out of the office without comment. She bunched her long skirt together in front to get back in the car, and the Indian held the door for her. They drove off in a quiet, regal manner, bumping up and down the ruts in the road.

My curiosity was too strong to sit patiently. I got myself up again and went over to the office. The door had been left open, and I could see the Commander sitting in the semi-light, puffing on a big cigar that he had just lit. He was obviously in deep thought, and so I turned to leave, but he saw me and waved his hand. "Come on in, Van Alan. I'm not going to bite you."

I made my way slowly around the counter and sat down in front of his big desk. "Is *she* going to give you trouble?" I asked.

"You could say that," he said. Then after a little pause, he added, "She's about to charge me with looting and breaking into and destroying archaeological sites. The Park Service is calling this kind of thing a crime and is committed to finding those responsible and bringing them to justice. They recently convicted and sentenced a man to six and a half years in jail and a forty-thousand-dollar fine."

"Wow, can you get her to back down?"

"It's not going to be easy. She's got the law on her side, and she knows how to use it."

"What's her price?" I said.

"Bottom line, she wants the camp to relocate." He shifted his weight in his seat. "Apparently, we're sitting smack dab on a bounty of antiquities. We're in the way of what they call 'historical enlightenment.' And with a hundred boys milling around here and there, kicking up ancient relics and climbing the cliffs rich in historic art, we are a menace to archeologists. The lady's going to use her influence to get us out ASAP. In her mind, we've been here too long—if we stay the rest of the day."

"Would the Park Service offer another site and money to help you relocate?" It seemed only right that the camp should be compensated for the expense of finding land and moving to new facilities.

"I doubt it," he said. "The government never seems to have enough money to carry out its own priorities. I doubt that they would have anything in their budget to offer us. They don't have to either. The law says they can move in and take over. And, if they did happen to have land that they might trade with us, it's bound to be out on the open prairie, nowhere near protected from the wind and storms like we have here."

"What do you plan to do?"

He sighed. "I don't rightly know, but I'm not of a mind to fight it much. I probably need to call Camps with Kids in New York, I guess, and tell them we need some added assistance. They foot the bills. Maybe they'll have some ideas."

I thought of Miss Abrams sitting in her office with the blown-up pictures of children of every race and color hanging on her walls. Maybe her boss could offer some kind of help. It didn't look like the Commander had many alternatives.

Tracy popped her head in the door. "I saw the Dragon Lady driving away with Geronimo at the wheel. What did she have to say?"

Commander Dougan gave her a rundown of his meeting, while Tracy stood and listened with a frown on her pretty face. He sounded more depressed, the more he talked.

"We might get a lawyer to handle things," he suggested. "He could develop a whole series of delaying tactics, but the government's power of eminent domain is likely to be too powerful for us to fight in the end." He looked up at Tracy. "What do you think?"

Tracy pulled up a chair to the desk and sat down. She looked very disappointed, but her manner seemed peaceful. "Why don't we just pray about it right now," she said as she folded her hands on her lap.

I glanced at the Commander to see his reaction. He was all ready to go with it. As for me, being a nonpracticing Jew, I was taken aback by the unexpected suggestion of prayer in the middle of our meeting. Tracy immediately began to speak to God, so I dutifully bowed my head, as Tracy had done.

"Oh, Heavenly Father," she started, with a heartfelt approach. "We come to You for wisdom and direction because we are truly unable to handle this situation which confronts us. You know that we have been ordered to pull up our tent stakes and find a new location for Camp Sage and Sand after so many years of working in this place to help turn boys into men. We love this very piece of land where You have placed us, but the government wants it now for its purposes. Show us what to do about this situation, Lord, and make things happen that will benefit these kids and fulfill Your perfect will in all of us. And, Father, we ask this in the name of Jesus Christ, our Savior. Amen."

The Commander said, "Amen."

I just remained quiet, mulling over the way Tracy had spoken to the God of Abraham, Isaac, and Jacob. She had made a clear plea without judging anyone, and her words had been so lovely that I was stricken with remorse that I had never been able to talk to God like that. She just went and spoke with him. I noted also that she had not given him any suggestions as to what He should do, unlike me who would have listed His choices.

After a moment of looking at each other, the Commander broke the spell. "That Dr. Armor has given us only one week to get back to her—or she promises to come back with the Park Rangers to find out why. She apparently carries a lot of clout, even as a consultant, and she obviously enjoys using it. For the life of me, I don't know what to do first."

I reminded him that he talked about calling New York. He agreed, even though we all knew that they were too far from the scene to help much, except perhaps if we were lucky, to offer us a little money to either hire an attorney or pay for our move.

I hobbled back to the clinic with Tracy while the Commander put in his call. Despite the clear possibility that she would have to undergo something her parents had spent years staving off, she was quite cheerful. I was surprised and told her so.

"Once you give your problems over to the Lord Jesus," she said, "there's nothing more to do than to sit back and enjoy the ride. You wait and see. He'll come up with something so 'out of the blue' that you'll be amazed. I can't wait to see what He's going to do now that He's working on it."

As for me, I saw her attitude as using prayer to get out of doing the real work when the going gets tough. My theory has always been to dig in and get the upper hand—or at least figure out the best compromise to come out ahead. "Don't you think it would be a good idea if you and I were to go into town and find the doctor, herself, and come up with a mutual agreement in which the Park Service and our camp would share the land? They could do their digging, and we could continue to teach our boys."

"No, it's out of our hands now. Not until we're given some clear direction. I'm sure you don't want to have the same thing happen as when you tried to fix the marijuana problem, do you?"

She had me there. "No, of course not. Would you have prayed about that too?"

"Yes, and as a matter of fact, I did."

"Well, it didn't work out very well for us, though, did it?"

"I don't think the entire incident is over yet," she said.

I had to agree, since the score was still Camp 0, Police 0.

The Commander came and stood in the open door of the clinic. "I talked to that Miss Abrams, up there at ENDCO headquarters. She promised to give all the particulars to her managers, but she said that usually in circumstances such as these, there is very little they can do to help out, unless it involves their insurance policy. But, personally, she also recognizes they are responsible for us—even if they have to oversee closing us down.

○◉○

After lunch, I lingered in the empty mess hall with the Commander. The clatter of glasses and plates and banter from the workers in the kitchen provided a steady background noise.

"What would it take to move the camp to a new location?" I asked.

"Not much," he said. "You should see this place when we close for the season. With the tents down and stored, it's pretty barren. The only real property is this big adobe blockhouse we're in now. It's crumbling and old, and the plumbing is about shot. There's no value in it."

"So, if we did find another location, perhaps we could move without much disruption," I offered.

"Affirmative, with one exception," he said. "Finding a suitable area with water would be our major need. Right now, I know of no other location within miles of here that has anything like our river here that we could build even a small pond for swimming."

I could see the problem. I had never been in a place as dry as this in my life. But then, I had never been out of New York before.

The Commander slugged down a last gulp of coffee and stood up. "Guess I'd better git to it," he said.

He took his cup to the kitchen, and the level of noise went up a couple of decibels as he talked to each worker, probably patting them each on the back.

I sat where I was, realizing that I was slowly finding myself being assimilated into this diverse family that had come together in the desert West to take low-paying jobs in order to reach out to a bunch of struggling junior-highers needing a healthy outlet within a very poor culture. The Commander intimidated me, the nurse encouraged me, the police bothered me, and the kids scared me. I had similar problems back East, except no one really cared much about me. I wondered if, somehow, I could eventually make a difference here.

Back at the office, a youngster was sitting at my computer, picking out something with one finger. He was about ten years old. His jet-black hair was filled with tumbleweed stickers, and he didn't smell too good, but he was going about his task with intensity, his little tongue sticking out of the corner of his mouth.

He glanced up momentarily. I thought he might run, so I said, "It's OK. Go ahead. What are you writing?"

He paid no attention and kept tapping out each letter on the keyboard. I came around and looked over his shoulder. It was a letter to his mom. I was intrigued at his ability to use a computer at his age rather than scribble with pencil on paper.

It read, "Deer Mommy. I lots of fun. I swin. Come see me. I love yu. Carlos." He looked up with a satisfied smile on his face and then pressed the print key and waited for his manuscript to come forth.

"Where did you learn to use the computer?" I asked.

"School."

"Do you know how to write with a pencil?"

"Sure, but I don't like to."

"I can see that."

He pulled the printed page out and held it close. As he started to leave, I said, "Do you want me to put it in an envelope?"

He handed it to me, and I rummaged around the Commander's desk, looking for an envelope. Then I sat down with a pen in my hand and said, "OK, what's your address?"

"I don't know," he said.

"Well, how were you going to send it to your mother?"

"I wasn't." He had this sweet innocent look on his face.

I put down the pen, folded his letter neatly into the envelope, and handed it to him. "There you go," I said. "I think your letter is very good. You can use this computer anytime to write to your mother."

He took the envelope and gave me a grin. It did something down deep to see that beautiful dirty face smile at me. Then he turned and ran outside, using his letter to fly in the wind like an airplane.

Chapter 11

THE THREE OF US took off the next day to scout out possibilities for a new site for Camp Sage and Sand. Not that we had any kind of plan, but we couldn't just sit idly without considering the inevitable move. The Commander was not going to fight it, and Tracy had turned it over to God. Commander Dougan took us in his SUV along the highway north of Cortez in hopes of spotting a canyon where there might be water. We were looking for any area not too far from town that appeared even remotely inviting.

I was entranced by the barren, maybe even hostile environment of this country. The hot sun pounded the outside of the car and occasionally blinded our eyes as it reflected off the metal. Here and there were scattered weather-beaten homes, many with one or two junked vehicles rusting in the yard.

"I don't know what we're doing out here," Commander Dougan said out of frustration. "Even if there was something of interest, I can't see that we could afford the land prices that they're getting now."

As we sped along, Tracy suddenly sat up and pointed ahead at a turnoff down the road. "Turn there!" she shouted.

Our hearts leaped as the Commander braked with lightning speed, skidding across the road in a desperate attempt to pull into an old side road without turning the car over. Once he came to a halt and stabilized us, he turned to her. "Are you trying to get us killed?" he said with exasperation written all over his face.

"I know this place! See?" she said excitedly, pointing to a crumbling wooden sign that was close to falling off its post. "I remember this is the same place my parents brought me years ago, and that's the sign they followed."

I could just make out the words "Ghost Town," but that was about all.

"What place?" the Commander asked as we started to bump along the potholed road toward a large outcrop of red sandstone boulders in the distance.

"It's an old town ... well, not a real town, actually. But here's the story: Back in the thirties, a Hollywood picture company came and built a movie set to film *The Last Sundown* with Gary Cooper. You know the famous actor? The producers went all out to make it authentic and hired the locals here to play the warring Indians who storm the town in the final scene. When the film was done, the company left all its fake buildings and main street to fall into ruin. Well, this young man and his wife from the production crew thought the place could be made into a tourist attraction close to Cortez, and so they bought the land from the film company for practically nothing, and turned it into a tourist ghost town."

"How did they do?" I said.

"Good at first. When the movie was fresh in everyone's mind, people came out to see the old town. Then, as the moving picture faded into memory, and the man and his wife got older, they had to depend on word of mouth and what little advertising they could do to get people to come.

"Eventually, she died, and that's when my parents brought me out here. The old man had gone into serious depression, and various people told the mission that he needed some kind of help. My father wanted to see what he could do to move him into town and get him a job or at least health care."

"What did you find when you got here?"

"It was like people said. I remember the man was very pale, and his hair was all white and uncombed, and his clothes were dirty. He scared me. I thought he was the ghost himself."

The Commander was being practical. "What do you want us to do here today?"

"Well, nothing, I guess. We're looking for a place for the camp. Maybe this old town could be a place to start. Who knows, maybe it's for sale. And, actually, I'm kind of curious to see what's happened to it since I was here last."

It was only a short two miles from the main road. As we approached the ghost town, we could see an overhead timber entrance that was partially fallen, a ticket booth, and a series of buildings beyond. We drove past the gate and stopped in an area once set aside for visitor parking.

"It's really authentic now," I said.

The hot wind carried some tumbleweeds across the road, and a small dust devil turned up a storm off to the side.

We left the cool of the air-conditioned SUV and started to walk the old street. I was handling my crutches pretty well by this time, putting more weight on my cast. An old wooden boardwalk ran the entire distance of the town on both sides, but we elected to stay in the dust for fear it would no longer hold our combined weight. The false buildings stood weather-beaten but proud. Doorways sagged, and broken glass littered the ground. Most of the paint was faded, but there was no doubting the intent of the set. We passed a barbershop, a sizable saloon, a two-story hotel on the first corner, an apothecary shop, a dress shop, and another saloon. I was fascinated by the town and how real it must have looked in the movie. Up close, it was obvious, however, that the storefronts were just that. Most of the windows, which were probably once adorned with lace curtains, were missing their glass and showed only the brown prairie through them.

There appeared to be no possible life left in the old town—or water to sustain it. A well at the end of the street went down only six feet and had never brought up water in its old bucket. The livery stable had long since been emptied of its horses, but a beat-up old car now sat in the corral. Its Colorado license plates were up to date, and we were amazed to see something so modern among all the relics of the past.

Next door, the country store seemed to have a bit more depth to it than the others. Out of curiosity, Tracy opened the door and called inside. "Hello? Is anyone here?"

Only the wind spoke back. Then, we all heard a muffled voice answer, "In here."

We crowded close together into the store with its rough, wide planking, hoping that it would hold us. Tracy called again, "Hello," this time a little louder.

We could hear some shuffling in the back, somewhere past the counters and tables that were strewn with junk, paper, and a heavy coating of dust. Suddenly a form appeared in the doorway against the light—short, white-haired, and ancient. We all knew at once the old man was still alive. Here he was, some twenty years later, probably well over ninety years old.

Tracy walked over to him. "We're just visiting the town today and saw your car. We didn't know anyone lived here anymore."

"The town's closed," the man said. "There's nothing for you to see."

"Of course," she said. "Now, are you all right? Can we get you anything?"

"No, No. I'm doing just fine. Thank you."

He moved spryly toward us. I was amazed at how healthy his skin color was. Obviously, he didn't worry about staying out of the sun. His eyes had a glint in them that showed he didn't take life too seriously. He seemed extremely friendly, for living the life of a hermit. "Don't see many people out here nowadays," he said with a smile. "What brings you out this way?"

Tracy said, "I was the one who wanted to turn here as soon as I recognized the place." She looked up at the Commander. "This man was good enough to oblige." She turned to us. "I'd like to introduce Commander Elliot Dougan and Melvin Van Alan, and I'm Tracy Palmer."

"The name's Pete," the old man said. "Peter Mays."

"I don't know if you remember my parents, Arthur and Edith Palmer? They brought me to visit you when I was just a young girl. They ran the mission in Cortez."

He thought a long minute. "Of course," he finally said. "I was just about ready to pack it in when they showed up. You could say they saved my life."

Tracy was thrilled. "They did? I'm so happy to hear it."

Commander Dougan looked concerned. "How are you doing now, old man?"

"Real proper," he said. "Real proper." He was silent as if the past had overtaken him. Then he perked up. "Say, do you all want some lemonade? I just made it up fresh."

We were all very thirsty.

Pete led us to where he lived in the back of the store.

When I saw his room, I was amazed how neat it was, having expected him to be living alone in some kind of squalor. "Nice place you have. You look quite comfortable," I said.

"I get along very well, and no one bothers me anymore," he said.

The Commander asked, "What do you mean? Because the ghost town closed?"

"No, siree," Pete said. "I mean none of them government people come sniffing around anymore. They finally left and didn't come back."

I took a long drink from my full glass of lemonade. It was made with real lemons and plenty of sugar. I couldn't remember having had such a refreshing glass. "What was their problem?" I asked.

"They was trying to put me out of here. Said I was encroaching on public land. They was fixing to tear down the buildings and return the place to the pristine splendor of the native country, as they called it. I'd call it barrenness." He smacked his lips as he took a long swig of his lemonade.

"What did you do then?" Tracy asked.

"Right here, missy." He patted a metal strongbox on the table. "Here was my answer to them. The BLM Merger Act of 1946. That was when the US Grazing Service and the General Land Office came together to form the Bureau of Land Management. Before the merger, I was already long since grandfathered on this land, so they couldn't do a thing about it."

The Commander had been listening intently. "So, basically, you stood up to the federal government and got them to back down."

"You got it," Pete said. "I didn't have to take it to court or nothing. They didn't have a leg to stand on, and they knew it. I was able to produce a title that gave me the rights to continue forever on these here ten acres, including the water rights. It's made out to the Vista Picture Studios and signed and sealed by the original Land Office. I got ten years on them before they even thought of setting up their BLM.

I had read somewhere that the Bureau of Land Management had charge of millions of acres of land west of the Mississippi. Its purpose was to keep cattle and sheep grazing and logging and mining in some kind of order for general recreation and wildlife refuges. I wouldn't have thought that ten acres made much difference to them.

"Do you think they had some other reason to put you off the land?" I asked.

"Sure," Pete said. "I'm right on their eastern border here. They was looking to extend it, and I was in the way."

"So you got them to back down?" The Commander was quite taken by the concept. I could see the wheels turning in his mind.

Pete pulled out a big album from his bookcase. "You want to see something that'll give you a kick?" he said. He opened the book and showed us an old photo of a young man standing next to a cowboy and his horse.

"You know who this is?" He proudly pointed to the young man. He giggled with an old man's squeaky laugh. "That's me with Gary Cooper."

We all crowded around to see the fading image. Peter Mays was definitely a good-looking fellow, standing almost as tall as the handsome young Gary Cooper. He had that same smile and twinkle in his eyes that were still visible on the old man's face today. "I was what they called a grip, and I actually played several bit parts in the movie," he said. "I'll never forget the fun we had that summer. But, Lordy, was it hot!" He looked serious for a moment, but then he brightened. "That's where I met Ginnie. She and me got to going together, and we never stopped after that."

Tracy asked, "Do you have a photo of her?"

"Glad you asked," he said. On the very next page, there was a snapshot of the young couple. This time, Pete had on a cowboy hat and western shirt and pants, and Ginnie wore a tight-fitting checkered dress with a silver gun in her hand.

For the next few minutes, we looked at old photos taken during the making of *The Last Sundown*. A wave of nostalgia got to all of us as we shared the good times that Pete had enjoyed so many years before. Later photos showed the early successes of the ghost town and crowds walking the main street, carrying cotton candy and bags of popcorn, as they inspected the movie set and had their pictures taken in the jail.

"You folks want a tour of the town?" Pete said hopefully.

"Thank you, but I guess we'd better be on our way," the Commander said kindly. "But we appreciate your hospitality."

Tracy put her arms around the old man and gave him a hug. "My parents thought you were a special person. I remember them talking about you."

"So were they," Pete said. "I'll never forget them. Are they still in Cortez?"

"No, they were killed a little over a year ago. I'm sort of in charge of the mission now."

"Oh, too bad, too bad," he said. "I'm very sorry."

"If you ever need anything, will you call me at the mission?" Tracy said. "I would be here in an instant."

"Thank you, missy," Pete said. "I'll keep that in mind. I got quite a few old friends who look in after me and help out with the things I need, so I'm not all alone. But I keep my will in the strongbox there, and you never know when it's going to have to be opened and read. I want to be buried next to Ginnie out there in the town cemetery next to the church. Take a look at it when you go by."

On that note, we moved back through the store and into the hot sun. The air-conditioning in the car would be very welcome. How Pete could stand the heat and the loneliness out here, I could not imagine, but after seventy years, it was probably second nature to him.

We drove slowly past the little cemetery with the wrought iron fence and looked at the headstones. No telling how many were fake and which one was for the real Ginnie. It had been an interesting meeting with a spry old man who had faced down the federal government agents so he could continue to live in peace. It was a lesson to think about.

○◉○

THE COMMANDER COULDN'T CONTAIN himself as we returned on the bumpy road to the highway. "I feel like a totally different person suddenly. If an old man like Pete can face down the federal government, there's no reason I can't—and that goes for all of us. I tell you, I'm pumped, as the kids say! That Dr. Riga Armor better watch her herself. Camp Sage and Sand is going to be staying right where it is."

Tracy and I exchanged grins, and we were pumped too.

When we got back, the Commander immediately started his daily rounds, talking to the counselors and the boys. I could see him shaking hands and patting backs. He was definitely a different person—alive again.

I had started to move my computer out of the office to the clinic when he showed up. He was all smiles. "Leave it there, Van Alan. I want you to get connected to the internet and start researching the American Antiquities Act, and whatever else you can find. We're going to get a handle on what that old battle ax used for her authority to try to force us off our land. I'm through being intimidated just because I don't know the regs."

The phone rang, and he turned from the counter to answer it. I tried to mind my business, but the Commander was so loud that the conversation was far from private. It didn't take me long to grasp that someone was calling to report that Marcus Dry Cloud was fully conscious at the hospital and was telling the police about the marijuana he had with him in the car crash.

When the Commander hung up, he said, "Well, it looks like you're off the hook. Marcus has talked, and the police have released you from suspicion of drug possession."

"That's great," I said. "Did Marcus reveal anything about the stash here at the camp?"

"They didn't say, but you can bet that's their next question."

I was still embarrassed by the incident that had kept the police from finding the stuff in Marcus's tent, so I didn't say more. On the bright side, I realized that I was free now to leave the camp and the hot southwest Colorado sun. I had a momentary feeling of the freedom it would bring. But, despite myself, I had become more involved in the success or failure of this place than I had expected, and now I wanted to be in on how everything would turn out. I silently resolved to try to be a better camper and pull my share of the load.

For the next couple of hours, I searched the web through a telephone hookup for anything that would shed some light on how Camp Sage and Sand could defend itself against the charges that Dr. Armor had leveled against us. It appeared that the mere presence of ancient artifacts in and about private land could easily trump the desires of the owners if there was any claim on the part of archeologists to take over the site. The US Department of the Interior had the final say as to who would ultimately occupy the property.

I reported what little I had found to the Commander. With a smile that made me think something was up, he said for me to be ready to report at a meeting he was setting up with all the counselors in the mess hall immediately following the evening meal.

For the rest of the afternoon, I went back and lay down in my room to get the weight off my aching leg. I realized that I had been on the go since early morning, and my leg was feeling the increased activity.

Chapter 12

We had sloppy joes, coleslaw, and pineapple in Jell-O, followed by watermelon for supper. Most of the boys went back for additional helpings of everything. The thing I observed was that the mission made it a point to provide as many helpings as anyone wanted. I asked Tracy about it, and she said that her parents had done everything possible to make the camp a place where every kid loved to come and stay. Even though the more secular Camps with Kids organization had taken over much of the financial burden, donations were still arriving from churches and individuals so that, in addition to skills training, teaching the Gospel to the children of the American Southwest would continue.

I had never been involved in any kind of church camp, so I wasn't aware of the work they did or even the reason for their being. In the short few days since my arrival, I saw little to suggest that I was in the middle of a bunch of Christians—nor had I been pressured to become one of them. So far, no one seemed to be concerned about my Jewish background.

As soon as the hall was cleared of stragglers and the kitchen staff was busily washing and stacking dishes behind the swinging doors, the Commander clinked his half-full coffee cup to get our attention. There were ten of us ready to hear what our leader had to say about the future of Camp Sage and Sand.

"I've called you all together to map a war strategy for our very existence," he started ominously. The military man was coming out in him. "Either we stand against those who would try to force us from these sacred forty acres—or we face extinction. We have no alternatives. There is no obvious place for us to go where we can accommodate at least a hundred young men with the same fine facilities that we have come to need and expect. We would simply have to shut down.

"Now, I believe within this small body is the makings of a plan of attack that will culminate in victory, if we do not allow ourselves to waver or be intimidated. I believe that all of you have been fully updated to the facts that we must deal with. Right now, I want us to start by synergizing our ideas and come up with a step-by-step battle plan for the future of Camp Sage and Sand."

He flipped the cover of a large pad of white paper on an easel and took up a marker pen. "Let us be clear about our objective." He wrote the word "Objective," and followed it with, "Keep CSS in its present location and establish future growth."

We all sat there silently mesmerized by the words of the paper.

"Come on. Come on," he coaxed. "Start giving me whatever pops into your brains."

Tracy was first. "Write the Interior Department."

The Commander wrote down, "Write USDI."

Steve said, "Hire a lawyer."

I offered, "Start a PR campaign." I thought our original idea of getting the public involved had a fair chance of slowing down or halting a bureaucratic steamroller.

"Have a joint meeting to stake out areas of responsibility."

The Commander said, "You mean, the camp would be restricted to one place and the archeologists to another?"

"Right."

The Commander wrote, "Restricted areas."

"Start fundraising."

The Commander wrote it down, sticking it just below "Hire Lawyer."

"Appeal to our congressman."

"Get a petition started."

We ran out of ideas pretty fast. There didn't seem to be many alternatives to choose from.

"All right. Now that we have these thoughts, let's prioritize them," the Commander said.

Tracy said, "I like the public relations angle. If people knew about the camp and saw the good work that we do, I think they might be willing to sign a petition or call our congressman. There must be some way for us to get people out here to see what we're doing—and maybe even get involved."

Steve said, "Maybe folks would come visit us if we had a good country and western band or something."

That seemed like a good idea to me. I knew of only one band, but it had broken up. That reminded me, however, that they had written and recorded the signature song of the latest craze in kid's TV programming. I knew the creator and animator of this phenomenal cartoon character whom I had last worked with in New York about three years before. *Magic Mike* was on par with the wildly popular *Captain Kangaroo,* which I had adored when I was growing up. Mike's cartoon adventures, created by my friend Eric Rogers, was already into reruns every afternoon on national TV and had just filmed a feature movie that was expected to make all kinds of money. To add to that, a newly produced *Magic Mike Show* was touring the country, making a big hit with both kids and adults.

I thought about what a great idea it would be to have Magic Mike visit our camp. The kids would go bananas—and so would the townspeople. Yet, right now I was a little shy about mentioning Eric's show for fear that I would be raising hopes of something that would probably be impossible to pull together. It would be a huge long shot to ask Eric to bring his cartoon characters all the way to Colorado on such short notice, especially to our little camp.

The Commander seemed to be pleased with our feeble efforts to think of ways to combat what we feared might be the inevitable end to the camp. He told us that we had given him some good routes to follow up for now. By his take-charge attitude throughout the meeting, I could tell that he had not forgotten Pete Mays at the ghost town, and like the old man, he wasn't going to go down without a fight either.

○◉○

I was anxious to call Eric as soon as possible at home, but my cell phone was completely out of range at the camp, so I waited to phone him from the office the next morning. I hoped that he would remember me. After all, I had been a part of the professional team behind the plan to go national with the *Magic Mike Show*, featuring all the cartoon characters he created from his local TV program. I had even been fortunate to capture a super spread in *Parade Magazine* with several color photos.

His secretary did recognize me and said that Eric was on the road somewhere in Illinois. She looked up his schedule of appearances to see if the traveling show might be in the western United States in the next few weeks. Unfortunately for us, once the show left St. Louis, their next appearance was to jump to Los Angeles, with a week off for travel and maintenance.

It had been more than I could have ever expected to have the show come to Cortez anyway—a little western town of eight thousand people. I don't know what I was thinking. I had gotten caught up in the excitement of the day, believing that I somehow might have a part in the rescue of this forsaken camp. The fact that I was from back East and knew a few people had clouded my mind to the reality of the situation.

I saw Tracy coming back from the swimming pool, and she looked really great. Her hair was still dripping around her shoulders and down her white bathing suit, and she wore a bright red towel around her waist. I watched her walk as she approached. Despite her high wedge sandals, she easily navigated the deep ruts as she crossed the roadway, hopping lightly from one flat spot to another. I thought how graceful she would look walking on Park Avenue in a light summer skirt instead of a colored towel. She had the deftness and assurance of a model.

When she saw me sitting outside the clinic, she smiled and waved, and for the first time I can remember, my heart actually skipped a beat. I mean, I couldn't believe it! She really seemed to be glad to see me!

I was probably grinning a bit too much when she sat down beside me.

"Whew," she said. "That's quite an uphill walk. I must be getting out of shape."

"Your shape is perfect," I said.

"Oh, you know what I mean," she laughed.

"I used to swim quite a bit a few years ago," I said. "I would love to be able to now, except for this heavy cast."

"I know. It must be hot in there." She gave it a tap.

"Luckily, not that bad. I'm trying one crutch a bit, and hopefully I can put more weight on it soon."

She looked closer and said with some surprise, "Somebody's written on it. Who did that?"

"That kid, Carlos. I helped him write a letter to his mother on my computer. He told me that it was bad to have a pure white cast. He took a marking pen and proceeded to write something and then drew this thing with wings."

Tracy turned her head at an angle and read, "'Angels are real.' Isn't that nice. That's an angel he drew."

I kind of smiled at the whimsy of the idea. "I wonder what he meant by that?" I said.

"You'd be surprised. Some of these kids are very special—I mean in a spiritual way. They're very secretive about it, but they've actually told me about having visions and hearing wonderful music. And, yes, some have said they've seen angels hovering over the camp."

That amused me. This would be the last place that I would figure angels would hover. Good grief. In my mind, this place wasn't very spiritual. There wasn't even a chapel. A chaplain came out only on Sunday mornings, to give a short Bible talk in the mess hall. I didn't expect these kids to have much religion, except maybe that of their native tribe. "Do you think some of them might be on peyote?"

"Who knows? I didn't even realize they had been hiding marijuana. It seems you were the first adult to discover that fact," she said.

"I don't know these kids. You would think that they should be mostly into food, swimming, horses, and softball, in that order," I said. "But there's no denying that something seems to be going on here. For instance, the amount of marijuana I saw was far greater than any kid or group of kids could afford to possess. Where would they ever get that much? Maybe one of the counselors is using them to deal."

"Absolutely not! I know them all, and none of them would do such a thing," she said. "It's got to come from the outside."

"Well, since the police raid didn't turn up anything except what the dogs picked up from the scent, let's hope that the pot is on the way out of here," I said.

"Yes, let's hope," she agreed.

The Commander came storming up. His face was red. "That woman! She's a witch, and you can spell that with a capital B," he fumed. "She calls me and says that she's been talking to some of the preservationists at Mesa Verde, and they're all excited about their new acquisition. Their *acquisition*—can you believe it? She was planning on bringing some of them here on an exploratory visit this afternoon, and I told her she could just go to you know where. They would not be welcome, and I would consider them as trespassers if they so much as set their foot past the gate."

I thought, *So much for our public relations campaign.*

Tracy backed up my thoughts. "You're not going to get anywhere acting that way."

"I know, I know," he said. "She just makes me so blamed mad with her superior high-and-mighty attitude. She doesn't even work at the cliff dwellings anymore. What she wants is to get a big fee for reeling us in after all these years, and I'm just not going to let it happen."

I tried to pacify him. "All the more reason to get the public on our side by showing them how the camp impacts their community in positive ways. When they see what the boys enjoy out here all summer without getting into trouble, we might double the number of boys who want to come."

He asked me then what I would suggest to bring the public out here.

At the present, I didn't have much to offer. "I've been sitting here thinking about it, and I'm going to put out a few feelers. If you approve, I might even call Miss Abrams to see if there is any money to put on an open house—perhaps with some fireworks and some local talent. Do you know if any of our boys can do anything special? We might just have a big talent contest to pick the best entertainer in the Four Corners. What do you think?" I was just winging it.

"These are just little guys," he said. "They wouldn't know talent if it bit them."

Tracy stepped in. "Don't underestimate them, Commander. Some of them might surprise us. We should at least talk to them and see if we don't get some reaction."

"OK by me. Why don't you make an announcement at noon today? See if anybody comes knocking at your door this afternoon."

"I will," she said. "And, Mel, you be there with me in case we have any takers. I'm going to need your expertise."

I didn't expect much response, but I was more than happy to sit all afternoon with Tracy, since of course, I had the expertise.

chapter 13

Just as we gathered for the noon meal, and grace had been offered by one of the older boys, I got a tug on my shirt. I looked down to see a serious young lad with a note in his hand. I took it and thanked him. The note had a phone number that I didn't know—and to call ASAP.

Once again, I was to be interrupted from a meal, but I figured I best go.

It turned out to be Eric Rogers in some suburb of Chicago. I was really pleased that he had been kind enough to call back so quickly. "Mel," he said with a bright voice, "when I heard you were in Colorado, I couldn't believe my ears. I thought you were permanently tethered in New York."

"Well, yes. I'm pretty amazed myself. It's a different world out here."

"Look, man, I want you to know that I owe you big-time, and I really appreciate it."

"Wow. What for?"

"That feature you got us in *Parade Magazine* opened up all sorts of opportunities," he said. "People started calling from just about everywhere, wanting to book us. Now we can hardly catch our breath between stops. And the crowds have been phenomenal."

"I'm so happy for you, Eric. You deserve the best."

"What can I do for you, Mel? Annie didn't give me any details." I gave him a quick rundown on how our little camp needed a PR makeover. I told him that an appearance from Magic Mike could possibly generate a wave of public support for our cause if we played it right. I said that I didn't suppose they could stop on their way to California.

"No, impossible," he said. "We're scheduled tighter than a pair of Hooter's cutoffs." He went on to describe the setup and take-down demands. "If we miss our built-in maintenance time, we're likely to fall apart."

"Of course, I understand," I said. "Really, I didn't even think there was any chance you could come."

There was a long silence, and I thought we'd lost the connection. "Now wait a minute, little buddy," he said. "Here's a new idea. I could pull Magic Mike out after St. Louis, along with Sparkle and perhaps Mr. Bob and come sailing past your camp, while the rest of the crew get some R and R. My sister lives in Denver, and I planned to see her and the kids anyway. How far are you from Denver?"

"I have to confess that it's quite a ways." At this point, I crossed my fingers.

"No problemo," he said. "It should be fun to relax in the sun out your way. I need a rest from the pace we've been on. "I know Mike would love it too."

I actually kissed the phone at this point. This was an out-and-out miracle! "Eric, are you sure?"

"Sure, I'm sure. Like I said, I owe you—and I meant it."

"When could you make it?"

He must have consulted his iPhone calendar because there was a moment of silence. "Two and half weeks. You probably want a weekend, right?"

"You bet," I said.

"Good as gold. I'll have Annie confirm by fax."

We didn't have that, but I gave him my email. "You don't know how much this means to us out here in nowhere land. I don't know if you realize that we are just a little camp for boys, but we will be forever grateful."

"It'll be great. Don't expect to put on the dog for us. We're just plain folk."

"Don't worry. I'll reserve a tent for you right away."

He laughed, but I don't think he realized how funny it was going to be if we happened to have a thunderstorm.

○◉○

I got back to the mess hall just as Tracy was winding up her pitch for young talent. From the list she had compiled in front of her, there were apparently some interesting volunteers. My heart was pumping from the unexpected phone call, and I couldn't wait to tell everyone.

I got Tracy to keep the boys a bit longer by whispering in her ear that I had an important announcement.

"Boys, Mr. Van Alan has an important announcement."

I rose and mounted my chair, balancing on one foot so I could be seen from the back. I cleared my throat and said, "Raise your hand if you've ever seen or heard of Magic Mike."

Ninety percent of the boys jumped with glee and raised their hands. Most of the staff looked at each other with questioning glances about who he was. No surprise, I guess.

"Magic Mike is very popular with kids all over the world," I explained. "As you know, when he gets in a tight spot, he can instantly become anyone he wants just by saying a few magic words. So he gets out of a lot of scrapes, and he saves other people at the same time."

I could see the boys were with me.

"Well, I've just had the most wonderful news. Magic Mike is going to come visit our camp in a couple of weeks. Isn't that great?"

The room broke out in cheers and applause.

I glanced down at Commander Dougan, and he too was clapping but staring back up to me with this "what is going on" look.

"We're going to have a super time," I said, and then I got down.

Commander Dougan stood and said, "Dismissed."

Every able camper was up and out the door within two minutes, talking to each other a mile a minute.

The crew at the counselor's table immediately started throwing questions at me.

Finally, the Commander's voice prevailed and everyone quieted down. "All right, Van Alan, what's going on?"

"I'm sorry that I didn't get your permission first," I said, "but I just talked to the creator of *Magic Mike and Friends*. Right now, he's in Illinois with his traveling stage show, and I got him to commit to a Saturday in a couple of weeks to fly out a few of his cartoon characters to be with us. I thought it would be a wonderful way to create some excitement at the camp, and in the community—especially among the kids—and have a big open house at the same time. What do you think?"

"I think it's downright bully," he said. "If these characters are anywhere as appealing as the Disney folks, I couldn't be happier."

Tracy turned and gave me a happy hug, which I really appreciated, and the other guys at the table shook my hand. Everyone was celebrating, but they had yet to realize the huge amount of work that lay ahead.

○◉○

OUTSIDE THE MESS HALL, I was surrounded by some of the lads who had waited to ask me some questions.

"Will we be able to talk to Magic Mike and maybe learn some of his tricks?"

"I hope so." I didn't want to get their expectations up, but knowing Eric, he'd make sure everyone who wanted to talk to his creations would get the chance.

"Do you remember when Magic Mike turned himself into a policeman?" one of the kids asked me.

"I sure do." Luckily, I had actually seen that one. "He took off after the robber and got him cornered down an alley after all the other cops were running the other way. He got all the money back to the bank too, didn't he?"

"Yeah," the cute little kid said. His eyes glistened as he recalled the scene. "How did he change into the policeman so fast?"

"He knows the magic words. Would you like to do that?"

"Yeah, yeah."

One kid added, "I'd be the next pitcher of the New York Yankees."

And one said, "I'd be a marine."

They all had something in mind.

"You can ask Magic Mike how he does it when he comes," I said. "But it may be a secret."

The kids moved off to their next class or whatever, and I got my crutches pointed toward the clinic. I hoped that Tracy would be there.

"You've certainly got the camp talking," she said. She was busy scrubbing the big sink in the main room.

"I hope it turns out to be a good time," I answered. "It seemed like the right thing. What we've got to do as soon as I get a confirmation on the date and times is to figure out the best way to use the cartoon characters to bring the community to us. That's when we can tell them our story and hopefully get everyone to rally around."

"You realize that no one here has any kind of experience putting together something as big as I imagine this could be. Are you ready to lead us?" she asked. She had stopped scrubbing and stood there facing me with her rubber gloves dripping suds.

"No, not really." She had just voiced my concerns. When I hung up the phone with Eric, I was so thrilled. But right after that, I panicked, thinking maybe I had just made a big, big mistake.

"You can do it. I know you can. And I'll help you."

And that's what I had been hoping to hear since I first realized it was going to be my show.

Chapter 14

I NAPPED AFTER LUNCH as deep as if I had not slept for a week. I dreamed about being fourteen again and standing in front of the synagogue at my bar mitzvah. I thought I was well prepared and rather proud of myself, but suddenly my mind went blank. I looked out at the congregation of smiling faces—especially my mother and father. I could see mother forming my leadoff words on her lips, but I couldn't make them out. All eyes were on me, and I was letting them down. I started to sweat, and it poured down my face. Then I realized I was crying. I was fourteen and crying like a baby in front of several hundred people! I wanted to run, but I was rooted in place out of the fear of not knowing what to do next.

I awoke suddenly, still experiencing the residual adrenaline coursing through my veins. I was fully aware what my dream meant. This wasn't the first time, arising from the high tension that came with fear of the future. I could usually come to grips with it when I would remind myself that my actual bar mitzvah had gone extremely well.

My dream was a call to action. I had to get on top of the dragon instead of letting it eat me. After splashing my face in cool water and combing my hair, I went back to the main office to read my email and talk to the Commander, if he was around.

He was on the phone with the parents of a boy who was standing in front of his desk with his head down and his hands behind his back. The Commander was telling them that it was necessary for him to deliver some discipline, and he was asking the father to come in to discuss it.

At first, I did my best to pretend I wasn't there, but since I had to wait until the Commander was free, I returned outside to admire the view.

Even though Camp Sage and Sand was located in a hot and barren part of a beautiful state known more for its impressive mountain ranges and snow-covered ski slopes, it possessed a unique beauty of its own. I spent a fascinating few minutes just looking up at the awesome cliff behind the camp and the multicolored strata that lined its sandstone walls. Various small caves were scattered in its rugged surface. I could see where climbing hooks were embedded to teach self-confidence and satisfy the climbing urge of growing boys as well.

For the first time, I really appreciated how the majestic pinnacle rock overlooked and protected the camp and how the little river that wandered by had been channeled into a wonderfully cool swimming hole below it. Tracy's parents had taken this gift of land many years ago and made it into the oasis where I stood today. They'd had a vision that was their legacy, and Tracy was still part of it. Camp Sage and Sand wasn't the mudhole that I first encountered. It was a truly perfect encampment that anyone could be proud of.

In only a very few days, I was becoming slowly immersed into a new role in life and actually beginning to enjoy it. I was starting to feel at home. The tensions that plagued me in New York City were more distant. The dry heat at the camp had become tolerable, the wilderness and its silence were less frightening, and the young boys were no longer a problem.

Commander Dougan and his disciplinee came out and joined me. "Luis, here, has been fighting with his tentmate, and he's going to be working in the kitchen a few days, aren't you?" the Commander said to Luis, for my benefit.

"Yes, Commander Dougan," he said.

"And, you are going to go right now to apologize to Carl and promise not to give him trouble anymore, isn't that right?"

"Yes, sir."

"OK. Go on. And don't let me hear that you're causing more problems. Are you listening to me?"

"Yes, sir." Luis ran off and didn't look back.

"Do you have much disciplining?" I asked the Commander.

"Surprisingly not. The counselors keep the boys so busy they don't have much time to think about getting into mischief. Oh, of course, there's the usual petty things—they may steal someone's personal stuff—but for this many kids, I'm pretty amazed myself that we don't have more squabbles. The counselors handle most of it unless it gets more violent. Luis here has had more than one run-in, and it's time we stopped it for good.

"Anyways, you're at the top of my list to see," he said. "What's with this Magic Mike, and where do we go from here?"

"I just came over to check my email and get confirmation that my friend Eric has actually given us a date for his show. It's totally awesome that he's willing to stop off here on his way to Los Angeles. I still can't believe it."

"You're going to have to fill me in on these guys. I've never heard of them. But, after seeing the excitement in the camp after your announcement, I'll take your word that this is a good thing."

I assured him it was as I led him back inside and over to my computer. It took a couple of minutes to log on and call up my email. I had only one message sitting there, and it was from magicmikeandfriends.com. The message read:

> Confirming Eric Rogers's conversation with Melvin Van Alan. Add new show date to schedule. Camp Sand and Sage; Cortez, Colorado; Saturday, July 4. Eric Rogers, Mike King (Magic Mike), Bob Banner (Mr. Bob), Michelle Nelson (Sparkle), and Daryl Wyatt (audio/electrical). Request three (3) nearby motel rooms, two nights, for performers, Friday, July 3 and Saturday, July 4. Electrical hookup needed at camp for Eric's RV and Daryl's audio/electrical unit RV. Sending stage dimensions and layout requirement, plus promotional materials for local rollout by Express USPS today. Show fee is $5,000 (for nonprofit camp). Call or email any questions Regards, Annie.

I was doubly excited when I realized that Eric had scheduled us on July 4. He was probably giving up his own holiday. We had not talked money, but five thousand dollars was a drop in the bucket compared to what they got on the road. What a wonderful gift from this creative crew. I was determined that we would make their visit worth their while.

I printed out three copies and gave one to the Commander and saved one for Tracy. We went and sat down to talk it over.

"OK," the Commander said. "What's next?"

"I guess the first question is, Are we going to be able to fund this extravaganza? I can only guess that our up-front costs could reach ten thousand dollars. We can make up some of it in ticket sales at twenty dollars each, if five hundred people came."

"We don't have anything near that in the bank, Van Alan," the Commander said. "We operate on a shoestring."

"Do you think ENDCO would help us finance it?"

"I put in a call to them, but they haven't gotten back to me yet on the camp takeover. I wouldn't expect so. They don't know that much about us out here as yet to put up such a large amount. You could call Miss Abrams yourself since you've met her personally. You might have a winning way with her. Who knows?"

Actually, I did think Miss Abrams had shown some interest in me. I sincerely hoped it would help.

"All right, I'll call her. Let's say we get a go-ahead financially. Eric has given us two and a half weeks to get everything done before his team shows. We're going to need posters and advertising, tickets, build a stage with electrical service, seating, lighting, food, and toilets. And because it's July 4, I think we should plan for fireworks."

"How can we possibly pull all that together in the time we have? Can we do it?" he asked.

"No, but we've got to do it anyway, don't you think?" I let out a huge breath. "It will be dependent on how committed everyone is when they're delegated a job. Can we get a meeting tonight with the key staff?"

"I'll put the call out now for after dinner."

I moved over to put some notes together on the computer, and then I turned back to him and asked, "Are you committed?"

"You can bet I am," he said.

○◉○

MISS ABRAMS WAS STILL in her office late in the day and accepted my call cordially. At the very least, I expected her to give my request a high priority after her invitation to call when I got back to New York.

"Oh, Mr. Van Alan, I'm so delighted to hear from you. Is everything going all right for you out there in Colorado?"

"Yes, it's a rugged old camp. Hot and barren, I must say, but I am beginning to fit in."

"I'm so glad, and are you teaching the young men all about riding?"

I decided not to get into explanations about the mix-up that brought me here. "No, actually, I had a car accident the first day or so, and now I have a cast on one leg. I've gotten into something else quite exciting, though, and that's the purpose of my call."

"How can we help, Mr. Van Alan?"

"Commander Dougan, our administrator, tells me that he has filled you in on some disturbing news that the US Park Service has expressed interest in taking over our location for archeological purposes. As a matter of fact, their consultant has given us one week to show cause why we might not vacate immediately."

"Yes, the Commander did notify us about this distressing matter. What is the current status?"

"We have decided to hold the fort, so to speak, and not comply with their demands. Instead, we plan to defend ourselves by raising up a community effort that we hope will force the Park Service to reconsider their position. We've already made contact with a major kid's show to appear here on tour July 4 and are inviting the townspeople for a big celebration. Our biggest need right now is to get up-front financing to put on a show of this magnitude. Do you think we could count on ENDCO to help us?"

There was a pause on the other side of the line. "How much are we talking about, Mr. Van Alan?"

"We're going to need ten thousand dollars to get us up and running," I said. "We'll be selling tickets, which I believe will cover it. Then the show fee is another five thousand dollars."

Another pause. "Mr. Van Alan, I've had a chance to discuss Commander Dougan's original situation together with General Enders … you know our founder and CEO? Well, he was quite interested in the whole affair, but told me that it would be up to the local camp organization to handle such matters. He is concerned for you, however, and has authorized me to tell you that you have the complete assistance from our legal department as you need it. And I'm certain that our insurance will cover your community open house against any liabilities. But, I'm sorry that ENDCO will not be able to provide additional funds over and above what it already budgeted for your annual camp program."

I was expecting her answer, so I didn't groan. "Thank you for taking our case to the General," I said. "We'll figure something out in the meantime."

"Well, I want to wish you and your workers out there all the success in whatever you come up with," she said. "I would love to be able to see the camp and meet all of you myself."

"Please come anytime—and bring the General. Thank you anyway, Miss Abrams," I said.

She hung up, and I sat there with the phone in my hand. My heart was heavy with knowing what Tracy and her family and the Commander had already invested in this worthwhile venture. In just a short few weeks, I, too, had come to respect these people and the little boys they wanted to mold into responsible men. We were so close to enlightening the community as to the importance of our camp program that I just couldn't see losing this great opportunity. Since I guessed Miss Abrams's answer in advance, I had already come to a decision. Sitting in the Bank of New York, was the eighteen-thousand-dollar inheritance from my aunt. I would simply make those funds available to Camp Sage and Sand, and no one else would be the wiser.

The Commander had taken a bathroom break during my phone call. He was back, and he couldn't wait to hear what had happened. "So, did they go for it?" he said. There was a little smirk on his face, which I could tell meant he considered the call hopeless in advance.

"You'll never believe it," I said with all the excitement I could muster. "They bought it! They thought our idea was worthwhile enough to commit fifteen thousand dollars to our celebration. They totally believe in us out here."

This caught the Commander completely off guard. He literally exploded. "It's a miracle," he hollered, waltzing around with both hands in the air. "That's a huge amount of money to spend on an operation way out in the boondocks like ours. Van Alan, I've got to hand it to you, you've got the Midas touch when it comes to putting together these deals. I don't know how you do it, but thanks to you, we've got a chance to rally the people around here and let them know we've got a cause worth supporting. I can't wait to tell everyone tonight that we are on a roll." Then he put his hand out ahead of him like a train moving down the tracks as he walked around.

After dinner, I handed out a list of jobs to each member with detailed descriptions and deadlines attached. Everyone had congratulated me for swinging the money for the big July 4 event. But, as the eight people attending read the list over, I could see their eyebrows go up and their spirits sink.

Steve asked, "How are we ever going to get all this done in the time we have?"

Everyone stopped reading and looked at me.

"We can do it. I know it looks impossible, but if each of you takes a major activity and follows through by the dates given, it will all come together. I promise you. I've done this kind of thing before. Of course, I usually had two or three months to do it in."

No one laughed at my attempted humor.

"Look, we've just been handed a fantastic opportunity to bring the people out to see Camp Sage and Sand. If we think the support of the locals is what we need to counter the misguided effort to get us moved out of here, this is our chance. Each one of us has to ask himself, 'Do I care whether the camp stays or not? Is our future important to the boys?' If you think so, there's no reason that all of these items can't be accomplished in plenty of time for the appearance of Magic Mike and his friends."

We began to go over the list again. I took the promotional job of advertising, Tracy took ticket sales and hospitality, Steve and Jesus Joe promised to get cracking on constructing the stage and installing electricity, Juan, the kitchen chef, took the food concessions, and I had to find someone to take care of the portable toilets. Within minutes, everyone had their job responsibilities, and the work didn't look as formidable as it had at first.

"What about fireworks?" I asked. "It doesn't seem right to put on a July Fourth show without them."

Tracy said, "The town has fireworks in the park after dark. We need to end our open house early enough so everyone can get back to town."

I was glad about that. Fireworks would be a huge expense. It was one big headache that we wouldn't have to face.

We concluded our meeting by promising to report our progress every two days or so after dinner. I was pleased with the results of our first get-together. Now the reality of success was spread among several others.

Chapter 15

I WAS BEAT AFTER a day of planning the open house. Despite my outwardly optimistic attitude, I wasn't certain it would come off as perfect as I wanted it to. There were still many details that we might not have covered, but right now, I was too tired to think any more.

After lights out, I had my towel draped over my shoulder for a much-anticipated shower as I negotiated the door of the counselor's bathroom. I was glad to see that I was alone so I could have room to maneuver my cast in the space available. After a minute, though, I realized I wasn't by myself. I could hear someone in some kind of difficulty behind one of the toilet doors. At first, there was a low moan, and then it seemed like struggles for breath and more groaning.

I went to the door and tapped on it. "Are you all right? Do you need some kind of help?"

The moaning increased, and then the Commander's voice croaked out, "Van Alan, I'm not feeling very well."

It was a shock to hear the voice of our all-powerful camp Commander in distress. "What can I do?" I asked him.

"I don't know. I'm having terrible chest pains. I'm afraid it's my heart."

My own heart about stopped when I heard that. I couldn't do much on crutches, and if he keeled over in the stall, I couldn't hope to lift him.

"Why don't you unlock the door and let me help you. Maybe if you lay down on the floor, you'd feel better. In the meantime, I'll get Tracy."

He was willing to go with that, probably because he had no better idea than mine. When the door opened, his face was a ghostly white, and I was shocked to see his ruddy features twisted in pain. Slowly, he came off the seat and hitched his pants up, as I guided him forward and down to the floor. He was pressing his hands against his chest. I was so scared that he might suddenly stop breathing, and then I would have to try CPR and beat his chest or something like they did on TV.

I bundled my towel and made a pillow. "Stay right there and be calm while I hurry to get some help," I said. And then I added, "You're going to be OK."

I grabbed my crutches and did a run-hop maneuver across the road.

Tracy's tent was close to the clinic, and there was still a light on inside.

"Tracy, are you awake?" I whispered in a hoarse voice. "The Commander's sick and needs help."

I could hear her rustling, and she appeared immediately at the tent flap in pajamas, holding a big Bible under her arm. "What's the matter?" she said.

"The Commander's in the men's latrine, and he's having some kind of heart attack. I got him to lay down on the floor while I came for you."

"Oh, Lord," she said. She disappeared into her tent and was right back, wearing a sweatshirt and pants over her PJs. She had her battery lantern with her.

"Let's go," I said.

"Wait a sec. Let me get some things from the clinic." She ran to the building and returned with a doctor's bag. She had put a stethoscope around her neck.

She reached the men's bathroom ahead of me, and when I got there, she was kneeling on the floor next to the Commander.

"Tell me what hurts," she said to him, as she got his shirt open and started to listen with the stethoscope.

He described it to her, and she continued to listen to his chest closely. Then she opened her bag and got some pills out and asked me to get some water. Gently, she lifted up his head and helped him swallow the medicine. "There," she said. "I've given you something to help the pain."

She looked up at me. "We've got to get him to the hospital. Go call 911 and tell them not to use their sirens here."

Once again, I did a run-hop on my crutches around the building to the office and the phone. The 911 operator was efficient and helpful and promised an ambulance as soon as possible. She seemed especially glad when I told her there was a medically trained person with the patient.

The guys with the ambulance were also kind and efficient. They bundled the Commander onto a rolling stretcher and loaded him quietly. He was groggy from the medication Tracy had given him. No one at the camp came to inquire about what was going on at the late hour.

Tracy went with them, and I stayed behind to act as a sort of officer on duty in case anyone else needed help the rest of the night.

○◉○

I WAS UP AND dressed very early the next morning to tell the counselors at breakfast what happened to the Commander. Each, in turn, was shocked and saddened by the news. Tracy had not called from the hospital yet, so I took this as a good sign that nothing worse had occurred in the meantime. We had no plans to pass the news of the Commander's health to the campers until we received word of his condition and prognosis.

I had a lot of things to do, and there was no reason to change what had been put into play. I anxiously awaited delivery of Annie's express package, so that I could get started with placing ads and other publicity for the show. Two weeks was pitifully little time to advertise our open house and get the public excited. I had to depend on the popularity of Magic Mike to make it happen.

Finally, the mail truck showed up about nine o'clock that morning, bringing a huge box stuffed with everything I needed to get the show on the road. It included promo tapes for radio and TV coverage, news stories and features, ready-to-imprint posters of various sizes, display ads, street banners, background articles on the show and its performers, photographs, ticket samples, direct mail flyers, and much more. I was totally delighted. Some of the materials I had actually created myself, back when Eric Rogers was one of my clients. My hard work then was paying off royally now.

What I desperately needed was for someone to get me into town, but I knew that if Tracy returned, she would be ready to crash. All the counselors had heavy responsibilities every morning. I put in a call to Bill Bradford at the paper and hoped he would be available. "Bill, I've got a great story for you," I said to him as soon as he came on the line.

"That's what everyone says when they have a self-serving story they want me to run."

I took it good-naturedly. "Better than 'stop the presses,' don't you think?"

"You've got something there," he said. "What's up?"

"What would you say if I told you Magic Mike was going to be paying us all a visit on July 4?"

"Who?"

"You know, Magic Mike of TV and movie fame? Don't you have any kids around the house?"

"Sorry, I'm a bachelor."

I filled him in with as much enthusiasm as I could dredge up. Pretty soon, Bill got a handle on the cartoon character. At least I hoped he did. Then I told him about the open house we planned and asked him if he would run a big feature story. I promised to take out some pretty big ads to back everything up.

"Get this stuff to me as soon as possible," he said.

That's when I told him I was stuck out at the camp. I invited both him and his advertising manager to come out for lunch and told him I would have everything they needed to fill a few pages. Boy, was I thrilled when he agreed to come and bring a gal by the name of Nicole Wayland with him. I was also hoping that they did printing and might produce our tickets and posters at the same time.

As soon as I hung up, Tracy called. She reported that the Commander was feeling better, having gone through some tests and taken more medication. He had suffered an angina attack, a lack of blood going to the heart, which indicated a possible obstruction somewhere in the coronary arteries. He had had an electrocardiogram that showed no heart damage. She thought he might need an angiogram to see where the blockage was. It looked like he would be in the hospital for a while.

I was relieved there had been no heart damage. "Are you able to come back to camp?" I asked.

"Yes, but I don't have transportation."

I told her that Bill Bradford was coming out at noon, and maybe she could catch a ride with him.

"That's great," she said. "You certainly work fast."

"Just lucky, I guess." I knew the Commander would probably call it a miracle.

Nicole Wayland stepped out of Bill's car first, and then Tracy emerged from the back seat. It was not fair to compare them, but I did. Nicole was in her early thirties, tall, and smartly dressed in tight designer jeans that accentuated her curves and brought out her best. She had a beautiful face, deep brown eyes, and smoothly tanned skin. Her shining black hair was long and pulled back with a turquoise and silver clasp. The rings on her slender finders were also of Navajo silver origin, as was her necklace.

On the other hand, Tracy had thrown on the first thing she could find last night, before she took off in the ambulance. She wore a pair of rumpled cutoffs, and her blouse was mussed. Her hair was not its usual tidy self. She probably had slept on a couch overnight. I felt sorry for her; she looked worn out.

Nicole swiftly came forward and introduced herself before Bill could get out of the car. "Bill told me that you are the genius who has drawn Magic Mike to our little town. You must be very well connected. His is the very hottest in kids shows right now."

"Oh, I know," I said, glad to hear that someone else knew about the cartoon phenomenon. I shook her outstretched hand with the silver and turquoise putting my eye out in the sun. "Your kids must have kept you up to date."

"No, no," she protested with the other hand. "I'm not married. But my neighbor's kids know all about Magic Mike. And, yes, they're wild about him."

Bill came up alongside her. "Nicole has been educating us on the way out here. It seems I should have been much more excited about your call this morning. I guess this is big news for Cortez, so I want to make sure we cover the story right."

"Thanks, Bill. We appreciate that," I said.

Tracy had been standing behind Bill. I was anxious to talk to her. "How's the big guy doing?"

"He's doing fine. More than ready to get back in the saddle. This is his first hospitalization, and he's not taking it very well."

"I can sympathize," I said. "How soon will he be able to get back to his regular duties?"

"It's going to depend on the tests that they're giving him. We'll know pretty soon. He's at least out of the terrific pain he was in last night."

She excused herself to get cleaned up, and I took Nicole and Bill on a brief tour of the camp.

"I've never seen the place, yet I've lived here for most of my life," Nicole said. "On the ride out, Tracy filled me in on how her parents built it after the land was given to them. It's an amazing location, isn't it, Bill?"

Bill had been gazing up at the huge sandstone cliff towering above us. "Absolutely. I'll have to get a photographer out here as soon as possible."

I showed them the swimming pond full of happy plungers, we walked around the playing fields and the tent area, and we ended up back at the administration building. In the meantime, we had stopped to talk to a variety of the little guys. They were respectful and shy, but they answered the various questions put to them. Each said he was very glad to be spending his summer here.

At the office, I pulled out all the promotional materials for a Magic Mike appearance.

Nicole was impressed and promised to give us a good break on the cost of the newspaper ads. Happily, they could print the rest of the flyers, tickets, and posters too. Since she also knew everyone in media in town, she offered to include local TV and radio spots, if I wanted. I was ecstatic not to have to handle it all myself.

Nicole put her hand lightly on my arm. "Enough of this business talk. So, Mel, do you ever get away from this bunch of monkeys to have a life of your own? I'd love to show you around our little town and take you out for a bite to eat," she said with one eyebrow artfully raised.

"I would enjoy that very much."

"Fine. Why don't I get all your costs together, and we can combine business and pleasure over a *Jambe d'agneau, avec polenta cremeuse* at our little French restaurant. Say, tomorrow night at five? I'll show you the town, and then it should be just about time for cocktails."

"A French restaurant, hmm? I'll have to get a ride, but I'll be there." Thankfully, I stopped just short of saying, "With bells on."

"You get a ride into town, and I'll bring you back, how's that?"

"Excellent," I said as I felt the electricity go up my back.

Bill slid a series of sheets forward from the promotional packet. "I've glanced at these articles, and they include practically everything I'm going to need to put together a nice feature for you this Sunday. Did you ever get anything personal from the kids that I can use about the camp?"

I handed him a file of short interviews that I had collected to start my own article. "This is a far as I've gotten."

He scanned them. "Looks interesting. I'll go over what I have and phone you with anything else I need. Besides the feature, we'll run a couple of promos on the open house and a map on how to get here. How are you fixed for crowd control and parking?"

Somehow, I'd failed to cover these items, so I made a note and hoped I could find someone to handle them. I had no idea how many people to expect. It made me wonder how many other critical areas I had forgotten to consider.

Chapter 16

At lunch, Tracy had pulled herself together, but she still looked tired. Nicole was dominating the conversation at our table, so Tracy didn't say much. She seemed to have other things on her mind. Bill was at another table, sitting with some of the older boys, notepad out, asking questions and appearing to have a good time. The boys were putting on a good show for him, and I could see him eating it up.

Our guests didn't stay long. They both had a lot to do to start the wheels turning for us.

After they left, I asked Tracy if there was anything I could do for her as she seemed so preoccupied.

She smiled at me. "I'm all right. The Commander's attack bothered me a lot. He's the rock around here, you know, and if anything happened to him, the camp would fold."

"I can see that," I said. "What about the other counselors, just in case?"

"I don't even want to go there," she said. "No one else has the overall administrative qualities and respect that he has. And we don't have the money to hire a new head. The Commander's been practically giving his services away. He's mostly living on his military pension."

Tracy's parents had started the whole thing. Now it was her responsibility to carry on. She would live with all the guilt if the place ended up closing. I know she felt like she owed it to them, and Camp Sage and Sand had now become her mission in life too.

I looked at her. "Isn't there anything you want to do, you know, just for yourself?"

"This is what I want to do. When I know these kids aren't getting into trouble, when they come here and learn about getting along in life, when they have a place to use up all their energy during the summer … to me, it's a spiritual calling in my life."

I didn't think I had a spiritual bone in my body, so it was hard to appreciate her passion. I was a simple person who had become used to getting on board other's ideas and aspirations because, I guess, I lacked my own. I wasn't exactly a wet noodle, but I had to admit that I'd never really sat down and come up with any of my own set of convictions. I'm afraid at thirty-four, I didn't stand for much, and now listening to Tracy, who was several years younger, I was a little embarrassed about it.

"What difference does it make, though?" I persisted. "This is such a small camp. You only connect with about a fifty or so boys for a little over two months. Maybe they act all right while they're here, but then they go back into the world when it's over. What about the other thousand local boys who don't get to come? Isn't what you're doing here just a drop in the bucket?"

"You don't understand, do you? We aren't responsible for every boy in the Four Corners area. Our job is to make a difference in a few, and then they go and make a difference in a few more. Hopefully it gets passed on. Our Lord only had twelve disciples, but look how many follow him now."

It was still hard for me to see the difference a little camp could make in an entire community when my training was in influencing the masses.

"Think of it as constructing a framework for the future," she continued. "The pieces are fragile. A few get put together, and you hope they stick so you can add a few more. Suddenly, one section breaks off, and you have to start working with them again. Patiently rebuilding, carefully holding it so the glue will stick. Slowly, a bigger framework begins to take shape, and more and more pieces stay in place. You start to get encouraged when you see something good happening. Slowly, the framework hardens and strengthens over time, and it becomes a way of life. Others are born into it and learn to hang on to it. The bigger the framework, the easier it is to add to because it stays up and becomes the accepted way."

Her analogy suddenly helped me visualize what I hadn't thought of before. Like how a few boys could come to camp, enjoy what they found, and go back home and start to live differently. Their positive experience just might affect others, and slowly the whole community benefits. It made sense, but it needed someone with a great deal of patience and perseverance. Something I didn't have. "How long does it take? To build a framework strong enough to hold up?"

"Who knows?" she said. "That's not my concern. I just keep adding to the structure that was started by my parents. We're not the only framework in town, by the way. What we do here gets added to what others are working on, and maybe we will connect somewhere. I pray for that. I pray that my little area of influence will help grow a strong, morally sound society.

I looked at Tracy in a new light. Most people I knew were more interested in what they were going to have for dinner in the short run or the place they wanted to reserve for the next vacation in the long run than pondering deeper and more involved thoughts. She had something about her that I admired, and I wanted to tap into it. "Maybe there's more going on around here than I realized," I said. "Where do these little guys pick up the values you seem to be talking about?"

"From their day-to-day contacts with the staff, the way they're taught to interact, the rules of the game, things like that. Some of them want to go a little deeper. They want to connect on a more spiritual level."

"You mean like smoking peyote and sweat lodges?"

Tracy laughed. "No, silly. Some become involved at home through family traditions, but here we study the Bible and talk about Jesus."

"Really?" I was a little bit skeptical. These were energetic young boys, after all. Where would they get the desire to read the Bible? And I hadn't seen much church going on. "You mentioned Jesus, the great teacher," I said. "I know about Moses and Elijah, but I don't know him too well. We didn't talk about him when I was growing up."

"I know," Tracy said. "Rabbis tend to exclude him. But you realize he was Jewish, and the first Christians were Jewish followers who believed in him."

"I know that you Christians seem to think he was actually the Son of God. I always felt that this was quite a stretch. Where do you get this except—from his own claims?"

"From your own prophets. One said he would be born in Bethlehem, and another said he would be born of a virgin who would call him Immanuel, meaning 'God is with us.' Together with the evidence in his life of miracles and healing, and his resurrection, which was actually seen later by hundreds, we have no trouble having a genuine faith and calling him the Son of God."

"These assertions are new to me. It makes me a little uneasy, but I'm curious enough to attend one of these meetings to see what goes on."

"You're welcome to come. We have them midweek, like tonight in fact. About twenty-five boys gather at the campfire back along the big rock. You've been there, I'm sure—where the men plan to erect the stage for the Magic Mike show.

I had seen the fire ring and some planks in a semicircle. I was interested to see how a half of the boys at the camp seemed to want to learn about things that were a bit more serious than cars and rock music.

We were interrupted in the middle of our conversation by the approach of the dreaded black Buick convertible again. This time, Dr. Riga Armor was alone. The top was up, but as she pulled up alongside us, she rolled down the window, expelling a wave of cool air-conditioning, along with a blast of her perfume. She killed the motor and reached for her camera. "I'm here to make a photo record of the area behind your campground. Don't worry. I won't be long."

"Oh, I'm sorry, Dr. Armor," Tracy said in a highly innocent voice I hadn't heard before. "This is private property, and you'll need a letter of authorization to take photos."

"Well, Tracy, since I'm here, why don't you just scribble a note for me?"

"You'll have to write a letter to the administrator, stating your purpose and the intended dates of your visit. I'm afraid I don't have the authority. And Commander Dougan isn't here right now."

"So I hear," Dr. Armor said. "When will he be out of the hospital?"

Obviously, the good doctor got around. She'd probably heard about the Commander's condition and was trying to take advantage of his absence.

"Hopefully tomorrow," Tracy said.

Dr. Armor turned her attention to me. "And who are you?" she said with a brittle attitude.

"I'm Mel Van Alan, one of the counselors."

"Oh, you must be the New Yorker who's trying to put this poor little camp on the map around here."

"What do you mean?" I asked. This lady was truly amazing.

"I heard you're setting up a kiddie show out here."

"That's true," I admitted, somewhat taken aback.

"You know, you two, this idea of trying to sell this pitiful campground to the public is not going to fly, don't you? The government is not about to allow these children you have out here to continue to desecrate the ground on which lies its national treasures—no matter what you do."

I could see Tracy struggling to hold her temper. "Our boys don't go anywhere near the area in question," she said. "They respect the land as much or maybe more than you do. You know, we should be able to come up with a mutual plan to allow the work of archeologists to operate here, while our boys learn from them—perhaps even help them uncover new discoveries. There's no need to have just one or the other; we can cooperate. You know there's a lot of acreage here to work in."

Dr. Armor gave her a frosty look. All Tracy's good reasoning made no difference with her closed mind. "I'm sorry, my dear. That sounds fine, but it's so naïve. We can't take even the slightest chance that any more artifacts are ruined or destroyed." She started the ignition. "Well, this isn't getting us anywhere. Please remind Commander Dougan that he's got only a few days more to comply with the department order or be closed." She made a slow circle around the parking area and finally left us alone.

"No wonder the Commander gets so riled when he has to deal with her. Does she actually speak for the federal government even though she's acting more or less as a free agent?" I asked.

"She certainly thinks so. I know she still has some pretty close friends at Mesa Verde, so we have to take her seriously," Tracy said.

"Where does she get all her inside information," I asked.

"Oh, she's Nicole Wayland's mother."

"You're kidding! So I'd better be careful what I say at dinner tomorrow. She must be the pipeline to the old bag herself."

"What's this about dinner?" Tracy asked.

I told her how I'd been invited to an evening out at a French restaurant.

Tracy's face clouded. "Well, you operate fast enough."

I held up both hands. "Whoa. She's the one that made the invitation. She said it was business. We're going to discuss the cost of the promotions for the show."

"Well, keep in mind that Nicole is divorced. She's quite the number around town, so if people stare at the both of you, you'll know why. But far be it from me to tell you what to do. Just look out. She's a smooth one."

I wasn't sure whether Tracy was a little jealous or not, but I decided it was worth watching myself with this Nicole woman.

○◉○

LATER, AT TWILIGHT, I waited to go to the campfire with Tracy. I didn't know what to expect. Why these young kids would want to spend their time learning about the Bible or hearing a sermon baffled me. Tracy hadn't detailed anything that went on, saying that I was going to just have to find out myself.

A nice big bonfire had been lit, and twenty or so boys sat in a semicircle on rows of logs. Several counselors sat among them. Their usual rough-and-tumble fidgeting was replaced with somber faces, waiting for the program to begin, almost hypnotized by the dancing flames. Tracy guided us around behind the group where we could sit on some large boulders that were still warm from the sun.

Steve and one of the older boys arrived with guitars in hand. I got the impression that they had been practicing together before they came because they were already tuned and had a list of songs between them.

The boys all stood, and Steve gave an opening prayer. I was becoming more and more impressed with Steve's versatility at the camp. There wasn't much that he didn't have a hand in. I was going to have to ask Tracy to fill me in on him later.

His prayer was more like a chat with God than an effort to intone favor and blessing from on high that I was used to hearing at temple. He just said something like, "Dear God, what a beautiful day you have given us today. How thankful we are to be here in your presence. You are awesome. Please come now and surround us with your heavenly angels and teach us more about our Savior, Jesus Christ. Amen." Then he took up his guitar and started to play some of the prettiest music I'd heard in a long time. For a while, the boys seemed to just listen, and then, little by little, they picked up the song and sang the words that they obviously knew by heart.

It was very strange to be hearing songs that extolled the "cross of Christ" and "the blood of the Lamb." These boys were singing about the very Jesus that had been eliminated from every religious experience in which I had ever participated. Now, he was the central figure of the evening, and every song and scripture pointed to him. It was weird, but I was transfixed, trying not to miss any of the words.

Slowly, but with certainty, what I would call the mood of the group changed. From a steady monotone to increased participation, the pace of the songs picked up, and at the same time, the boys began to move and sway with the music. I found it hard to just sit, being affected by the spirit of the meeting.

Suddenly, Tracy raised her hands to the sky as if in surrender. I turned to look at her and saw that her face had taken on a kind of serenity that I had only caught a hint of before.

Now, some of the boys were moving about, away from their places. I wondered if the counselors would tell them to sit down and come to order again. A few had taken to wander from left to right and back again, some with their hands in the air like Tracy's. I was both moved by their independence, and at the same time worried that the campfire gathering was getting out of hand. It became even worse when one boy started shouting out in the middle of the music.

This was a major disruption to me, yet no one stepped forward to stop him.

One song followed another, accompanied with clapping or a quiet bowing of heads, depending on the type of music. One of the campers moved forward and beat on a hollow log in rhythm to the music, and the deep resonance added a new dimension to the sound of the guitars.

Finally, the singing stopped for a moment, and in the dead silence, one of the counselors suddenly spoke out in a loud voice, "The Lord says that he is pleased with us tonight. He has looked upon us and our praise is a sweet sound to his ears. His hand is over us and blesses us. 'Come close,' he says. 'You who have been far away. Let me put my arm around you and give you peace. You have been wandering. You don't know me. You don't know how much I love you. You are my lost sheep. I want to draw you near to me. I want to bring you into my fold and be mine forever.'"

There was a murmur as several answered with, "Praise you, Lord. Thank you, Lord."

As for me, I was left sitting there stunned. What I had just heard hit me in the middle of my stomach. Every word had shot through me. I really didn't know if what I had heard was genuine or not, but the wandering stuff was all too true. It could have been some kind of hoax or hype. I didn't know for sure. It was so unexpected. Just for a second, I couldn't help thinking that God had actually said something to me. But then, I decided that it couldn't be. This campfire wasn't organized for me. I was merely visiting, and I really didn't belong here.

Tracy was looking at me. I caught her concern in the light of the big bonfire. "Are you all right?" she asked.

"Why?" I said. "Don't I seem OK?"

"You have this funny look on your face."

"My stomach's upset. I think it might be something I ate," I lied.

She knew better. "Would you like to go talk with Steve about it?"

"What's there to talk about? You're the nurse, for crying out loud." She was making me irritated.

"I'm sorry," she said. "You do what you think is best."

The meeting continued along the same lines as it had started.

What they were calling "the Spirit" seemed to energize the participants, and the boys were now calling out at random. Various ones thanked God for the day spent swimming and in sports, thanks and praise for the camp itself, praise for God and his goodness and more. Then their words changed to requests. Prayer for a brother in prison, another for an alcoholic father. The list was long and serious: an aunt with cancer, a brother in the military, a little sister who had been thrown from a horse, and several for the health of Commander Dougan. I'd never seen anything like it, and coming from young junior high and even younger boys, I was greatly impressed at their apparent maturity.

The continuous prayers seemed to cause the "spirit" of the gathering to escalate. Some of the boys fell to their knees, some started crying, and one or two fell flat on their backs. I was dumbstruck. Never in my life had I ever witnessed such a strange scene. I could only imagine that some of the boys might be on some kind of drugs. If this were the case, I felt the camp counselors were perpetuating a terrible crime, and I wasn't about to be a part of it. I slipped off my perch on the rock and started for the edge of the path.

"Are you leaving?" Tracy asked.

"Yes, I can't stand this. It's turning my stomach."

"Look, why don't you let me explain?" She took my arm and guided me away from the campfire and directed me toward a grove of pinions. "I think I understand a little of how you feel. After all, this is new to you, isn't it?"

"You bet it is," I said. "I can't stand the hijinks, and if there are drugs involved, I don't want anything to do with it.

"I can assure you, there are no drugs," she said. "The first time I saw what we refer to as the 'manifestation of the Holy Spirit,' I could hardly believe it was real either."

"The *what*?" I said.

"For reasons only known to God, the boys at this camp have been touched with something very special. It started last summer, as far as I know, and continues now almost every time we have a praise meeting at the campfire. These boys are very genuine. They become totally oblivious of everything around them, and they receive a beautiful blessing directly from God. What you're seeing is the real thing, Mel, believe me. I don't know why our camp, but the boys are being very blessed."

"What do they do, black out and see colors and have weird psychedelic manifestations and such?" I was totally not believing a word she said.

"No. For one thing, they are seeing angels, sometimes hundreds of them, they say. They are seeing events in the past and in the future. They are seeing Jesus. I mean, this is real, and they are being very, very blessed."

"How do you know all this?"

"I've talked with them. They are eager to tell me what they saw and heard. Sometimes it's glorious, and sometimes it's very scary, but they always come back for more. They experience things at their age that we may never get the chance to learn in a lifetime."

I was skeptical to say the least. No one ever told me about such things, and it reminded me of a couple of parties I attended in Greenwich Village where the people got very turned on.

"I don't know," I said. "I'm going to have to think about it."

The sound of taps wailed throughout the camp from the scratchy record over the PA system. The kids reacted slowly as the counselors grouped them and helped them shuffle toward the tent area. They appeared to be a little drunk, and I was a bit worried for them. At their age, I had never acted like they did, except maybe when I would twirl enough times to make me stagger. Was this some kind of cult thing? The only assurance was that I trusted Tracy enough to believe that she wouldn't have condoned something that would harm these boys. She loved them too much for that. Still, I was totally confused by what I had seen and heard throughout the evening campfire, and it would be a long time before I would get over it. As for the thought that God had spoken to me, I dismissed it. The thing was, I didn't think He cared.

Chapter 17

THE DOCTOR DECIDED COMMANDER Dougan needed to stay at the hospital another day, so the next afternoon, Tracy went to visit him, and I hitched a ride to town with her. I was wearing my lightweight pants with an open-necked sports shirt. The left leg just barely fit over my cast. I was sporting only one crutch.

"I can't wait to hear how your date with Nicole goes tonight," she said with a tiny smile on her face.

"This isn't a date," I said somewhat defensively. "We're just going to talk about the Magic Mike show."

"Oh, OK. If you insist. But I'll bet she wears something really, really low cut and can't keep her hands off you."

For the moment, that didn't sound so bad to me.

Tracy dropped me off at the newspaper, and I went in to look for the seductive advertising manager. I was shown her tiny office in which to wait. There were various folders scattered over her desk and on the top of the file cabinets. I had to lift a box off the only seat in front of her desk.

As I waited, my mind started reviewing the events of the previous evening. I couldn't help thinking that maybe I should talk to Steve. Teaching this type of religious stuff to innocent boys was very offensive to me, and I wasn't sure if their parents would approve.

Nicole swept into the office, breaking my reverie. How Tracy could have known how low Nicole's blouse would be, I hadn't the slightest idea, but it could have easily used another button at the top.

"Well, well, well. This is a pleasure," she gushed, with her hands in the air, as if she was just drying her nails. "I don't have the pleasure of such a fine-looking man waiting for me in my office all that often."

I refrained from saying, "Shucks, ma'am." Instead, I managed to get up and stand on my good leg and try to act the part of the sophisticated New Yorker that I was supposed to be. "Thank you, Nicole. You flatter me."

"Not in the least," she said, indicating for me to sit. "You wouldn't believe the cowboys around here who don't think to dress up for the ladies when they know they're going out. You are a refreshing oasis in the desert."

"Well, the whole purpose was to go over our promotional plans," I countered. I didn't really expect to turn the evening into a night on the town.

"Oh for sure," she said, reaching under a couple of folders on her desk. "I've been getting all sorts of quotes." She scanned some entries on a yellow pad and nodded her head. "There's plenty to discuss. Do you want to begin now?"

"That would be great," I said.

"All righty." She pulled out several sheets from the folder. "I'm going to give you what I'd call our optimum exposure, and then you tell me if we need to pare anything down as we go." She handed me the pages and made a check mark on her list. "First of all, I think you need to take several full-page ads running in the entertainment section over the next few days. This would absolutely guarantee the highest visibility. A full page will give you space to run plenty of copy, ticket prices, a little map to the camp, and pictures of Magic Mike and his gang."

I froze when I saw the black and white page rate for just one insertion and calculated the amount for several more. All the money I had to spend was my eighteen thousand dollars, and somehow, I had to cover the five-thousand-dollar show fee, staging, lighting, housing, and who knows what else. I could see that the advertising costs were going to swallow a big chunk of it. "Give me the rest before I comment."

Nicole sweetly checked off the printing of tickets, posters, and handbills and hanging the street banner. Each received a big check mark with a flourish as she went down her list. "So, what do you think?" she said when she got to the end.

"I think you've amazingly covered it all." I was impressed with all the work she'd done in such a short time. "Tell you what. Let me get a look at our other costs and estimate how much we might bring in from ticket sales. I'll be able to give you the go-ahead in a day or two. Would that be all right?"

"Perfectly OK with me," she said. "We're committed to helping you make a success of your open house. We still have the time—if you get right back to us."

"I will. Believe me."

Nicole put down her pad, stood up, and smoothed her dress. "So, now that we're done with business for a while, what say we enjoy ourselves?"

I stood and pulled back my chair to let her move around the box on the floor and followed her out through the office and past the receptionist.

"I'm leaving early, Joyce," she said. "Mr. Van Alan and I are doing the town."

Joyce looked up and gave me a slight wink.

Outside, Nicole guided me to a sleek red sports car at the curb. "There's really not much to see, but that's OK," she said as she slid behind the wheel. "I have fun showing people around."

Her enthusiasm was contagious. I had been to the hospital several times, but I had only taken a quick glance at Cortez. Now, I was a bit more interested because she was the tour guide.

She wanted me to know about her too. "I've lived here most of my life. Both my parents were archeologists, so this was their Eden," she said. "Daddy died when I was a teenager, leaving Mother to carry on their work alone."

I tried to picture Nicole growing up under the thumb of the infamous Dr. Armor.

We passed the Cortez Cultural Center on Market Street. "Here's where you can learn more about the native people and their customs. The center schedules a lot of interesting activities.

"The cliff dwellings at Mesa Verde are the big drawing card, of course," she went on. "It's put our little city on the map—and given me a chance to meet people from all over the world who are curious to see how the ancients lived. You may not believe it, but I've never been farther than about five hundred miles from here, so I get a real thrill talking to people from the outside world. I'm so hungry to travel and see other places."

This shone a new light on this businesswoman who appeared to be so in control. I saw her now as really a person in need—someone who was probably lonely. I was feeling sorry that she had not taken advantage of going to other places—until it suddenly occurred to me that I, too, had only recently broken out of my own little corral. I had to laugh.

"What's so funny?" she said.

"Well, until last month, I had never been west of New York City. Unlike you, though, I didn't even care about it. I was just a happy little clam living in a stagnant pool."

She smiled. "Really? I would have thought you were very worldly."

"Sorry to disappoint you," I said. "To be honest, I've experienced very little of the world around me. But now, I'm learning a little something new every day."

"Well, I still want to know about the big city. I can't wait to hear what it must be like to live there."

We drove around a few roads until we got to a pleasant area that featured many Southwest-style homes. "There's where I grew up," she said, pointing to a rambling adobe ranch, flanked by a beautiful array of large cactus and yucca plants flourishing up a long driveway.

I was impressed. "It's very nice. Is this where you live now?"

"Oh, no. My mother still does. I have my own place. She and I don't always see eye to eye."

"I met her briefly," I said. "I can see there are differences."

Nicole was the one to laugh now. "Tell me about it. I guess I'm more like my father. I'm really glad because I loved him so."

"He must have been young when he died."

"Only thirty-five. He fell while he was opening a new shaft in the cliff dwellings. Mother saw it all. It was terrible."

"I'm sorry," I said. There wasn't much I could think of to add at the moment.

We drove back toward town, passing the hospital on the way.

"I hope never to darken that door again," I told her as I recounted the visits I'd had, including the car accident.

Nicole listened with her mouth open. "I can't believe it. A car crash? So, that's what happened to your leg. I was going to ask. You must be a very lucky person."

"Not really. Maybe you shouldn't even be driving me around right now."

"I'm not afraid," she said. "I'll take my chances."

○◉○

The time was just past six o'clock as we pulled into a parking lot next to a small building on Main Street.

"This is my favorite place. You're going to love it, that is, if you like French food."

"Sounds wonderful." It was hard for me to imagine a French restaurant in the middle of Cortez, but I was certainly famished and eager to have something other than chili and hot dogs and hamburgers from the mess hall.

Chez Claude beckoned us.

The pleasing smells of cooking that met us inside the door set my stomach to growling. Not many diners were here yet, so we had our choice of seating.

A nice-looking young girl gave us menus and ushered us to a table in a back corner.

"Bill usually won't let me take the locals out to dinner here on our expense account, making you very special, I'll have you know," Nicole said. "Just don't look at the prices."

I scanned the menu and saw what Nicole meant. They were what I might have expected in New York.

"How do they keep in business out here where tacos and beans are the preferred meal?" I asked.

"Oh, you'd be surprised. Wait'll you see the people who come here. There are lots of wealthy residents. This part of the country has attracted a large population of Californians and Texans who want the best, and they can afford it. They have big houses and ranches scattered all around here.

"I guess I'd be wise not to typecast all the people based on the kids we're dealing with at the camp," I said. "I've hardly been out of my surroundings since I got here, so I'm a bit sheltered."

I left it up to Nicole to offer suggestions and to order for us. She was very sweet to the waiter, and they appeared to know each other. Her mouth turned up slightly at the corner, revealing a cute dimple. Her eyes were bright and animated. I found it rather nice to watch her.

Next, she turned to the wine menu. She wanted to know if I would like a bottle, and I agreed. Never before had I had such an attractive woman—or any woman for that matter—order for me, and it was fun. The pressure of pleasing someone on a first date was all hers.

That being accomplished, I got back to our business discussions. "So, do you really think our promotional efforts will bring out the local folks to our little camp?"

"Yes, I really do," she said. "First of all, I did some checking with a variety of age groups I personally know—granted, a very small sampling to be sure. But, with few exceptions, they all know Magic Mike and immediately got excited when I told them he was coming to town. They wanted to know where and when and begged me to get them tickets. I think that should please you."

"Oh, it does, believe me. The only thing that really worries me in a good way is whether or not we can handle a large crowd out there. I don't know what to plan for."

"Plan big, I should think," she said. "When the kids get their parents involved, everyone is going to want to come. Especially on the Fourth of July."

"What does the town do on the Fourth of July anyway?" I asked. "Aren't we going to be competing with their usual plans?"

"That's the other thing I checked on," she said. "The mayor is a pretty close friend, and I wanted him to know what was going on. I was also concerned that you might be getting into some kind of trouble by not having the right approvals for the open house and fireworks. Administrators are funny about getting their stamp of approval, especially if crowds are involved."

I hadn't thought of that. "What did he say?"

"He was a little annoyed that you hadn't called him first, I'm afraid, but then I guess he got to thinking about it. He called back to say he had run it by some of the council. The Magic Mike appearance worried him because it could have the potential to draw people away from their own celebration. The last thing he wanted was to have fireworks in town, and no one come. Instead, he even said that the town might be willing to put on the fireworks at the canp that night—if you wanted. He talked about the camp location as being especially unique up against the mountainside, and that it might make quite a show for the people, as a change of pace."

My mouth dropped open. I couldn't believe our luck. The idea of fireworks had really scared me because of the cost, and here was an unbelievable opportunity to save a huge amount. Plus, we would receive the town's blessing and publicity and maybe even crowd control.

"That's incredible! You amaze me with all you've done."

"I know. It's probably my mother's influence. I get onto something, and I can't leave it alone."

"Did you know this whole thing is a result of your mother's efforts to shut down Camp Sage and Sand?"

"I'm afraid so, and I'm sorry too. She's been sniffing around that property as long as I can remember. I think she's finally taken it on as a project because of the government's increased concern over the desecration of antiquities out here. We've had some recent cases where looters have taken and sold pottery and other valuable items. It's ended up in some big fines and prison time. That's why she probably feels that this is her best time to strike."

"Pardon me for asking, but don't you have a problem talking about your mother like this?"

"No. Not really." Nicole tilted her head slightly and firmed her chin. "Her career always came first as I was growing up, and now I see her for what she's become. I still love her, but I don't spend much time with her."

"How does it happen that your last name isn't Armor, like hers?"

"My father was Myron Wayland. When he died, she took back her maiden name. That happens to be another disappointment—that she wouldn't carry on his name. She's just another classic example of the in-your-face feminist."

Our wine arrived. We watched as the sommelier carefully showed us the label and pulled the cork ever so gently. Then he gave each of us a taste, and Nicole nodded her approval.

Like her mother, Nicole was the typical career woman, but not demanding, and certainly much more cooperative. There was no doubt that she took charge, yet she made the ride a pleasant one. I liked doing business with her.

"Now, I'm dying to hear about you," she said. "I'm terribly curious how I would find a sophisticated person like you working as a counselor at a small boys' camp in this dusty little town. I mean, what were you thinking?"

I was amused by her bluntness. I hesitated, partly because I hardly knew what I was doing here myself, and so I didn't exactly know how to explain it. And I was too embarrassed to reveal that I thought I would be teaching writing.

"OK, bear with me," I said. "I heard about working with kids on the radio, and it seemed like a unique opportunity for me to do something for someone other than myself, for a change. I think I really like kids, but I don't know much about them. I was never treated like one in growing up—more like a short adult. Plus, my father didn't make himself available to teach me all the sports things that most boys like. So, I became an intellect, and I thought I was doing just fine as a loner with my cat—until I saw some of the people I grew up with getting married, having families, and raising children. I began to feel left out.

I paused a minute to see if I was boring her.

"So, I signed up in a rather big rush, got in my rusty car, and took off across the Great Plains without really thinking about what I might find. I just needed to get away and perhaps discover what I wanted to do with the rest of my life along the way."

Nicole sat without comment, waiting for me to continue.

"The camp wasn't what I expected," I went on. "Yes, the mud comes up to your ankles when it rains, and the midday heat is unbelievable, but I've become strangely attracted to the place. I found some people who want to make a difference in the community. Not only in a physical way, but in the hearts of a bunch of small boys who need to grow up to be leaders.

"Things got off on the wrong foot, literally as you can see. After my accident, I wanted to leave so bad, I couldn't wait to get the next plane out. But after I was forced to stay, I got the chance to learn of the commitment these people have for the camp, and now I've taken on some of that desire myself. Does this sound hard to understand?"

"No, of course not. I'm very impressed."

"Well, I'm in it up to my ears now. Magic Mike is coming, and I'm the only one who really knows anything about what it's going to take to stage it. I'm having second thoughts that I may have gotten the camp into something that we may be unable to handle. And I don't know if it will keep us from having to move, even if it is successful."

Nicole smiled. "If people learn about what all you are doing out there and have a good time on the Fourth to boot, how can it hurt?"

"I don't suppose it can—unless something unforeseen happens. I confess that I have a tendency to be negative. It doesn't help things, I know."

Nicole reached over and squeezed my hand. "Nothing bad is going to happen. Just expect the best. The fact that your friend even considered stopping here with Magic Mike is a good sign. I can see you have a lot of good experience, and I think you were sent here to use it. Now, put any negative thoughts behind you and start inspiring us all with your winning ideas."

Her encouragement made me realize what I lacked most was for people to believe in me. I certainly had trouble myself. It was good to have a kick in the pants from time to time to get me back on target. My spirits were beginning to revive. Maybe it was the wine, but I was beginning to lose the fear of failure I had been harboring. More likely, it was the company.

The food came, and it was excellent. We ate in silence for a while, savoring the special sauce with the lamb dish Nicole had ordered for both of us. The chef must have saved us the most tender pieces of meat. I had trouble not smacking my lips with pleasure as I ate.

"Whoever could have decided to open a French restaurant way out here?" I asked.

"Claude is a maverick. He's not concerned with making a name for himself in some big city. In fact, he was born here. Most people don't think it's strange for a great artist to want to live where there's open skies and a lot of room for free thinking. You know, like Georgia O'Keefe? Why should it be any different for a great culinary artist?"

"I suppose you're right," I said. I hadn't thought of the similarity, but it made sense. "You, for example, should live anywhere you want to." I was thinking of Nicole's hunger for new places. "Why are you still here?"

"Circumstances have kept me from leaving. Perhaps you heard that I've recently been divorced."

"I'm sorry," I said.

"No need to be. We had rarely spoken the last two years. He and I grew up together, but then we started moving apart shortly after we were married. Some things just don't work out the way you think they should." She put on an "I'm all right" smile to assure me. There wasn't much more to be said.

Our dinner was over. We both were too full for the rich desserts they offered or even coffee. We didn't linger since people continued to fill the little restaurant, and they needed the table.

As we left, the young hostess asked us if we had enjoyed our meal. I was very happy to tell her that it was the best I'd had in a long time. I would certainly come again and perhaps bring the Commander and Tracy for a special getaway.

Nicole pulled next to her and said, "Tell me, Diane, have you ever heard of Magic Mike?"

Her face lit up. "Of course. My little brother wouldn't miss him on TV."

"What would you think if he were to come here for a day?"

"You're kidding. Really? When? I've got to tell my brother."

"He's going to be here on the Fourth of July. Tell your little brother—and bring the family. It'll be in the paper this week," Nicole said.

"All right!" Diane gave Nicole a high five while the people in line looked on. They had overheard Nicole and smiled at each other as if they had been let in on a secret.

"The news is going to travel fast around here," Nicole said as we stepped out on the sidewalk. "There aren't many celebrities who come through, so I predict this will be a big event. You better plan for it."

"I know," I said. My stomach tightened, which didn't help my digestion any.

On the drive back to the camp, Nicole pumped me for information about New York. She wanted to know what it was like living in the city. How expensive the apartments were. If I thought she could get a job. If people were friendly or hard to get along with.

Having been so used to the New York way of life, I had to work to put myself in her place and visualize how she might face such a big cultural change.

"I think it all comes down to attitude. If you are ready to take on a different lifestyle and willing to treat it as an adventure, you'll do perfectly fine, whatever comes your way. I won't kid you, though. It's a lot more difficult living there with all of its frustrations. After the initial excitement wears off, the daily grind will become real. People get in a huge rush, and they don't always look out for the other guy. They usually don't mean to be curt, but sometimes you wonder where they learned about being a member of the human race. Yet, at the most unexpected times, you wouldn't believe how much heart they have."

She listened with interest. I didn't know if she had plans to leave her nest in Cortez anytime soon or not, but she apparently had few ties and could take off whenever she wanted.

"I hope if you're in New York when I get there, you'll show me the ropes," she said.

"I'd be glad to. The big city can be a lonely place."

It was still light when we pulled into the parking lot at the camp. A crowd of young boys converged to admire Nicole's red sports car. The dust had already dulled the shine, and she was going to need another car wash when she got back to town.

Nicole listened while I thanked her for her initial planning and for making so many contacts in such a short time, especially with the mayor. I was grateful for someone who knew how to put together a campaign of this magnitude. I told her how wonderful the dinner was. It was truly a special treat. She was being so quiet that I got the idea she hated to drive off and leave me.

Suddenly, she leaned over and gave me a big kiss. I was so startled I didn't know what to say. I had thought the evening had been intended for business, but clearly Nicole had something else going through her mind.

She saw my reaction and said, "I'm sorry. I didn't mean to shock you. I just felt a rush of affection for you. Was that too silly of me?"

"No … really, I'm flattered," I said, trying to think of something else to add.

"It's just that you're so sweet, coming all the way out here to volunteer with these boys. And you're so naïve. I don't think you know the half of what it's like in their homes. I just want to thank you for being here and bringing some fun and excitement into their lives."

"Oh, Nicole, you give me too much credit. I haven't done anything yet. And to tell you the truth, right now, I wish I were back in New York. It'll only be with talented people like you that we'll ever pull this thing off. So, thank you too." I opened the door and got my good leg out to stand on while I retrieved my crutch. Then I leaned back in to her. "I'll call you tomorrow after I go over your proposals. And thanks again for dinner. You're wonderful."

Nicole smiled and gave me a little wave. She steered her car in a wide turn to miss a cluster of kids gawking at us and drove away.

Chapter 18

TRACY APPEARED TO BE deep into doing some kind of paperwork when I entered the clinic. She looked up, "Well, you're back early."

"I didn't expect to be out late. It was only a business dinner."

"Do your business meetings always end with a kiss?"

"Aha, so you were spying on us!"

"Not in the least." Tracy looked squarely at me in all innocence. "I want to keep an eye on things."

"The truth is, Nicole kissed me. I didn't kiss her."

"Believe me, I don't really care," Tracy said. "That's between the two of you."

I was surprised by her reaction, but rather than extend the conversation, I went to my little room and sat on the bed.

"She's got everything figured and ready to publish when we give her the OK," I called back. "I'm beginning to think we might have a large crowd."

Tracy came and stood at the door. "That's wonderful. Have we got enough money to do it all?"

"I've got a budget in my head, but it'll depend on what the other needs are. These things always run way more than you intend. Actually, I think, posters might be the most efficient way to go. The word is already starting to get around. Maybe a couple of promo ads in the newspaper. A little radio. No TV. And guess what? The mayor is moving the town's Fourth of July fireworks here. Can you believe that?"

Tracy's face lit up. "Incredible! However did you get him to do that?"

"It was all Nicole's doing. She's taken the bull by the horns."

"There's always a big crowd for the fireworks. Even if they miss Magic Mike in the afternoon, there will be another group that night."

"Right. So what we need to do now is think of how to get these people to rally for us after it's all over. We have to assume that Dr. Armor is going to follow through on her threat to evict us. Maybe we can have the kids take petitions around to be signed at the event. We should also have brochures describing the camp and its history and suggest how people can donate. I think if we can just get people to know we might have to move and sign on with us, they'll help us fight to stay."

Tracy's face was radiant. "Mel, I can't thank you enough for what you're doing. My parents would be so pleased to know someone like you." Her eyes started to tear up. "Camp Sage and Sand was so important to them. God certainly sent you all the way from New York at exactly the right time."

"I don't know about that, Tracy," I said. "I've fumbled a few things since I got here. Believe me, I'm running by the seat of my pants. It could all blow up, leaving us very embarrassed, if things don't go right. And, just to let you know, I don't feel this call from God. I wouldn't know him if I met him on the street."

"That's really not how he shows himself," she said. "God is spiritual and his call is a spiritual one. But I can tell you this: He moves and works through men to accomplish his purposes. If you ask him to direct you in the upcoming days, you'll see him work in your life, and I know he'll prove it to you."

I heard what she was saying, but it was hard to think of giving control to some unseen being. After all, I had my degree and plenty of experience. That counted for something. But sweet little Tracy was no dope either. I would keep an eye on how things progressed spiritually just for her.

The bed was soft, and I lay back. Tracy saw that I wanted to be left alone and quietly pulled the door shut. I'd had a full day. It felt so good to just relax.

I dreamed that Nicole and I were in my New York apartment. I took her into my arms and began to kiss her with a passion that I hadn't experienced before. She was hungry for making love and responded with a fire that drove me to pull her down on the soft cushions of the couch. She molded her body against mine. I started kissing her neck.

Someone was knocking at my apartment door. I ignored the rude interruption. If it was the lady from downstairs, she would eventually go away.

But the knocking continued. "Mel, can you open up?"

I finally realized that someone was at the outside clinic door.

Tracy always locked it when she left. There were too many tempting drugs in the closet.

"Hold on, would you!" I called back. I was angry and in no mood to end my dream. Pulling my crutch toward me, I grudgingly made my way to the door and unlocked it.

Steve stood there with an apologetic look. "I'm sorry to bother you, but the Commander has had another heart attack at the hospital. He's critical. Tracy wants to include you in our prayer vigil right away."

My first thought was to wonder why she thought I could help pray with a bunch of Christian believers. Hadn't she heard me? I'd just told her that I didn't feel anything spiritual. But Steve was so anxious for me to join him, that I set the lock and pulled the door shut behind me.

I was surprised by the large gathering in the mess hall. My bad attitude melted away when I saw everyone. Not only were all the counselors there, but quite a few of the older kids. They had formed a ring around the walls, standing somberly hand in hand.

Steve and I were the last to join the assembly, and two boys broke apart to bring us into the circle.

We stood there, and the room was deathly silent. I saw all heads were bowed, so I followed suit.

Tracy said, "Juan, would you pray?"

The big cook took a deep breath and expelled it. He shifted his feet, and I saw his hands take on a renewed grip with those next to him as he prepared himself. "Oh, Father God, you are our protector, the master of heaven and earth, our guardian in time of trouble. We are here to ask you to show your mercy upon our beloved brother, Commander Dougan, who is right now clinging to life. Touch his body. Raise him up again. Bring him back to lead us in the difficult days ahead. You know, Lord, how he has saved so many of us from the pit of hell on earth. He took me from the streets where I was lost, and he gave me a job and put his arm around me as I struggled with my addiction. He saw me through it—and not just me neither. There's others of us who will testify to his care and concern. Father, don't let him die! We love him, and we need him to keep these boys on the right path—so they don't fall into the same pit I was in. Do a mighty work, Lord. Heal him now. I ask all of this in the name of your Son, Jesus Christ. Amen."

Several of the assembled repeated, "Amen." I saw tears running down the faces of quite a few men and boys. Even I got a lump in my throat as I thought of the big man who was lying in the hospital right now. He had already made a strong impression in my life that would stay with me. I couldn't imagine how this camp would operate without his energetic leadership.

Tracy's voice broke the silence again. "I'd just like to say that the Commander has been like a second father to me. He was there for me when my parents died, and he has more than capably handled all the responsibilities that my parents left undone. Whatever happens, I know that it is God's will for us. We have to rely on him. We cannot know his plan, but we can praise him in the midst of our fear. The doctors say that the next few hours will be critical ones for the Commander. He may return here—or he may not be able to lead us anymore. But God will still be watching over us. I'd like to ask each of you to go to your bed now and kneel down and thank him for Commander Dougan. Pray that he will be healed—and go to sleep knowing that everything is all right. We have given it all over to God. Put your arm around those boys who are not here and encourage them. We are still a family, no matter what happens next. Good night, everyone."

With those loving words, the group stirred and quietly started moving out of the hall. Several counselors hugged the boys who seemed most affected by emotion. I hadn't realized the impact that the Commander had brought to individuals around the camp. It was apparent that he was a father to more than a few of the boys.

I went over to Tracy and said, "I'm so sorry. I hope he's going to pull through."

She looked up at me, and instead of defeat in her face, she had a sort of glow. I could see that her faith gave her strength. Her resolve was infectious and made me calm.

"I hated to bother you, but I felt you would want to be a part of our gathering. You are an important member of this camp."

Her remark pleased me. Up until now, no one had affirmed my being here. "Yes, thank you for including me," I said. "I want to do what I can."

She smiled. "For now, we're going to have to wait on the Lord. We might as well go and get some sleep."

We walked back to the clinic in silence, and she brought out her key.

I took it from her, and our hands lingered together just for a second. Then I unlocked the door. "Let me know if anything more happens," I said.

"Of course. I'm going to stay in the office near the telephone," she answered. "If it rings in here, don't let it disturb you."

"You know it will," I said. "But I am concerned."

We lingered another moment, and I wanted to take her in my arms and comfort her. But then the moment passed once again, and she turned and walked away.

○◉○

The sun was already streaming through the window in the door of the clinic when I woke. For the first day since I had been at the camp, reveille had not sounded over the ancient PA system, and it was late. I rose and washed and shaved as quickly as I could. I was anxious to get the latest news on the Commander's condition. Again, no news was good news. I also wanted to know what effect his illness was going to have on our plans for the big open house on the Fourth of July.

Breakfast was coming to a close when I arrived in the mess hall, but all I wanted was a cup of coffee after last night's rich dinner. The majority of counselors lingered at the adult's table. I studied their faces as I took a vacant spot to see if there had been any serious announcements.

Tracy was quick to get me up to speed. "He's holding his own. The doctor is cautiously optimistic. He says he's a 'tough old bird.'"

I was encouraged. Perhaps the worst was over. "Where does this leave us?" I asked the table at large. "Where do we go from here?" I guess I was the one to voice what was on everyone's mind. I hoped that I hadn't overstepped anything, but from the nods I saw, perhaps it was time to face the future.

Steve said, "The Commander's been gone on occasion, but not for any length. We're going to need someone to run the everyday operation … that is until he's ready to come back."

All heads nodded again.

He went on. "I don't know if any plan has been made, but I think Tracy is the only one who knows the daily ins and outs of the place. The rest of us have our hands full with our various responsibilities. If I had a vote, I'd say we should look to her to lead us for the time being. I'd be more than glad to have her telling me what to do."

Each of the members at the table expressed agreement as they went around the table.

As for me, I was heartily in favor of Steve's suggestion.

"All right, all of you," Tracy said. "I didn't want this, but I realize it's really the only way. Believe me, I'm not ready to take on anything more, but I've been here long enough to know what needs to be done, so I guess I'm it. But I'm going to need everyone's help, especially when it comes to laying out discipline. Most of the kids have a healthy fear of the Commander. I'm not sure how they'll take me."

"They already love you," Jesus Joe said. I was surprised to hear him speak up, as he was a man of very few words.

Don, the industrial arts counselor, added, "That's true. I think they'll respect your authority—and we'll make sure of it."

"Well, let's hope it won't be for long," Tracy said. "I'd rather not be the administrator."

There was a short pause among us, and I knew it was time to ask the question that had been plaguing me. "I hate to bring this up now, but are we still on track for the Magic Mike appearance? I need to know, as this is about our last chance to cancel."

Tracy looked around at the group for confirmation. "I don't see things have changed. Dr. Armor isn't going to let up. She may even be encouraged if she thinks the Commander is out of the way. But if she thinks I'm a pushover, she's got another thing coming."

Steve said, "The lumber for the stage is on order. It's being delivered tomorrow."

"I think we should go ahead," Tracy said. "This is just too good an opportunity for us. I know the Commander would want us to keep at it."

"OK. I'll call the paper and schedule the advertising," I said.

There was a general murmur of agreement. With that, the staff rose and began to leave for their work areas.

Chapter 19

I PHONED NICOLE FROM the office. Her voice was soft and sultry. "Thank you for such a wonderful time last night," she said.

"No, it was you who made it wonderful. I enjoyed the dinner and your company very much."

"People are already asking me who was that handsome man I was with. They want to know if it was business or pleasure."

"Both," I said. "It was fun, but I'm especially pleased at the plans you put together for us. That's why I'm calling you so early. We need to get the show on the road."

"Good, I'm ready. Tell me what you decided."

We reviewed her proposals, and I gave her the go-ahead on most of them. She planned to have some ads and poster layouts to see the next day. I told her to leave off any mention of fireworks until I could confirm our plans with the mayor. She wanted to know how much we would charge for the tickets. That threw me, but I gave her a figure for adults and children and hoped it would be fair. I also came up with the showtime for the middle of the afternoon. It was all guesswork, and I tried not to get panicked.

"Mother called me last night when I got back," she said.

"Oh, did she see us together too?"

"It's a small town. Someone told her."

"What did she say?"

Nicole gave a quick little laugh. "She's so transparent. She knew who you were, of course, but she pretended not to. I told her you were a volunteer at the camp, and then all of a sudden, she remembered seeing you. She said you didn't say much.

"That's true. I left her for the others to handle. It wasn't my business at the time. I did try to be nice to her big Indian bodyguard, but he told me to get lost."

Nicole giggled. "That's George Silver Bear. He's big, but he's harmless."

"He sure fooled me. Anyway, what did the good doctor say?" I asked. "Anything about the camp?"

"Not really. She and I don't talk business much. I think she wanted to know if I was getting involved with you. I told her we were discussing advertising."

"And that's true. You just know how to make it more interesting," I said. "But I really do appreciate your taking this load off my back. Look, I'd better go—so call me when you have something to show me."

"I'll get right on it. Bye for now."

Tracy had come into the office as we were talking. "Did Dr. Armor get after Nicole for cuddling up to you?"

I made a face. "She's not doing anything like that. Dr. Armor only admitted that she knew who I was. I guess she and Nicole keep their distance."

"Well, that says something for Nicole."

Tracy idly pulled out some drawers of the Commander's desk, glancing through his files. "I don't know really where to start. He's got a system all his own."

I watched her frustration. "I'd suggest you let things just happen for now—unless you know of some kind of report or bills that are due. Maybe the Commander will rally, and you won't have to get into it after all."

"Oh, I hope you're right. I never considered the camp operating without him. I feel so lost." She stood up at the desk and suddenly put her hands up to her face.

Without hesitating, I came around the desk and held her. She was so in need of someone to encourage her. She was struggling under a weight that she had tried to avoid. The Commander had been right there to take over when her parents died, and now he was gone—at least for the time being.

"It's going to be all right," I said. "You're not alone here. We're going to be just fine."

That's when she broke down and really cried. Big tears gushed down her cheeks, and she tried to pull away to mop them up. I just held her close and wouldn't let her go. She needed to get it all out. Finally, she began to calm down. She was probably embarrassed. After all, she had been so self-confident since I'd known her.

In a minute, she moved away and hurried over to the Commander's little washroom. I could hear the water splash as she rinsed her face off.

Her face was red, and she wouldn't look me in the eyes when she came out. "I'm sorry. That was foolish. I'll be fine. I keep thinking of how much my parents loved this place. I know it doesn't look like much." She glanced out the window. "But you should have seen it at first. Truly sage and sand."

"I'm sure it's come a long way," I said, just thinking about the job of getting the creek dammed for the lake. I knew she was right.

The phone rang, and we both jumped. She picked it up rather cautiously, probably expecting bad news. She said very little, looking directly at me the whole time. Then she thanked the person and hung up.

"Well?" I said. I steeled myself for the worse.

"He's going to be all right. Oh, thank you, God! With rest and care, he's coming back. And no operation either." A big smile lit her face, and she slumped into the Commander's battered chair.

○◉○

ABOUT AN HOUR LATER, after Tracy had done some work at the desk and left to get some rest, I was fiddling at the computer when little Carlos came in.

"You here to write another letter to your mother?" I asked.

"I think so," he said.

"Well, come on over. It's all yours." I moved aside to let him sit in my chair.

He plunked down and put a little finger up to his mouth. Slowly he began to look for the right keys to begin his message.

I was fascinated, standing over him, wondering what he was going to say, letter by letter.

But my attention was diverted to his neck. His thin shirt had pulled back, and I saw that there was a rash all along his hairline and down his back. Looking closer, I saw red spots around his ears, and his cheeks were bright red.

"Wow," I murmured. I put my hand on his forehead, and it felt way hotter than it should be—even for summer. "Are you all right?"

"I barfed up my breakfast," he said.

"Oh, brother. We'd better get you over to see Tracy." She had just gone to lie down, but this kid seemed to be coming down with something.

"Let's go." I took his hand and pulled him from the computer and around to the clinic. The door was locked.

Carlos leaned over with a cramp, and I thought he was going to vomit again. He gave a dry heave, but nothing came up.

"Let's go to her tent," I said, maneuvering him back across the road. I hated so much to disturb her, but I called softly, "Tracy, are you in there?"

She immediately answered and stuck her sleepy head out. "What is it?"

"You'd better take a look at Carlos here." I pulled the boy closer. "I think he's got something."

Tracy came outside the tent and squinted against the bright sun. She had Carlos bend his head forward to where I was pointing and pulled his shirt back. Then she examined his forehead and cheeks. "You're right. This boy has the measles."

I immediately felt like I needed to wash and wished I hadn't touched him so much. I didn't remember ever having the measles.

"I want to look at your tentmates too," she told him. She took him firmly by the hand, and they walked rapidly down to his tent, with me following on my crutch.

"Where are they?" she asked, seeing the bunks were empty.

"I don't know," he said. "Over at the field, I guess."

Tracy scanned the names located in a plastic holder. "Why don't you see if you can locate Jay and Ben?" she said to me. "I'm going to take Carlos. And when you find them, bring them to the clinic right away."

I went to look for them. Being midmorning, most of the kids were usually in some kind of class, but Carlos had pointed to the corral, so I started there. I asked a bunch of kids who were sitting on the rails, watching the horses. Thankfully, the two were there. "You both need to come up to the clinic with me. Tracy wants to examine you for red spots. Carlos has them all around his neck." I glanced at one of the boys, and he looked fine. "Have you felt sick to your stomach at all?"

He shook his head no, but both left the group and went running ahead of my slow hobble.

Carlos was sitting on the examining table with his shirt off. His upper torso was busy with spots.

"It's measles, all right. He's one of our little guys from Mexico," Tracy said. "He may not have had the MMR series of shots." She took a look at Carlos's tentmates while she was talking. "They don't look infected, but I need to check their files."

She pulled the folders from a metal drawer. "I don't have immunization data on any of them. I guess I'm going to have to confine them for at least a day. It's normally three days, but Carlos has gone for at least one. I don't know where he became infected, but we can't afford to have an outbreak."

She went to the phone. "I'll call his father and at least alert the public health nurse in town."

Tracy looked tired. She didn't need any more problems than she already had. A lot had suddenly descended on her in the past twenty-four hours.

Carlos's father was unwilling to take him, seeing he had a night job. What to do with three energetic boys who had to be isolated for two days or so? Tracy was searching my face with that look in her eyes that I'd come to read like a book.

I threw up my hands. "What can I do? I'm not a babysitter."

"You can read adventure stories. Play on the computer. Take them for a walk. Bring their meals to them and have a picnic. Just keep them away from the general population for a while. You can do it."

I was totally uncomfortable with any of it. This would also keep me from planning the Magic Mike show. I felt overwhelmed. No, I'm sorry, I couldn't do it.

Tracy saw my reluctance and said with a sigh, "OK, I guess I can take them. Let me just get a few things pulled together."

I couldn't stand the guilty feeling that came pouring over me. There was absolutely no way that Tracy could add one more layer to the weight she was already carrying. Besides, how could I face her when I had relatively little to do around camp? "Wait a minute," I said. "Let me see what I can do after all. You've got enough to handle." I didn't have a clue as to what I was going to do next. I was just going to have to take a chance that I'd had the measles vaccine way back before I could remember. I envisioned my face covered with red spots in a couple of days.

"I'll get someone to spell you," she said. "The time will go fast."

I could see that she was really very grateful.

She pulled the boys together and put her arms around them. "Now, Carlos has the measles. It's not serious, but you guys are going to have to stay away from the other kids for a couple of days so that it doesn't spread to the rest of the camp. Mr. Van Alan is going to keep you company. You do what he says, OK? I'm depending on you to cooperate. He's a wonderful friend."

My heart leaped. I didn't know if she really meant it down deep, but it was music to my ears.

Suddenly, I was energized and quite able to take charge of the boys if nothing else but to prove myself. I opened the door. "Come on, you guys. Let's see what games we can find on my computer."

Tracy gave me a big smile and helped me herd them outside.

Chapter 20

JAY, BEN, AND CARLOS were now my responsibility.

"So, guys, how about a soda?" To start out, I figured it would help us to relax with each other.

"OK," they said.

I took their orders and went around the building to the machine next to the dining hall while they crowded around the computer.

They seemed to be engrossed in a complicated game when I got back, so I sat in the Commander's chair behind his big desk to watch. In a few minutes, I started looking for reading material. Only one of the desk drawers offered any promise. There was a thick *Naval Officer's Handbook on Leadership,* a wholesale catalog for institutional tables and chairs, a bird-watcher's guide for the Southwest desert, and a museum appraiser's guide of antique pottery with prices for the current year. I was mildly interested in the latter because of Dr. Armor's claim that the Commander was stealing ancient Indian artifacts for gain. It was ridiculous for him to be doing such a thing, but there were check marks next to several items in the guide. I got up and compared the pen and ink drawings to the actual pottery in the little office showcase. They were close, I thought. And then I saw that the appraised prices ranged from five thousand dollars to twenty-five thousand dollars each, depending on condition. There must have been close to eighty thousand dollars' worth of pottery in this one display!

No wonder Dr. Armor had been on the Commander's case so intensely. Her trained eye had obviously spotted the valuable cache of antiquities, and she wasn't about to let him get away with having any of them, let alone selling them. He was obviously well aware of their astonishing value but had not made a move to sell them. That would definitely have jeopardized the camp.

By this time, the computer game was causing some squabbling between the boys.

I closed it down and got them to do some drawing while I went to the mess hall to get their lunch.

Sitting with them close around me in the office, eating grilled cheese sandwiches and chips with milk and an apple apiece, I realized I didn't know anything about these boys. Jay was the oldest, about thirteen maybe, and Carlos was the youngest. They looked a lot alike, with deep brown skin, jet-black hair, and big brown eyes, but I knew from their files that they each came from totally different backgrounds. "Tell me," I asked Jay. "Where are you from?"

He looked at me out of the corner of his eyes, curious maybe as to why I should be interested. For a moment, he didn't answer, and then he must have decided it wouldn't kill him. "Shiprock," he said.

I knew that was in New Mexico Navajo country because I had spent some time perusing a big area map taped to the wall.

"That's quite a ways," I said. "What made you come here?"

"My dad knows Jesus Joe," he said.

"Oh, he told you about us?"

"They want me to make jewelry."

"Is that what you want to do?"

"It's OK."

"Is your family Navajo?"

"Yes."

"Do they make jewelry?"

"They weave rugs."

"I've seen some beautiful ones." I pointed to a colorful example above us on the office wall. "Something like that?"

"Yep."

"How long would that one take?"

"Oh … three months maybe."

I was fascinated. It was rich in detail, with large and small turquoise and gold diamonds against a dark, earthy background.

"What about you, Ben? Where are you from?"

While Jay had been a little shy, Ben looked at me directly. He had a captivating smile. "A few miles."

"Navajo?"

"Ute."

"Oh, so what are you learning here?"

"To be a rodeo rider."

"Really?" I said. "What kind?"

"I don't know. Broncs."

"You had any experience?"

"Daddy was a rider." The smile left his face.

"He's not riding any longer?"

"Naw. He was killed by a bull."

"Oh my!" I was shocked. "I'm sorry."

"Yeah." He turned back to eating his sandwich.

I was at a loss to know what to say next. After a second, I said, "Do you want to be a rider like he was?"

"Ma says no."

"I can imagine, but wasn't it just an accident?"

"Too dangerous, she says."

I looked at Carlos. "So, what about you, Carlos? I hear you're from Mexico."

"Yep," he said. The red spots had now fired up on his cheeks.

"Do those itch?" I said, pointing to them.

"Uh-huh."

"Don't scratch them, OK?"

He had a bottle of white lotion that Tracy had given him. "I use this," he said.

"How long have you been in the US?" I asked.

"Not long," he said.

"Both your mom and dad live here?"

"Just Daddy. Mommy is coming soon … I hope."

"Any brothers or sisters?"

"Seven brothers and two sisters."

"Wow, where are they?"

"Juarez. My big brother is here."

He was pretty sharp for a ten-year-old, I thought, but small in stature and a little frail. "What are you learning here, Carlos?"

"Nothing."

"Aren't you in some classes?"

"A little."

"Well, what one do you like best?"

"God."

I was totally lost. "What class is that?"

"Ain't no class."

I didn't understand what he meant at first. Then I remembered seeing him at the Wednesday-night gathered around the fire. He had been right in the middle of the older kids with this angelic look on his face and his hands waving in the air, free as a bird. I could still picture it.

I stopped eating and mused. Carlos was just so innocent. He really captivated me with his big brown eyes. Then he pointed the final bite of his grilled cheese sandwich at my bum leg and said, "And the angels too."

I looked down, and there it was. He had been the one to draw the little angel on my cast with the words: "Angels are real."

"Yeah, I've been wanting to ask you about that, Carlos," I said. "What did you mean?"

"Mister, I see them."

Jay and Ben nodded solemnly. I guess they had seen them too.

"Well, tell me about it, you guys. Is this some kind of Indian ceremony that you go through?"

"No way," Jay said. "Angels are real."

Ben said, "Yeah."

I couldn't help thinking: *What have they been eating or smoking?* "You mean to say that you've actually seen angels? Are they flying around? With harps? Do they wear long gowns? What do they look like?" I was joking with them.

Carlos looked sad. "Maybe you don't believe, but we see *beeg* angels—very *beeg*—and they tell us things."

"What kind of things?" I composed myself. This was so amazing, I hardly could believe it, but with three boys all soberly agreeing with each other, I wanted to know more.

"Like what's going to happen," Ben said.

"You mean tomorrow or next week—or what?"

"They show us things that are to come—to prepare."

"Really? Prepare for what do you suppose?"

"When people will be bad. I don't know," Jay said.

"That's already true," I answered. "There are places in the world right now where many are beaten up and jailed for their beliefs. Jews, for example, and even Christians. I've seen end-times TV shows that are like that. Anyway, it's a long way off."

"No, no, the angels say it's soon. They say to prepare."

Jay was getting a little dramatic, I thought, but I didn't want to throw cold water on his exuberance. "So, what do you have to do to prepare?" I asked.

"To tell everyone about Jesus. He's going to take care of us when things are really, really bad."

They all agreed. It was like they were reading off the same page, and I was amazed at their mutual insight. I wasn't sure it was normal for kids of their age, which made me even more curious. "So, what about those who don't believe in Jesus?" I was half thinking of myself.

Ben said, "They are chained in a pit of fire."

This was getting ridiculous. No one believed in that anymore. I couldn't understand these boys being told such stories.

I looked at Carlos who had been quiet for several minutes. "And what do you say, Carlos?"

Carlos looked at me with those big eyes of his. I could see he'd been watching my reaction to their stories. "Don't you believe us?" he said.

That was definitely the question. Did I believe them? These three kids had really no reason to try to make a fool out of me. They seemed very genuine. I should be flattered for their confiding in me. But, no, I didn't believe them.

"I'm sorry, Carlos, but it's hard to believe all this about angels. I don't even believe the stories that Jesus is the real Son of God. I hope you understand."

"You're wrong, mister." He stuck a stubborn jaw out and sounded just like my own father used to when he and I didn't see eye to eye.

"All right, kid," I said, getting just a little bit annoyed. I thought we'd better discuss something else because there are some subjects

I don't want to talk about, especially with kids who are much too young to know about such things. My religion was very personal to me, and I didn't want anyone messing with it. Over the years, I had concluded certain things, based strictly on what I wanted to believe, and to hear something so entirely alien to me from the mouths of babes was not an option. I hadn't liked the Wednesday night campfire gathering, and this confirmed it. Obviously, they were getting indoctrinated by some of the more radical counselors—and Steve was probably the chief.

"Let's just agree to disagree," I told the boys. "Let's talk more about your families."

But, somehow, the boys had lost their enthusiasm. They seemed to be saddened. I hadn't gone along with their strange visions. Adults had acted that way to me before when I didn't buy into their business ventures or go to their home parties. Unfortunately, I'd lost what little trust I'd started to build with these kids—at least for now.

Steve walked in. All three of the boys looked happy when they saw him, and the atmosphere improved abruptly.

"So, what are these little truants doing here?" he asked with a wry smile. "We're short of some good ball players this afternoon."

"I guess we should have told you," I said. "Tracy wants them kept aside for a couple of days because Carlos here has the measles."

"The measles!" he said. "Wherever did that come from?" He started inspecting each of the boys in turn.

"Tracy figures Carlos picked it up before he got here. Probably never had shots. She doesn't have records on any of these other guys, so she was going to start calling around."

"All right. I guess it's a good idea to keep them confined," Steve said, "but we're going to need you two fellows back out there, so don't you both go getting sick on me." He squeezed both Jay and Ben on their shoulders. "OK?"

The two nodded seriously, but Carlos stood with his head down.

"And you're going to be all right too, Carlos. Just don't go scratching those spots and making sores. It'll be all over in a few days."

I watched Steve as he talked with the boys and felt envious toward his easy, friendly manner. I could see how the kids enjoyed being around him. At the same time, I was bothered by knowing he was pumping his religion into their innocent minds and filling them with that ridiculous fire-and-brimstone stuff. Better he stick to his counseling, I thought.

"Steve, you and I have got to talk sometime soon," I said. "I need to ask you some questions about different things going on here."

"Anytime, Mel," he said. "Glad to have a chance to get to know you better. As a matter of fact, I am really impressed by the way you jumped in so quickly to help keep the camp afloat. You've only been here a short while, and bam, we have Magic Mike coming on the Fourth of July! I can't tell you how much we all appreciate it."

"Well, thank you, Steve. It's nice of you to say so. It's been truly amazing to see how things have started to work out."

"We can thank the Lord for that. It's an answer to prayer. He's using you in a special way."

He sounded just like Tracy. The thing was, I was amused that Steve didn't seem to understand what plain luck it was that I'd thought of calling Eric Rogers, who had a sister in Denver he wanted to visit, and who just happened to be willing to stop off in Colorado for a little R and R.

○◉○

In the meantime, Tracy found that both Jay and Ben were immunized against measles, so they were released to go back into the camp population. Carlos stayed with me. Thankfully, I had no symptoms yet.

For the next couple of days, Tracy set up a sleeping cot for Carlos in the clinic, and we had our meals there. Although, at first, I anticipated the boredom of sitting with one little Mexican boy all day long, trying to think of ways to keep him occupied, I now began to see that this eight-year-old was pretty exceptional. The more I was with him, the more I came to love his simple thoughts, which were sometimes rather profound.

I asked, "Carlos, what is it like to have seven brothers and two sisters?" Growing up without any of my own had left me happy to be the center of everything and equally as sad to be the center of everything.

He thought a minute and said, "Momma says if you are nice to the baby, he wants to sit on your lap."

I had to think a moment too. "You mean that if you are good to someone, they care more about you?"

"Uh-huh."

"So, you were taught to love and take care of each other so that, in a big family like yours, everyone would get along well."

"Yep, we do."

"Why did you come here instead of staying with your mother and the rest of the family?"

"Daddy came to work here. I wanted to come too so I hid in the truck, and when they found me, it was too late to go back."

"Was your father mad?"

"He talked to the mission, and Miss Tracy brought me here."

"Where did you learn to speak English so well?"

"We always talk English. Mommy is very smart."

Yes, I thought. *She surely must be smart to have taught this kid to speak so well and think like an adult.* His level of maturity amazed me. "So, you wanted to come here. Why was that?"

"I want to be American."

"Have you found that America is a good place for your family?"

"I want to be somebody. So do my brothers and sisters."

It was true, and little Carlos had been fortunate. His father had probably come illegally. They might get deported, but in the meantime, he was at this camp whose mission was to help kids like him prepare for a better place in life. And now that I had become a part of his future, I determined that I wanted to make him want to sit on my lap. Most of all, I wanted to pass on something of value to him like the other counselors were doing rather than merely serving as his babysitter.

I wasn't sure just where to start, so I asked, "What do you want to learn at camp?"

"To tell stories about America."

Boy, was I pleased. *That's why I came here in the first place.* "Do you want me to help you tell your stories?"

He broke into a smile, surprising me with his pleased reaction.

"I can do that," I said.

Chapter 21

STEVE WAS RIGHT ON the ball and brought in a volunteer crew of men from his church who started building the stage for the upcoming show. They were a great bunch of guys with a terrific sense of humor. While they kidded around a lot, they got a lot of work done.

They worked from a set of plans included in the kit that Annie had sent. It was to be a modest size to keep the costs down, but it was certainly going to look impressive when it was finished. I was intrigued to see how a secret trapdoor was built into the middle of the stage, hidden from the audience. Here's where Mike could instantly become anyone he wanted to be and change his appearance before their very eyes.

The men said they could use my help, so I took the job of running the overhead power saw while Carlos sat on the sidelines and watched. As they measured lengths of board, I cut them to size from bundles of pine board that sat nearby. In this way, the construction moved ahead at considerable speed.

During break time, one of the men wanted to know what church I went to, and when I told him I was Jewish, he was interested in hearing more. I said that I no longer attended services, except rarely on High Holidays. The guy told me, "You know, at our church, we pray for Israel all the time."

I was mystified as to why they should care a hoot about such a tiny Middle Eastern country that was no bigger than New Jersey. "What does this have to do with your Christian religion?" I asked.

"Oh, in the book of Psalms, David said, 'Pray for the peace of

Jerusalem: that they shall prosper that love thee.' We know that if we stand with Israel, the Lord will bless us and Israel as well. We just feel greatly connected to the Jewish people because we believe we are 'grafted' to the tree of Abraham, Isaac, and Jacob. Does that make sense?"

I didn't think it made sense at all. What right did Christians have to take on the ancient Jewish traditions that could not possibly belong to Gentiles? From my standpoint, they wanted the blessings of God's covenant with the Jews—and then added Jesus on for good measure. "I guess I'll have to think about it a bit," I said. "It's a bit confusing to me."

"If you would like to come to our Bible study, we'd love to have you. We can answer any questions you might have."

I figured he was interested in converting me, and it was the last thing I wanted. "Right now, I'm pretty busy with the Magic Mike program, so I can't take on anything more."

That didn't dissuade him a bit. "OK, I'll check with you after the Fourth of July. I know you'd like the guys I meet with."

Thankfully, we needed to get back to work—so our conversation was over.

○◉○

Tracy declared Carlos out of the measles-giving business a couple of days later, so he went back to his tentmates, but he had already started to write about what he saw in America for his family back home. I was eager to continue working with him.

Unfortunately, that had to be put aside since we had only two weeks to get everything ready for Magic Mike. And, yes, I began to stress out! There was so much yet to do. I had received proofs of both the ads and posters from Nicole and had given them an enthusiastic go-ahead. Both jobs were wonderful. The paper's artist had come up with some very bright graphics and eye-catching headlines. I knew it was going to excite anyone who had ever heard of Magic Mike and intrigue those who hadn't. I still had to coordinate with the mayor, but Nicole told me the town council had eagerly approved the combined fireworks program at the camp.

I called an after-breakfast meeting of my committee. Steve was well on his way with the staging, generator, and lights. The ads and posters were coming out in a day or two. Tracy would have tickets in plenty of time and had enlisted a couple from the mission staff as cashiers. She was also seeing to the lodging of our guests.

Juan was planning on cooking more than a thousand hot dogs initially—with another several thousand ready to go—plus all the trimmings and paper products. He thought this was an area in which the camp might even make a profit. Three independent concession trucks of soft drinks, candy, and popcorn were coming from town.

Jesus Joe had accounted for twenty portable bathrooms to be set up the day before the event. I was going to visit the mayor and police department to organize the traffic, parking, and security. A large rough area outside the camp would be used for parking—as long as we had help in moving people in and around the boulders and cactus plants. The crowd would be encouraged to bring blankets or tarps and sit on the ground or in lawn chairs.

"Now, what have we forgotten?" I asked.

Each person sat quietly, thinking. We didn't have any additional thoughts, but there were probably many smaller details we would have to face in the days ahead.

Afterward, I walked with Steve to the stage. It was coming along beautifully, and I was impressed by the professional job his guys had already accomplished. There would be no need for a curtain. The backdrop was the tremendous red sandstone cliff that soared hundreds of feet overhead. I wondered if this might create an echo, but Steve didn't think so. The men were in the process of constructing a canopy of crossbeams over the stage to shade the performers from the sun and protect them in case of an afternoon rainstorm.

Steve had to hurry along to his morning class, so I was left alone. With my crutch, I mounted the side steps that had just been put in place. From the height of the platform, I wanted to see how many people would be able to view the performance from various angles. I went to the center and looked out over the expanse of rough ground. It was a great location, practically an amphitheater, where the grade gradually rose from the stage front to the farthest edge and back of the field. The sides were bordered by large rocks where people could also sit.

"Ladies and gentlemen," I announced to the hopefully sellout crowd. "I give you Magic Mike." And with a sweep of my hand, I turned and pretended to introduce our famous guest who would appear from the wings.

And suddenly, I knew there was something I had forgotten: the master of ceremonies! Who would introduce the show? Who would run it? Who would be good enough to be like the ringleader in the circus—full of fun and excitement? My heart went up into my throat. Not me, I thought. No, I couldn't face such a big crowd. I had no experience, but I couldn't think of anyone else at the camp who could do it, except perhaps the Commander, and he was currently unavailable. Then I was relieved to think of the one person who could get me off the hook. Eric Rogers, the creator of Magic Mike himself. *Yes,* I said to myself, *he is outgoing, upbeat, and energetic. I'll get him do it. Whew!*

But someone still had to talk about Camp Sage and Sand. Someone had to convince the audience that this little camp was worth continuing into the future. This was the entire reason for the big event. We couldn't blow this great chance to secure the community support when it was going to probably be needed soon. Who could effectively take our case to the public? Right now, I seriously didn't know. Once again, I hoped it wouldn't have to be me.

○◉○

Just before noon, Tracy and I got into her little car and went to see the Commander in the hospital. We found him sitting up in a private room with oxygen at his nose and a drip line in one arm. He was pale and looked like he'd lost some weight since I saw him last. His hair even looked a little grayer.

Tracy went over and gave him a kiss on the cheek. "You look wonderful," she said. "What did the doctor say today?"

"He's satisfied with my condition. Wants me to start getting up and around today. I feel pretty weak, but it's not my custom to sit."

"Everyone is looking forward to your being back at the camp, sir," I said. "We're all hoping you will be a part of the Fourth of July celebration."

"I plan on being there, Van Alan," he said. "You couldn't keep me away. Trouble is, I'll have to displace you from the clinic. I won't be able to stay in my old tent. What do you think of that?"

"I'm ready to move, gladly," I said. Now that my leg was getting better I was actually becoming a little embarrassed about having such a privilege anyway. I needed to get into a tent like the other counselors. By now, I was more accustomed to roughing it at Camp Sage and Sand, and I wanted to be in the trenches with the other men.

Tracy sat on the edge of the bed and held his hand, and I lowered myself into a lounge chair. We filled him in on the progress of the upcoming events.

As he listened to all the details, he perked up, and his eyes took on more intensity. "You people amaze me with your energy. Looks like our sleepy little camp is going to be the center of attention in a couple of weeks. Dr. Armor's attack may actually draw us closer to the community. I hope your efforts will help us combat what she started. I commend you all for being so proactive."

"We also plan to have some of the older boys carry around petitions for people to sign," I told him. "It'll give us something to hand the government if they try to use their eminent domain."

"Good, good," he said, as a nurse came in to take his blood pressure.

Tracy looked at her watch. "I'm afraid we've got a lunch meeting with Mayor Evans. I hate to leave you," she said, still clinging to his hand.

"Go on and git," he said. "I'll probably just nap."

"Good to see you doing so well," I added. "I know you'll be up and back with us soon."

"I expect so." He made a deep sigh as if the thought might be a little too much to bear right now. I realized then that this heart attack must had taken a big toll on him.

On the way to the restaurant, I voiced my thoughts to Tracy. "Once he returns, we've got to make sure that we don't put the weight of our world back on his shoulders."

"Just what I've been thinking," she said. "I may look into fixing up a little house near the mission where he can spend most of his time. If he comes back to camp, it's going to be difficult for him to avoid the problems that come up. Just for a while, at least."

"I know he won't like that, but you can try. He's probably stubborn enough to want to be back into the saddle before he should be. It might kill him to be put up in a little place where he doesn't have anything to do."

"I know," she said. "But it might kill him to come back to us too soon."

○◉○

We found the mayor talking with some townsfolk outside the little café where we were to meet. He was at the center of their attention and telling a funny story when we walked up. The group burst out in laughter, and I wished I'd been there to hear it.

Dave Evans looked to be about forty. His hair was dark except for a streak of white, combed back at the front. He turned to us as the others moved away. "I was telling them about the week I was staying at a Western Mayors' Conference in one of your more ritzy hotels in Los Angeles. They'd put a sign on the back of the door in my room that said, 'Have you left anything?' I changed it to say, 'Have you anything left?' They got a kick out of that." He put his hand out to me and said, "Dave Evans, I expect you're Mr. Van Alan. I know Tracy. How are you, beautiful?"

Tracy smiled shyly and said to me, "Dave and my parents were close friends for many years."

"I'm glad to meet you, Mr. Mayor," I said. "Call me Mel. I apologize that we haven't contacted you before this. I know Nicole Wayland has at least filled you in on what we are planning out at the camp. This whole opportunity came up so suddenly, and we didn't know just what to do first."

"No problem, Mel. We're excited to hear what's going on. You know, I have three kids, and they are absolutely nuts about this Magic Mike character. I've seen him on television, and I like it because it's wholesome kid entertainment, so I'm pleased they're coming to our area." He put his arms slightly behind us both and said, "Come on.

Let's go in and get a table. I've been watching for Barry Knox, our chief of police, who's going to join us. He must have been held up."

I wasn't sure if he was making another joke, but I chuckled. I liked this guy and thought we would get along well with him.

The café was crowded with the lunch crowd, but the mayor headed for an empty table in the back that I figured was probably his everyday spot.

An elderly waitress immediately came up behind us and said to Dave, "The usual?"

"You bet, Martha."

She poured him a cup of coffee from a pot she had brought with her. "What'll you all have to drink?" she asked us.

Tracy and I both ordered iced tea.

Without hesitation, I said, "We were blown away with your offer to move the city's fireworks program out to the camp on the Fourth. It was beyond our expectations."

He said, "Well, it so happens to solve a problem of our own. We have a major landscaping and reseeding program going on at the park, so we've been in a quandary as to what we were going to do for the holiday. We kept putting the decision off, and time was running out on us. Nicole called and suggested we think about going outside of town for a change. At first, we couldn't picture it, but honestly, I think this Magic Mike thing is pretty big. Who knows? Half our kids will probably be involved. We decided that once we're there, we should make it a day—with your permission of course."

"We have tons of space," Tracy said. "The ground is a little rough in places, but it's a great opportunity for us to let people see what we've been doing all these years, as well as provide a beautiful place for celebrating the Fourth. I think it's going to work out extremely well."

"There are quite a few logistics that need to be covered," I said. "I'm hoping you'll put us in touch with the people we need to coordinate with."

The mayor took a sip of his coffee. "That's why I wanted to start with Barry. Most of what we're talking about will be his responsibility. There are a few others, such as the fireworks crew, but he's our main guy."

As if on cue, the Chief made his way swiftly through the tables to grab the seat we'd saved for him. He had about the same build as the Commander with the same large barrel chest. He had a pleasant look that turned serious for the moment. "Sorry I'm late. I just got a long-winded talking-to from one of our esteemed citizens—and you know who."

Mayor Evans nodded and made a face. "Barry, let me introduce Tracy Palmer and Mel Van Alan. Do you know Tracy from the mission?"

"Of course. How have you been doing since your mother and father's accident?"

"Fine, thank you, Chief," Tracy said. "You were very kind to all of us."

The mayor said, "Mel, here, is from New York City, like I was telling you. He's a volunteer out at Camp Sage and Sand and the one who's bringing Magic Mike to town."

The Chief stuck his hand across the table to shake. "Well, you must be quite the promoter. We don't usually get that kind of Hollywood stuff here. What's the occasion?"

"Mike's creator, Eric Rogers, actually runs his operation out of New York. That's where I've worked with him in the past. He's doing this as a special favor." Here was my chance to explain the real reason behind what we were doing. "This whole thing comes out of some brainstorming that we did to raise awareness about the camp. Our director, Lieutenant Commander Elliot Dougan, a retired naval officer, has recently been threatened by someone close to the federal government that Camp Sage and Sand may be forced to shut down because it lies directly on or near an undeveloped Anasazi archeological site. A letter given to the Commander stated that it is unlawful to injure, destroy, or remove any prehistoric object of antiquity from public lands or lands adjacent to United States National Parks. The person bringing the charge is very serious about it, and we think that if we don't come up with something rather soon, we might suddenly find ourselves without a campground."

"Who is the person bringing the charges?" the mayor asked.

"Dr. Riga Armor," Tracy said. "Do you know her?"

"Know her? Nicole's mother? Of course. Who doesn't? We know

her very well," he said. "Isn't that who you were referring to just now, Barry?"

"Oh, yes," he said with a laugh. "We have our run-ins from time to time here too. Today, she was after me to install larger signs to identify the Trail of the Ancients. I told her that wasn't my department, but she insisted that I get someone to do it."

"She was on me last week for the same thing," the mayor said. "I told her exactly whom to contact, and it wasn't you."

I said, "Dr. Armor has been after the acreage out there since it was given to Tracy's parents. She's accused Commander Dougan of desecrating the land for even touching the pottery that he's found. We don't object to archeologists coming into the property, but we're not about to give it up completely. Instead, we feel it could be a great opportunity for us to work closely with these experts to teach the history and care of the land to our kids. And, who knows, we could be developing some future archeologists in the process."

"So you think that community awareness is the way to keep the good doctor from closing you down?" the mayor said.

"Exactly. We want the public to know what we've been doing all these years and rally behind us. During the program, we hope to announce some kind of plan to stimulate that support," I said. "Right now, we're just thinking as we go along."

"From what little I've heard so far," Chief Knox said, "it sounds downright evil for the old lady to be throwing you guys off your property by using the power of the government. What does she want anyway?"

Tracy said, "She's been angry for years that the original owner gave the property to the mission. Now that she is no longer associated with Mesa Verde per se, I think she's been looking for an opportunity to put herself in charge of a new development site to boost her ego and use federal funds to establish her own organization. We don't know how many treasures this piece of land has buried on it, but it probably does have some since we've discovered many bits and pieces scattered all along the base of the rock formation."

"Well, for my part, you can have all the cooperation my department can give you," Chief Knox said, "as long as the mayor and city council say it's OK." He looked at his boss for his concurrence.

"Absolutely," the mayor agreed. "I especially like your idea of cooperating with the government to develop the land and train your boys to respect it. I don't believe any one individual should take it over for personal gain or exploitation—if that's what Dr. Armor has in mind. What can we do to help?"

Tracy and I looked at each other and grinned.

"You've already committed more than we could have imagined possible," I said. "If you can help us with the parking, traffic, and crowd control, and perhaps if you were to speak at the evening event, Mr. Mayor, that would be tremendous. The fireworks display is another generous offer from the city."

"Jim Burns is heading that crew. He told me he's familiar with your place and is already excited by an idea to stage a waterfall of sparkling fire cascading down from high up on the sheer wall. He's aching to get a look at the terrain since he's a weekend rock climber, so I want to put him in touch with your guys out there as soon as possible."

"That can be arranged immediately," I said. "Just have him give us a call."

After a quick meal, our lunch meeting broke up with handshakes and backslaps all around.

Tracy and I were absolutely pumped. As we walked to the car, we shared our thoughts.

"We've come so far in such a short time—it's a miracle." Tracy said. "A couple of weeks ago, I was really discouraged by what might happen to us. Now, I actually believe we may have a chance to keep the camp alive and bring about more involvement—plus add a whole new area of archeology and history to our program. I know there are some of the kids who would be thrilled with this training. And, I take back anything I said about Nicole. That woman has truly paved the way for us with the town far more than I could have ever expected. They seem willing to provide anything we need."

I was thinking the same thing. "Nicole's a dynamo. We need to go over and see if she's ready for us to finalize the work she's done."

Chapter 22

Nicole was in her office. The box was back on the chair, so I had to lift it off and bring in another chair for Tracy.

"Well, did you have a successful lunch with our esteemed mayor?" she asked.

I hadn't remembered telling her we were meeting him. "Very," I said. "Thanks to you, both he and Barry Knox were two-thirds sold on the Fourth of July celebration. Now I believe they're fully behind us. We're excited by the whole prospect for the camp."

Tracy added, "You've been such a great help, and I want to add my thanks too."

Nicole looked at Tracy with a pleasant smile. "If I hadn't met those sweet little boys of yours, I would never have appreciated what you've been doing out there. I think it's important that other people get to meet them."

I made a memo to myself to make certain that visitors on the Fourth got a chance to interact with the boys.

"Well, things are beginning to come together," I said. "How about the advertising?"

Nicole pulled a file folder from the biggest stack and took out several items. "OK, here's the Sunday full-page ad."

It was eye-popping, with stars and stripes and details in big cloud bursts. Magic Mike was prominently pictured along with fireworks and popcorn and candy.

"It's tremendous. I like it. It'll get everyone's attention," I said.

Tracy agreed wholeheartedly.

Nicole brought out the poster that duplicated the ad.

"I can get the Boy Scouts to put these up for a donation to their Fall Jamboree," she said. "They will guarantee to get it in almost every store window—plus the added benefit of coming themselves."

"You don't miss a trick, do you? That will be great." I began to form the idea of hiring Nicole to come work for me as soon as I returned to New York.

She brought out a box of tickets that were already printed, and Tracy grabbed a bunch. "These are super," she said. "I just hope we have enough, now that we've gotten the city involved."

"I had an extra thousand printed," Nicole said. "It was nothing, once the press was rolling."

"It looks like you've thought of everything, Nicole," I said. "I'd say we're ready to go ahead on all this stuff."

We agreed to run the big ad twice in the next two weeks and a smaller one on a daily basis. The price was high, but I was depending on the revenue from the tickets to cover it.

When we got up to leave, Nicole hesitated. "There's one more thing. I'm not certain, but I think my mother has something up her sleeve. I can't imagine what it is, but she was being very secretive last night on the phone when I said something about the Fourth of July being moved out of town. She said, 'Humph. We'll see about that.' I tried to get her to clarify that, but she changed the subject. So, I'm warning you to be ready for just about anything. I know her."

"Thanks for the heads-up," I said, a bit concerned. "I guess there's not much we can do until she makes a move. She told the Commander he had one week to comply with her demands, and that time has passed already."

Nicole walked us to the front, and we left. "I hope nothing happens between now and the Fourth," I told Tracy. "We've got a lot at stake now."

"I'm not afraid of her. What could one old lady do?" Tracy said.

○◉○

On Monday, the day after the full-page ad appeared, the special events phone line that Tracy had set up in town started to ring continuously. A volunteer committee at the chamber of commerce office began selling tickets, and the line snaked around the building. In a couple of days, the posters increased the excitement even more. Finally, Tracy had to add another ticket office at the storefront where the mission sold used clothes.

The Commander's health continued to improve, and it looked like he might be back with us by the end of the week. He would have nothing to do with the idea of being sheltered in a little house away from the action. However, he did promise to take a back seat for a while—if we allowed him to join us at the camp.

The performance stage was complete, and when I got together with Steve, I told him that he had outdone himself. It was like an immense veranda, in the Southwest style, with heavy lodge beams jutting forward from the roofline. The sides had been adorned with green plantings set in giant barrels in raised levels. The cliff backdrop towered above everything.

"If we're going to have the whole town out here, I figured it better be good," he said. "My guys really enjoyed themselves coming out here and giving their time. A couple of them particularly wanted to come back and teach construction next year."

This warmed my heart. My reaction was like perhaps what the Commander would have had. Instead of being a simple volunteer from New York, I was growing increasingly grateful for whatever people were willing to do. It began to dawn on me how much I had become attached to this place. "They were a great bunch of men," I told him. "I hope they all come back because I want to get to know them better."

"They liked you too, Mel. Of course they did get a kick out of some of your eastern ways."

"Like what?"

"Oh, your accent, for one. The New York sound. And being a little standoffish. You know, appearing to be just a little superior. And being very particular, such as trying to get each and every board cut perfectly, and throwing away the warped ones. And—"

"Enough already," I said.

He laughed. "No, really, they loved you. They want to talk with you. Most of them haven't had a chance to travel and want to hear about the East Coast. You are not only a curiosity, but you have a genuine spirit about you that wants to come out. These men have tender hearts, and they love nothing more than to deal with each other as brothers. They want to include you too."

I had never known what it was to know men like this. Having no brothers of my own and only one or two close friends in college, the most contact I'd had with men was purely business. The one exception I could think of was Eric Rogers, who now was on his way to spend a couple of days with me. He had always been downright generous, and, yes, I could see now that he really meant it. I had wrongly thought he wanted my professional help without paying the high fees of the bigger agencies, but now I saw he was the real thing. I was moved by these thoughts, and I wanted to think more about it.

I also began to look at Steve from a different perspective. He didn't have to bring me into his close fraternity of friends. Others wouldn't have bothered. I was an outsider, and he knew I'd be leaving in a few weeks. There was no reason for him to spend any extra time on me, and I was really pleased that he wanted to include me in anything.

Another person who changed my perception was Jesus Joe. Primarily because of his name, I had assumed that he was a humble Catholic man. He certainly appeared to approach life with the simple manner of a monk. But I found out differently when we met in the afternoon to finalize our electrical needs.

"I am Navajo," he said when I asked him if he went to the same church Steve did. "I see the sky, the earth, and the wind."

I took this to mean that he marched to a different drummer. I decided I would ask him more about his religion at a later date. For now, he was our chief electrician. "Did you get a generator for the stage and lighting out there?"

"No need," he said. "Rural Electric people brought in a new line. Plenty of juice, all hooked up. All ready for your 'magic' people."

The show information had specified that they would furnish all their own lights, sound system, and special effects. All we needed was a source.

"And how about lighting for the audience, the paths, and the parking areas after dark?"

"Steve wants torches everywhere. No electricity."

Wow, I thought. *Now that will be spectacular. The whole area lit by flaming torches after dark that cast a beautiful glow over everything.* It was a great idea, and I couldn't wait to see the effect. "Sounds like you and Steve have this area well covered," I said with gratitude. "You guys can certainly be depended upon." I couldn't help but think of some of the union problems I'd had in setting up various exhibits at Jake Javits Convention Center in Manhattan. At times I wanted to tear my hair out just getting a little help, and it was rare for me to be assigned someone who cared enough to think ahead for our needs.

○◉○

HAVING MET WITH OUR events committee—and feeling greatly that we just might pull it off—I was eager to walk around the camp and talk to some of the boys about getting them to mix with the townspeople when they came for the Fourth of July. I wasn't sure what I was going to tell them, but I hoped it would come naturally.

I wandered toward the corral where I could see a bunch of kids sitting on the fence rail. I asked several of them, "Are you looking forward to Magic Mike being here?"

"Yes," they all said excitedly in unison.

"Can we get his autograph?" one of them asked.

"I'll bet you can. And did you know that lots of other people are coming to see him too?"

They looked confused. They thought Magic Mike was coming just for them.

"It's true," I said. "There's going to be a big crowd from town, and we're going to want you to welcome them. Do you think you can do that?"

There were silent, probably wondering what I was getting at.

"When the people come, we're going to want you to talk to them and not be shy. Tell them what you're learning here, and answer any questions they have. We're going to give every one of you a new camp T-shirt to wear too, so they'll know who you are. You can show the folks around. Maybe even take them to see your tent and the mess hall and the corral here. Now, do you think you can do that?"

"I guess," one of them said, "but do we have to?"

"Well, it's like learning how to welcome someone to your house. This is your home for right now, isn't it? You are called the host, and the people are your guests. What you do is make them comfortable and happy they came. And you make them want to come back. And you also want them to tell other people what a super place this is. That's why you don't want to be shy. You take people by the hand and show them around."

"Yeah, but what if they don't want to come with us?"

"Well, of course you only take them around if they want to go. So, the best thing to do is walk among them in your camp shirts; they're your guests, and you smile at them and say hello. You can even say, 'Welcome to the camp' if you want. I can tell you they'll really be pleased to hear you thank them for coming."

"Can we invite our parents too?" one of the younger ones asked.

"Absolutely. Call them or send a letter home right away to tell them to be here on the Fourth of July." I suddenly thought of an idea. "Your mothers and dads and sisters and brothers can come free! If you give us their names tonight after dinner, we'll save some tickets for each of them. Won't that be neat?"

"Yeah," they said—and they meant it! It was so great to get their positive reaction. I could see them getting behind the idea of talking to people. *Tonight, at mess, I am going to say this whole thing again for the rest of the campers to get them as excited about being good hosts. I hope I can do it. A lot depends on all the kids being sold on it.*

Steve turned to me, after I got through giving the same little speech to the entire assembly later at dinner, and said, "That was very nice, Mel. You have a nice way of talking to the boys. I think they understand now that we definitely want them to be a part of the program. Encouraging their families to come is also a great idea that I hadn't thought of. Most of their parents are struggling, but they support what we're doing here, and perhaps I should add, they should be."

"Thanks, Steve," I said. "We need to mobilize every possibility."

"We'll, I've got to run," he said. "I've got Wednesday-night praise and worship to lead." Steve turned to leave. "You coming again this week?"

"No, I don't think so, Steve," I said. "I've been wanting to take some time to talk to you about it when things weren't so hectic. Let's just say that I don't really agree with what I saw happening out there last week, and I just can't be a part of it. Please understand that I'm new here and shouldn't be getting my nose into established programs, but I wasn't happy to see how those innocent boys were being whipped into a religious frenzy to the point of talking with angels. I can't be a part of such cultish goings-on."

Steve's mouth opened, and his eyes went wide with shock. "Mel, Mel, you've got it all wrong. I have nothing to do with what you saw last week. Believe me! I am as astonished by it as anyone. What I am doing out there is standing by, learning as it happens. Honestly, it's all out of the blue. I never saw it coming. You've got to believe me. This started the first time we met as a group this year. I had plans for nice worship songs around the campfire. Things have taken a huge turn, but—I can tell you this—I am not going to stop it or stifle it. Not when I believe it comes from God's Holy Spirit. I believe it's the same manifestation as happened in Acts 2 that we know as Pentecost. I mean, this is totally amazing."

He had given me an earful, but without hostility. I had already begun to see that Steve was totally committed to the welfare of the boys and did excellent work. I had no reason to doubt his sincerity. Yet, how could he lead me to believe that he had nothing to do with what I saw that night? It was impossible to imagine how a bunch of little boys could act the way they did without being directed by an adult.

"OK," I said. "I'm sorry if I made some rash assumptions. However, for me, until there's some good explanations, I can't be a part of it."

"Fair enough." He held up a hand. "I understand what you're saying. In the meantime, you might want to read the first part of the book of Acts of the Apostles in the New Testament and see for yourself. It could open your eyes to what I'm saying. Tracy keeps a Bible handy in her desk." He gave me a warm smile and left.

The mess hall had emptied except for the kitchen crew, but I stayed a minute to reflect on our conversation. I had seen the biblical reference to Pentecost at one time or other, but I couldn't think where since I had never read the New Testament. *Is this what he meant by the Acts of the Apostles?* The apostles were the close friends of Jesus, so this was outside my knowledge. There was still too much to do in the days ahead to bother with thoughts of religion. I only hoped that what the boys were delving into would not affect the outcome of a successful celebration, which was now only a little more than a week away.

Chapter 23

COMMANDER DOUGAN SURPRISED US all and returned to the camp the next day. He was greeted by a small group hastily gathered at the administrative office, and a big welcome sign had been taped on the outside wall.

As Tracy drove into the area, the Commander waved from the open car window like the president. He was weak and had to be assisted out of his seat, and a gasp went up as he almost lost his balance against the car door.

Embarrassed, he straightened up and made a brief statement in a thin voice. "Thank you everybody for being so nice for coming to greet me. It's wonderful to be back. I hope to talk with each and every one of you to find out how you're doing. In the meantime, I will be staying at the clinic, so come and see me. God bless you all." He made another quick wave and headed for his new bedroom with a hand on Tracy's arm.

I had taken my few things from the clinic and moved them back to the tent where I had started. The canvas walls no longer seemed hostile, the wooden floor kept me from the dirt, and the cot was comfortable. I felt very much at home now, compared to the first night I arrived. I no longer cared if it rained—except for July the Fourth, of course.

The Commander was propped up on his freshly made bed when I returned to see him. "Are you up to hearing all the details of our celebration?" I asked.

"By all means, Van Alan. Tracy filled me in on ticket sales before she left to swim. It seems that we have a best seller going on here."

"Yes, we do. And I expect you heard that the city's fireworks program is going to be here that night too?"

"Downright amazing." He was nodding with approval. "I don't know how you managed to pull it off, but I must say, you are some kind of publicity man."

"I can't take credit for that. If you know Nicole Wayland at the newspaper, she's the one to thank for the city contact. She's helped us quite a bit, as a matter of fact."

"I know she's nothing like her mother, and for that, we have to be thankful."

For the next few minutes, I filled the Commander in, so he would be a part of it all.

"It doesn't seem like you've missed much. With help of the local police, we just might fit all the people in and move traffic in and out. That's my greatest concern," he said.

"Mine too. But you know, the Army Corps of Engineers are even going to bring in a temporary bridge up a ways from the stream crossing to provide a second lane for outbound cars. All this is being done without us lifting a finger. It's as if we're being handed a miracle."

"It is a miracle, boy, and don't you doubt it," the Commander said.

Suddenly, I was aware of someone standing at the clinic door. I turned, expecting to see Tracy. A guy in a blue shirt, jeans, and cowboy boots came forward to the little bedroom. "You Commander Dougan?" he asked me.

"No, that's him," I said pointing toward the bed.

"This is for you, Commander," the man said as he handed over an envelope. "Have a nice day."

The Commander looked surprised, but he put out his hand to accept the letter.

The stranger turned and left without another word.

"Who was that, Van Alan?"

"I have no idea. I've never seen that guy before."

The Commander slit the envelope with his thumb and drew out a sheet. He read it for a moment and then handed it over without saying anything.

It was a summons from the Twenty-Second Judicial District Court, Cortez, Colorado, referencing Camp Sage a.k.a. Camp Sage and Sand. It said we were in violation of provisions of the American Antiquities Act of 1906 and are now under a stay order barring activities scheduled to occur on July 4 at said camp to prevent further damage to property of immediate interest of the United States federal government. The order was signed by a magistrate judge for the district court.

I handed it back to the Commander. I felt sick to my stomach. "So the wicked witch has struck," he said. "Our celebration provided the perfect timing."

"What are we going to do?" I wondered aloud.

"Well, over the years, I've learned not to rush around with our heads cut off. I know this magistrate, and he's a pretty good fellow. Maybe he'll take my call and give us a little advice from the bench."

○◉○

I FOUND TRACY AT her daily swim before the kids took over in the afternoon. She was gracefully doing laps, and I watched her athletic body rhythmically pulling along from one bank to the other. The more I saw of her, the more I treasured who she was and how she dedicated herself to others. There were no hidden pretenses with her. What you saw was what you got.

And what I saw was very, very nice. Her natural blonde hair, now tied up in the back, usually was combed out, which enhanced her natural beauty. She never wore makeup that I could detect, but she did use some kind of perfume that I had yet to identify. I liked it a lot.

I sat at the edge of the pond, happy to be quietly alone with her, and I took off my shoe to dip a bare foot in the water. Yikes, it was cold! How she could stay in for more than two minutes beat me. Pretty soon, my foot began to get used to the water temperature, and it actually felt good.

Finally, Tracy slowed her pace and stood at the shallow end. She took off a pair of goggles and saw me. "Well, hello, how long have you been there?" she said.

"Quite a while," I lied. "You have such a smooth form. I envy you."

"I've been swimming in this pond for so long it's become part of me. I don't know what I'd do without the peace and calm that this place brings. I can wash off any trouble right here."

I could use some of that peace and calm right now, I thought. "There's nothing like this where I come from," I said. "Nothing where there isn't a score of other people flopping around. It's not calming in the least."

She waded over and sat next to me. Her skin was covered with goose bumps from the midmorning breeze, and she quickly threw a towel around her shoulders.

After a moment, I said, "I've got a bit of bad news."

"Oh no, I don't want to hear it."

"OK. Suit yourself."

"All right. What is it?"

"The Commander just had a visit from a process server. We've been slapped with a stay order from the local district court to put a stop to our Fourth of July celebration. Dr. Armor must have given the judge enough justification to close us down for the day. I'm only surprised that she didn't have him extend it indefinitely."

"Oh, no. What are we going to do? I hope the Commander's all right because we can't let him be burdened with handling this mess."

"He knows the judge. Maybe he can clear it up with a phone call."

"Hopefully," Tracy said, "but Dr. Armor isn't about to let it go without a fight now that she's gone this far."

"Probably. I just wanted to alert you so we could get with the Commander to figure out what we should do together … after he makes a call."

As we got up, Tracy gave me the edge of her towel to dry my bare foot. We walked quietly back to the clinic.

The Commander was just putting the phone down. "Just talked to Judge Randolph. He confirmed that the wicked witch and her lawyer had paid him a visit armed with a stack of federal documents regarding the protection of antiquities. She showed him how we fit the category, and all Ben could do was to issue a stay order, pending hearing our side of the issue. She told him there would be thousands of people out here swarming over the area, and the entire site must be protected from destruction of ancient artifacts. He said we'd better git ourselves a meeting with him ASAP if we want the order lifted in time for the Fourth. He recommended we bring a good lawyer because she had a pretty hot one."

"Who do we know who's a good lawyer?" Tracy asked.

"Go git Steve," the Commander said. "He's from town and knows people."

I went looking for Steve and found him in class, teaching the rules and courtesies of baseball.

"Can I speak with you a minute?" I whispered from the doorway.

He told the kids to hang on and slipped over to see me.

"A judge has issued a stay order to keep us from having the public out here on the Fourth. We need to see him right away with a good lawyer. Do you know anyone who could help us?"

"Funny, I just talked to this young guy Sunday, and he said if we ever needed any help, to call him. Talk about the Lord's provision! He's just come into the area and plans to set up an office. He seemed very sharp. Let me think of his name, and I'll come up to the office right after class."

"Thanks, I really appreciate it. And we're at the clinic."

It wasn't long before Steve joined us. "The guy's name is Mark McGuinness. He's about thirtyish and looking for business. I think he said he's a Stanford graduate. Anyway, I can try to find him through some of the guys at church. They'll know where he's staying. I'll get on the horn later and have him call you."

"*Now*, Stephen," the Commander commanded.

With that, Steve took the phone and started making some calls. Fifteen minutes later, he had Mark on the line. Steve filled him in briefly and started to hand the phone to the Commander, but Tracy shook her finger at him.

"Have him talk to Van Alan," the Commander said.

I took the phone, introduced myself, and told him about the stay order.

Mark was very nice, and since he had nothing else pending, he'd get out to the camp right away.

"Another miracle?" I said to the Commander.

"Another miracle." He smiled.

Chapter 24

AND, YES, MARK KNEW all about Magic Mike.

The Commander was pleased. "Well, son, I expect you'll do just fine. I can remember when I was just out of college and going into the navy. There wasn't anybody or anything that I couldn't tackle and win. You're up against a pretty tough cookie, so don't underestimate her. She's testing our mettle, trying to get this property using the federal government's clout. She may have put together some big backers like state senators and maybe even the governor, who knows? She's been cozy with some of them for years. Just keep a cool head and think outside the bureaucratic box."

We all shook hands as Mark left. He lingered with Tracy just a bit, and for some reason, it made me irritated watching him get close to her.

Steve walked the young lawyer out to his car and talked for a while before he drove off. Our hopes for a successful Fourth of July went with him.

○◉○

MARK WENT TO WORK right away, and we were granted a court date for early the next week. After his review of the facts, Mark told us he thought that Dr. Armor's case was flimsy since her assertion that the camp was sitting on a gold mine of artifacts was not backed up by tangible proof. The Commander's little display would be difficult to use as evidence since the pottery could have come from anywhere.

The fact that she merely suspected the early presence of the Anasazi on our property would not stand up without better evidence. The lawyer couldn't see how that could be enough to convince the judge to continue his stay.

Then the bottom fell out. Mark called back an hour later to say that Dr. Armor's lawyer had revealed she had access to written material that proved the presence of an actual ceremonial kiva located at the base of the great rock formation. Josiah Hobbs, who had donated the land to Tracy's parents, had detailed this discovery and presented these facts in a diary he had given to the Mesa Verde Library at his death. Dr. Armor had been waiting for just the right time to bring it to light. Now she was determined to keep the public off the land and remove the camp as soon as possible so she could start excavating the site.

This news was extremely depressing. It appeared Dr. Armor had the evidence that would undoubtedly force the judge to put a stop to our celebration. It was no longer her word against ours. Old Josiah Hobbs had apparently found some actual ruins on our property.

"I never imagined she would come up with any real proof," Tracy said. "Mom and Dad certainly didn't know a thing about it—or they would have told me. And they would have done whatever it took to protect the area from being desecrated. I've been all over that area and never seen anything even slightly resembling a sacred site."

Having found the catalog in the Commander's desk, I made the assumption that he already knew more than he had told anyone. As if he were reading my mind, the Commander spoke up. "It's time I told you all. I've known there was a kiva out there for several years now, Tracy. I should have told you and the folks as a courtesy. My thinking was this, and you may fault me for it if you want: I've never known such honest people as your mother and father. I knew that if I told them what I'd found, they would feel bound to inform Mesa Verde and other historians around here, and we'd never hear the end of it. What I feared then is what is happening now. The camp is being threatened with imminent closure to make room for the archeologists who are now going to swarm all over the place. My mistake was in bringing in some of the pottery from around the kiva and putting it on display. I even toyed with the idea of selling some of the pieces to bring in funds for better facilities, dorms, classrooms, and whatever, but I stopped that idea the day the newspapers reported what happened to some guys who tried the very same thing."

"I don't know why I never saw a kiva," Tracy said.

"It was filled with dirt and sand. I recognized the circular stone outline and started digging around it. That's when I came across the pots that I have. There's probably a lot more where they came from. Anyways, I covered it all over again so no one would spot it."

"This is going to kill us for sure." Tracy moaned. "I thought we might have had a chance with Mel's community support plan. All of our work will be for nothing now."

"Look, let's not give in too soon," I said. "Mark seems to be a clever kind of guy, and maybe he'll come up with something. It's true that Dr. Armor has some pretty solid stuff, more than we thought, but perhaps we can still work something out with the federal government. It's going to take a long time to get through the bureaucratic mill before they move us out, and a lot can happen in the meantime."

The Commander let out a sigh. "I'm tired. Right now, what you both need to do is git back to Mark McGuinness with what I've told you. We'll know soon enough if we are going to even have a case to fight sometime in the future, depending on what Judge Randolph decides about next weekend. You need to figure out how we're going to keep from disappointing a lot of kids who are looking forward to a good show. I wish you well."

Chapter 25

I CALLED MARK BACK and told him everything we knew. He was philosophical. "OK, so we have some skeletons to deal with. Thanks for the update." We set up a time to meet him an hour prior to the hearing on Tuesday. I hoped he had a plan.

The second full-page ad appeared as scheduled on Sunday. As I read it, my stomach tightened. Since we were still advertising, there were going to be a lot of disappointed kids if we didn't get the judge to vacate the stay. We needed an alternate site for the Magic Mike show and fireworks if we lost. The mayor and the chief of police had to be contacted right away.

I set up a Monday-morning meeting with them, Nicole and Bill from the newspaper, plus Tracy and me. The mayor offered his office.

After small talk with coffee and doughnuts, we got seated.

Nicole patted a place on the couch next to her. She moved close so that our arms were touching.

Despite the distraction, I took a deep breath and did my best to fill everyone in on our problem, starting with the court order. I confessed that we didn't have a very good case, now that Dr. Armor had proof of the existence of ancient ruins on our property. And the government might indeed want to keep a large crowd from converging there.

"I just knew Mother had something planned," Nicole said. "Didn't I tell you?"

Mayor Evans was not happy. "So you're telling us that everything might have to be moved to another location for next Saturday? Is that right?"

I swallowed and said, "It looks that way right now."

"When's the hearing?"

"Tomorrow at 10:00 a.m."

"Is there any chance that the judge might rule in your favor?"

I squirmed in my seat. "It's impossible to say. Our lawyer is trying every way to beat this. Judge Randolph did tell Commander Dougan it seemed a shame that the public might be restrained from coming to two of the biggest events of the summer. He hated to be the one to disappoint them."

Chief Knox spoke up. "Offhand, I don't know of any other place big enough to accommodate that many people, not with the park torn up. Maybe the airfield?"

"Check on that, will you, Barry?" the mayor said. "We need an alternate lined up immediately."

The Chief pushed back his chair and took his coffee with him to make some calls.

Tracy looked downcast. "I am so sorry that we've put you in such a tough position," she said to the mayor. "We had no idea that this was going to be thrown at us."

"Don't worry about it, Tracy," he said. "Look, we can't help what happens when people start to push their own selfish agendas. We'll just have to stay flexible. That's been my life's two-word philosophy: stay flexible."

Bill Alexander said, "We can easily inform the public if there is a change of location to the airfield because it's on the way out to the camp. Plus there's still plenty of time. Just call us as soon as you're certain. Nobody's going to blame the camp or even Dr. Armor if we give a reasonable explanation for the move and promote the fun they're going to have wherever they end up."

"Thanks, Bill," I said. "You've been a big help. We have no intention of canceling the Magic Mike show. There's too much already invested in it. I know these performers. They're used to putting on a good show just about anywhere."

Barry Knox stuck his head in. "The airfield's out until after dark. Too many unscheduled private flights."

"Keep looking, will you?" the mayor said. "I'll start checking around too."

Our meeting broke up with a decision to find a place for the Fourth—even if it had to be on desert land. We knew that would be awful, but we were feeling a bit desperate.

Nicole moved even closer to me. "I'm sorry for my mother's narrow mind. She's committed to saving even the smallest piece of history, and that's not all bad. She does have a good side, but it's hard for her to show it."

"I know. We're involved in our own little world too. I would like to see a compromise, however, rather than what she's proposing. There's no need for the camp to close."

"I agree," she said. "And if I get the chance to talk straight with her, that's what I'll say."

○◉○

BACK AT THE CAMP, the Commander surprised us when he suddenly appeared driving a beautiful white electric golf cart, making circles in front of the administration building. "Neat huh?" he said as he swung by.

"Where did that come from?" Tracy called back.

He pulled up beside us. "This is a gift from General Robert Enders of Camps with Kids. He phoned me at the hospital last week to offer his condolences. I guess I forgot to tell you."

"Well, what a wonderful thing to do. I had no idea he was so aware of your situation."

"I told him that my greatest desire was to be back with the kids, but I wouldn't be able to git around like I used to. They just delivered this baby half an hour ago. I'm going to go in and phone him right now to let him know he's the greatest."

It was pure pleasure to watch the Commander glide around the lot, especially as he bounced over the ruts. The color was returning to his face, and his beaming smile made me glad. I realized how much I had come to respect this guy, and I was very happy for him.

"General Enders wanted to know how we'd resolved the problem with the Park Service," the Commander said, back after his call to New York. "I told him we were going to be in court tomorrow, and I'd let him know the result. He repeated his pledge to place his legal department behind us."

"That's good, but I think Mark can take it for now," I said. "We'll find out soon enough."

Chapter 26

Tracy and I were ready and in the car shortly after breakfast. The Commander hadn't joined us at the table, but the staff prayed for us there. I found comfort in their support, but I still had this sinking feeling that we were preparing for the inevitable.

We joined up with Mark at a little café across from the courthouse. He had lugged in a couple of heavy books and a briefcase full of papers. It always amazed me how much paperwork legal proceedings seemed to generate, and our little case was no exception.

He was bright-eyed and ready to take on the dragon. "Look, you guys, we don't have much to refute Dr. Armor's claims, now that she's come up with some pretty convincing evidence, but my appeal is going to show that we can adequately protect the area from public harm during the Fourth of July—and as long after that as necessary. The town attorney said they'd have no trouble helping us police the area. If either of you have any better thoughts, I'd like to hear them."

I couldn't come up with anything.

Tracy was more thoughtful. "We've got to remember that God is in control. Let's see what he wants to work out."

I gave Mark a hand with his books crossing the street. As Tracy moved ahead, out of hearing range, he said, "Isn't she something? Tell me, is she going with anyone that you know of?"

Once again, I felt myself becoming slightly irritated. Was it because he was moving ahead where I wanted to go?

"Not that I know of, Mark," I answered him. "She's been rather secluded out at the camp."

We watched her walk ahead of us, each with our own thoughts. We met with Judge Randolph in his cramped office, located in the rear of the second floor of the courthouse building. Dr. Armor and her lawyer were already talking with him when we arrived. A court stenographer sat back in the corner. We found another chair or two and waited for the judge to begin.

He smiled at all of us. "Welcome to my little abode. I hope we can keep this short. In the case of *Armor v. Camp Sage*, I would like to bring this hearing to order. Let me say that on Wednesday, June 24 of this year, I issued a writ in the name of Dr. Riga Armor, of this town, the plaintiff, and an unofficial representative of the United States Park Service, against Camp Sage, formerly Camp Sage and Sand, the defendant, to cease a proposed open house at said boys' camp on Saturday, July 4 of this year. The purpose for this stay order was to ensure the safety of certain irreplaceable ancient Indian artifacts on the defendant's property that could conceivably be damaged, moved, or even stolen during this public event. We are now gathered to hear the facts of the alleged ancient cache at Camp Sage and allow the defendants an opportunity to present their side of the inquiry. At this time, I would like to ask the attorney for the plaintiff to lead off with a description of the items in question and the reason he would ask us to order this stay be made permanent."

Dr. Armor's lawyer cleared his throat and began to repeat much of what the judge had just said. He went through a short history of Dr. Armor's verbal attempts to forewarn Tracy's parents and later, Commander Dougan, that they might be harboring endangered artifacts belonging to the people of the United States and that they stood in possible confrontation with the American Antiquities Act of 1906. He said, despite this, the camp had done nothing to rectify the situation, and in fact, would not allow a representative of the National Park Service to investigate or take pictures of the land in question after repeated requests.

Then he dropped his bombshell. "My client, Dr. Riga Armor, has a diary in her possession, written by the previous owner of the land in question, a Mr. Josiah Hobbs, following a detailed search through the archives at Mesa Verde. The library had been aware of the existence of this diary, but had never made a connection to the case in which Dr. Armor had personally been investigating for so many years." He pointed to his client who raised an old leather-bound album for all to see.

The judge said, "Let us mark this diary 'Exhibit 1,' and leave it in the hands of Dr. Armor for the time being. The defendants will be given ample opportunity to peruse this exhibit before they complete their case."

The lawyer went on to show one of the Sunday ads from the newspaper, announcing the Magic Mike show and Fourth of July celebration. "This is what my client wants to avoid. Now that there is compelling evidence of an ancient ruin, plus pieces of pottery known to be in existence at Camp Sage, it is imperative that the public not be allowed to come within close proximity—not now and not in the future—until everything is charted, photographed, and documented. It is therefore imperative that this so-called celebration not be allowed to continue for any reason. That is our statement, Judge Randolph."

The judge said, "Very well. Thank you." And then he turned to us. "I am now going to allow one hour for the folks from Camp Sage to review this exhibit, and then we'll continue this hearing. However, at that time, if they feel that they need longer to prepare their case, we will adjourn until another day." He tapped the end of his pen against the desk as his gavel.

Mark rose and went over to receive the diary from Dr. Armor. She said, "Be careful with this, young man. It's an important piece of history."

"Yes, ma'am," he said, and he lifted it from her lap.

Before becoming a rancher, Josiah had obviously been a professional field observer and created a remarkable diary from his notes, which were carefully written in a beautiful script that must have flowed from a faithful old fountain pen. The early pages had yellowed, but everything was readable. We turned to a section that had been bookmarked by Dr. Armor, for details of a kiva and signs of ancient life located in a raised terrace somewhere below the great rock structure. Josiah had drawn a sketch of the ruin, establishing how he had found the area buried under accumulated sand and dirt and tangles of growth, which he later cleared. There was no doubt that this was the very kiva the Commander had described to us privately.

We briefly discussed our options with little optimism.

When the judge called us together, we told him we were prepared to continue.

Mark had just started by conceding that the old diary did indeed show evidence of archeological findings, when Judge Randolph's secretary tiptoed in and handed him a message.

The judge held up his hand. "Just a moment, young man. It seems you have another member of your team waiting in my outer office. He wishes to testify. Let's have him come in and see what he has to add to this little hearing."

We turned to the door as Commander Dougan stalked in, followed by an older white-haired gentleman, slightly bent-over, nervously holding an old straw hat in hand. The room was already crowded, so I rose and gave the Commander my seat, while the older man and I stood along the bookcases.

"Sorry to barge into the meeting, Judge," the Commander said. "I don't know how far you've come in your deliberations, but we have some fresh information that's just come to light. I wanted to git in on the record before this meeting was over."

"Your timing is impeccable, Elliot," the judge said, calling the Commander by name. "The defendant's side is being heard at this very moment. Speak up. I'm sure the others are as curious as I am to hear what is so important."

"All right, listen up. Last night, I woke from a sound sleep with a remarkable new thought from the Lord. I pondered it for a while, gitting more and more anxious to investigate my inspiration. Just after light, I called Fred Roberts here." He pointed to the older man. "Well, after a bit of prompting, I got Fred to jump in his car and git out to the camp. Fred had done the original property survey when Hobbs donated the forty acres of the camp to your parents, Tracy. Within the hour, we actually found the ruins that we were told had been reported by Josiah Hobbs in a diary. Fred walked all around it with the copy of his survey."

Turning to face Dr. Armor, he said, "The upshot of this confounded mess you tried to start here, lady, is that Fred, here, located the very stake he put in the ground that marks the corner of Camp Sage and Sand, and I'm pleased to tell you that the old ruins are actually sitting outside our property by several hundred feet. This stuff is not on our land and never was!"

Tracy and I looked at each other with amazement. If the kiva wasn't on our land, it meant our land could not be confiscated by the government. We were free of Dr. Armor. And we were free to have our celebration on Saturday. It was a totally unexpected surprise that had come out of the blue.

Dr. Armor's neck stiffened, and she stared at the Commander in disbelief. "I've known for years that when Josiah Hobbs gave that land to you religious people, there had to be archeological artifacts all over that property. That tower rock was sacred to them, and it stands guard over many other confirmed sites. Hobbs proved it in his notes." She stood up and pointed an accusing finger. "That land was meant for scientific purposes."

The judge rapped his knuckles on his desk. "Now, now, we're not going to turn this hearing into a shouting match. Sit down, Dr. Armor, and control yourself."

Instead, she moved over to the window and stood looking out at the city.

"Fred," the judge said, beckoning to the old man, "I've personally known you for years, but for the record, let's hear from you. What are your credentials, sir?"

Fred Roberts moved forward a couple of steps and said, "I'm a licensed property surveyor, Your Honor. I've been in the business in this county for forty years, and my father before me. I was hired by the Reverend Arthur Palmer to set the boundaries for the boy's camp for his nonprofit tax application."

"And did this property include any archeological ruins, as far as you could tell?"

"No, sir. They were way to the east, like the Commander said. The camp property doesn't even go up to that part of the big rock."

The judge sat back. "Well, it appears that the original complaint does not match the property in question. And if the ancient site is not within the boundaries owned by Camp Sage and Sand, I'm inclined to vacate this stay order at this time—unless I hear an objection."

Dr. Armor's lawyer had moved over to the window and was speaking in low tones with her. Finally, he turned to the judge with his head down and spoke in a quiet voice, "No objection, Your Honor."

Tracy and I couldn't help applauding. I did a high-five with the Commander, and I shook Mark's hand. I told him we hoped to see him on Saturday at the camp.

He said he wouldn't miss it for the world.

This ordeal was over for Camp Sage and Sand. Now we could get on with the other challenges that were facing us.

The Commander was next to me as we walked into the hall. He appeared very tired suddenly after putting in such a tremendous effort this morning.

I was hoping he hadn't overdone it so soon after his heart attack. I put my arm around his back. "So is this another one of your miracles?" I said.

"*My* miracle? No," he replied.

Chapter 27

We celebrated at the mess hall that night. None of the campers had been let in on our recent worries, so they were no doubt mystified with our high spirits.

The Commander stood just before the boys were dismissed and made a little speech. "I want to thank God for his blessings on this place and on me tonight. We adults are celebrating a victory that we had today in the courthouse over in Cortez. In the past few weeks, we have been going through a challenge from people representing the government to move us off of this beautiful piece of land because they thought we posed a threat to the security of certain archeological ruins and artifacts located at the foot of the great rock. Today, with God's help, we were able to prove that these relics are not within our boundaries. This decision, while freeing us from immediate responsibility, does not mean that we are not mindful of the presence of such a valuable lode of antiquities. This weekend, during the Fourth of July festivities, we will see that a guard is placed at the site, and in the weeks ahead, we will build a fence on our boundary line to keep people from straying over.

"And later, we hope to start negotiations with the United States Park Service to allow us to set up training programs where those of you who are interested will be able to discover your talents in archeology by helping in the dig that is sure to begin. I want to also thank God that my heart attack has not stopped me from being back with you boys so I can watch each of you become leaders in your homes and the community. It's so good to be here again."

There was applause and whistles. The kids liked the Commander, despite his tough appearance and leadership. He had affected me the same way in just a few weeks.

"Now, I want Mr. Van Alan to give all of us a final look at what we can expect come this Saturday. I'm sure he's going to need the cooperation from each of us to make the day one that will always be remembered."

The Commander caught me off guard, but I had brought my check-off list, and I knew this included about everything. So for the next ten minutes, I covered the various people who were in charge and the areas where the boys would be asked to help. I told each of them how much we wanted to meet their parents and relatives and that we would take time to talk with them, even though we would be very busy. I encouraged each camper to enjoy himself, but to remember he was representing all of us, and that he must be on his best behavior. I reminded them that one major need would come in the cleanup phase where they could be a big help. Finally, I wanted them to remember all the good stories that happened so we could come up with a big write-up that would go along with the photographs we would be taking.

I hoped they were catching some of my own enthusiasm as I was telling them about the events to come, but it was hard to see it in their faces. I took it on faith that they would do their part when the day arrived.

Tracy was the one who showed real excitement. She grabbed my arm and squeezed it as we were leaving together. "This is all so wonderful," she fairly bubbled. "To think we were merely hoping to have an article in the newspaper, and now this! I can't believe how it's snowballed. Mother and Father would be so pleased."

"It amazes me too," I said. "I never expected things to progress so far or so fast. But since our original purpose has changed, maybe we should review what we want to say to the community. How about a little fundraising?"

"Oh, no. Not unless someone offers. To appeal for money after people bought tickets wouldn't be right. Besides, God has always provided so generously."

"Wouldn't you want to make improvements in the camp?"

"Of course," she said. "When we need something, we always ask the Lord. That way, he's in charge—not any of us."

"I'm just saying that we've got all these people coming—"

"I know," she interrupted. "I promise to think about it, OK?"

"OK with me," I said. "Whatever you want to do is fine."

We dropped the discussion. I knew better than to push her into anything. It's just that my marketing background made it hard for me to pass up the opportunity, while she saw it as "using" the opportunity.

The sun was low, sending out bright rays over the desert, as we walked from the mess hall. We had to shade our eyes to see our way, but the colors were absolutely glorious. The early-evening shadows created a rugged landscape among all the mesas surrounding us and revealed cuts in the rock structure that I'd never spotted. It was a breathtaking close to a very successful day.

I wanted to take Tracy's hand as we walked, but I was aware of the boys all around us who would love nothing better than to make something big out of it. Besides, I knew many of them were already in love with their only female counselor and nurse at the camp, and they were very protective of her. Mark McGuiness had wanted to know if Tracy was going with anyone. His question had set off my own serious thoughts. She was like no one else I had ever known. Aside from her comment about Nicole's kissing me in the car, she had done nothing to make me think she might give me a second thought. A few minutes ago, she hugged my arm, and her touch had sent a thrill soaring through me.

Not wanting her to leave right away, I steered her down the path and over to a log seat that overlooked the swimming pond. The place was alive with running, jumping, and splashing kids who were making the most of their free time before bedtime. Several boys called out, "Hi, Tracy" as they ran by, and a little group came over and sat at our feet.

Tracy joked with them and touched a couple lightly on their heads. It was a beautiful time as I watched her talk and reach out to them with such affection.

Finally, the lifeguard began to clear the pool. A few stragglers had to be pulled out and marched away against their will.

Tracy said, "They love this time so much they don't want to quit."

"I do too," I answered. "It's so peaceful. The day is winding down, and the sunset is so unbelievable that it makes me want to just sit here and meditate."

"I'm glad you came all the way from New York to share this place with us," Tracy said.

I agreed. "You know, back there, I got so caught up in the rush of making a living that I almost never took the time to sit and enjoy life like this. It's beautiful—even more so with you beside me."

Tracy took a small breath as I took her hand and squeezed it. She didn't pull away, but she didn't squeeze back. She gave me one of her warm smiles. "I like you Mel, but you're not going to be here long, and I'm committed to this land. I can't get involved. I hope you understand."

"I just want to be close. What can I say? You are so sweet, and I love to be around you."

"I like you very much, but we don't have the same religious beliefs either. That's important to me too."

"I understand. Even though I'm proud to be a Jew, I'm still searching for what it really means. Being out here in the West has made me think more seriously about spiritual things. The vast openness and the beauty of nature do something to a person that's hard to describe. I don't feel so in control of my own future anymore. Who knows what the summer will bring?"

Tracy shifted toward me. "I do like sitting with you and holding hands. I like hearing you talk about things I'll probably never see. I like your newfound compassion for the boys. I've never been with anyone who is both as amusing and smart as you. If we could leave it there without going deeper, I would dearly love it," she said.

"I'll have to settle for that right now, I guess. But I'd really like to kiss you."

Her face fell. "And that's just what I need to avoid. I'm sorry." She let go of my hand and stood up.

Just then, the sound of taps from the old trumpet hit the loudspeakers. We had to wait until the last note to continue.

"It's time I was getting to bed and doing some reading," she said.

"This has been a fantastic day and a lovely evening. I have a lot to thank you for."

"Don't thank me. Besides, we still have a lot to do in the next three days. I guess I'd better turn in too."

We walked in silence back to our tent area and said goodnight.

I was disappointed in Tracy's response to me. The camp was quiet by now. It had been a long day, and I was anxious to get a good sleep.

○◉○

ERIC ROGERS CALLED THE next morning. "You got everything ready for us?"

"Everything we can think of," I said, trying to sound positive.

"We'll be there Friday. You got lots of people coming?"

"I think we've sold four thousand tickets."

"All right!" Eric was impressed. "Nice going."

"Just be ready for a bit of rough living. This is not the Big Apple."

"*No problemo.* I'm looking forward to it. So is the cast. We haven't disappointed anyone yet. The show's a good one."

"I know it will be," I said. "I can't wait for my kids to see it. This is the biggest thing some of them have ever seen."

"Got to go," he said. He gave me his cell number if I needed it and hung up.

I went over my list, looking for anybody who needed to be contacted again. I'd checked and rechecked each and every person responsible. Today, the army bridge was due to be brought in and set across the creek for the extra outbound lane of traffic. Portable toilets already sat in a row near the designated parking lot. Signs were printed and ready to be erected on the main road from town. The police had been out and made their final plans. All the hot dogs and food items were in the kitchen freezer. The weather report was excellent. *Is there anything I've forgotten?*

I was scheduled this morning to have the plaster cast exchanged for a lighter walking cast.

Juan, our bighearted cook, had offered to drop me by the doctor's office in his truck and pick me up after he did some shopping in town. He was always so busy in the kitchen that we had never said more than a passing "hi" at meals and some brief discussions about the food for Saturday's community event. He and his wife worked together to serve us, and they were both good people.

"So, how big is your family?" I asked after we got underway.

"Alena and I have eight kids and two grandkids. Both our parents are living with us, and my sister just moved in."

"Wow," I said. "Have you worked at the camp long?"

"Oh, yes. Alena and I have been here going on ten years. This is our summer gift to God."

"What else do you do?"

"I have a carpet-cleaning business. My two sons are taking over now that they are old enough. But we have always given our time to the camp when it is open."

"That's wonderful," I said. "What got you started?"

"My twin boys went to camp when they were eight. They came every summer for the next five years and couldn't wait for it to start every year. Alena and I began to volunteer, and we've never stopped."

"You actually mean you don't take a salary?"

"No, sir. God takes good care of us. It is our pleasure to give it back to him. We've never gone hungry, and my kids are all happy and obedient. Who could ask for anything more?"

He was totally unselfish. I knew how hard Juan and his wife worked, driving out to the camp before sunup and leaving at twilight every day, seven days a week. They were always smiling with a good word for everyone. And here I thought I was so noble for giving up a couple of months or so out of my life.

"Let me ask you something," I said. "Your boys have been here and know what's going on. You and your wife do too. I'd like to get your perspective on something that's happening that I don't understand."

"I'll try to help you ... if I can," he said.

"Some of the kids seem to be having visions and see angels and stuff. Three of them told me that these angels are talking to them, and I don't know what else. This happens when they have their midweek prayer meeting. I went a couple of weeks ago, and the whole thing confused me. Tracy tried to tell me that it was all right. Is it some kind of cult thing that's going on here that might get out of hand?"

Juan took his eyes off the road to look at me for a moment, possibly to judge my sincerity. He smiled a bit and said, "I wouldn't worry about it too much. Your concern is worthy, but I guarantee it's no cult. It doesn't come from anything man started.

"This is a surprise from God, Mr. Van Alan. I am Catholic, as you may know. The Commander, Steve, and Tracy are Protestants. We have talked about it and agree that it is truly a blessed appearance. We don't know where it's going. We agreed to do nothing except embrace it for now since it started less than a month ago—even before the camp got going. We don't want to make a big thing out of it or mention it to outsiders because it might start something we can't handle. Nor do we want to stop it, do you see?"

I liked his clear-cut answer. He wasn't going off in spiritual language; he was stating the facts as he saw them. "Have you seen it yourself?"

"Alena and I like to leave as early as possible, but we stayed once. We were amazed to see those little boys who run around the camp so wild every day become transformed into powerful prayer warriors in front of our eyes. The next day, they were their same mischievous selves. It was hard to imagine."

"So you think it's genuine?"

"What else could it be, Mr. Van Alan? Those boys know nothing about things like that—not at their age."

"You're probably right," I said. "But it seems so fantastic. Angels and things? Why here?"

"Who knows? The angels at Fatima spoke to children too. Children are very innocent and are willing to accept such things, I think."

I agreed with that, yet I was much too cynical to believe such goings-on without more proof. "Well, I wanted to get your take on it. I have to admit that I've been blaming Steve and his Christian friends for inciting some kind of fantasy out here in the desert. It's just that it's kind of new to me."

"Steve is as surprised as anyone, and that goes for me too, Mr. Van Alan. Alena and I are not willing to make any quick judgments."

"Sounds like good advice, Juan," I said.

We arrived in the center of town, and Juan pulled up in front of the doctor's building.

Not knowing how much time either of us needed, I proposed to meet him across the street at a little outdoor café. "That looks like a good place; there's no rush to pick me up," I said.

He let me out, and I got my crutches out. I thanked him, and he drove off to do his shopping.

Changing my cast was easier than I thought. The doctor took an x-ray and slapped on a lighter boot with a heel to step on. I came out of the office with a cane in case I needed it.

○◉○

ACROSS THE STREET, I ordered a coffee and a roll and found a nice table under a bright umbrella. The midmorning air was still cool in the shade. I took a deep breath and thought how wonderful it was to experience such a splendid peace in a place where the people were relaxed and friendly as they passed by, and the scenery was absolutely breathtaking. Had I been sitting outside a Manhattan café, even in Greenwich Village, the throb of commerce, the taxis, the truck traffic and their exhaust, and the throngs of people hurrying to who knows where would have filled me with a certain tension and urgency that I, too, needed to be rushing about. Not here, though.

I was readjusting my chair to get a bit of sun when I heard a car horn. When I looked up, Nicole had pulled up across the street and rolled down her window. "Well, look who's taking a day off in the big city!"

I waved and called, "How are you?"

Without an answer, she pulled a beautiful U-turn in the middle of the block and swooped into a parking space in front of the café. She left her car and walked up to my table. "Would you be open to a little company—or do you want to be left to your thoughts?"

"No, no," I said. "It's great to see you." I stood and helped her to a chair. "I should have called you before now."

"Yes, you should have," she said with a big smile. "If you buy me a cup of coffee, I might even forgive you."

I signaled to the waitress, and she brought Nicole a steaming mug within seconds.

"So, you're having a party out at the camp on Saturday after all."

"You'd better believe it," I said. "The court appearance better be the last of it."

"Mother is not too happy."

"Why should she be mad? It turns out those ruins are on government property, and now she should be able to have her cake and eat it too."

"I don't know what her beef really is," Nicole said. "I think she probably pictured your forty acres set aside for her exclusive use. Maybe to set up headquarters in your administration building and have a groomed tent area complete with pond where she could bring in a bunch of young eager workers to explore a brand-new archeological site. Who knows?"

"I hope she's through with her harassment. The people out there have had enough of her."

"Well, at least you're going to be able to have Magic Mike and Fourth of July. Are you ready for us?"

"As much as I can think of."

"People are coming. I hear it all over town. I can't wait myself." She fairly jumped up and down in her chair. "You are a phenomenon, you know? Those people at the camp could never have dreamed of having something as huge as this without you. Do you realize that?"

"I can't take all the credit. It just snowballed, and you are largely responsible, don't forget," I said.

Nicole raised an eyebrow and put her hand on my arm. "I think you and I make a great team, don't you?"

"Yes, I do." I laid my hand on hers. "You know, I've been thinking about when I go back to New York …"

Now, both her eyebrows went up. "Tell me."

"Well, I've always worked alone, keeping my promotions business small, but I think I could see adding a person like you to work with me and learn the ropes."

"Oh, goodness, do you really think it would be possible?"

"I've been thinking about it."

"Oh, I'd love it. I'd love it. Working in New York City—and having a job with the big guns? When are you going back?"

"Well, not for a month or so. You know. The summer's not over yet."

"I don't think I can wait. Oh, I don't know how I can stand it."

She was getting too excited. I needed to lower her expectations. "How about you and I getting together once a week or so, and I can go over the things you would need to know. Kind of a New York training program. Then you'd be ready for the big city before you got there. Maybe the time would go by a little faster for you."

"That would be perfect! Oh, thank you. I am so thrilled."

"Don't go quitting your job here—or anything like that, Nicole," I said. "Let's take it one step at a time, OK?"

"I won't even tell Bill. He'd kill me anyway if he knew I wanted to leave. You're right. I guess I can manage to wait, but I don't know how. When can we start?"

"How about next week? Things will have returned to normal."

"Wonderful," she said. "I can cook us supper. I'm not a bad cook, and we can talk about all sorts of things. How about a week from tonight?"

"It's a deal," I said. I had nothing going on. My only problem might be getting transportation, but I'd figure something out.

Juan pulled up behind Nicole's sports car, and I signaled to him. "Join us for a cup of coffee?"

"Oh, no, sir. I need to get back for lunch."

I turned to Nicole. "That's my transportation. I'd better be going. It was great seeing you. I'll watch for you Saturday."

"I'll be there early. I don't want to miss a thing," she said.

○◉○

On the way back, I got to thinking that I'd done a dumb thing by spilling my thoughts so soon to Nicole. Now, there would be no peace the rest of the summer. I had no doubt she'd be good at the job, but I wasn't sure how close I wanted to be to her yet. *Oh, well. It's too late now.*

Juan was in a good mood. He had turned on the radio and was humming along with the music. I liked it too. I suddenly realized how many new sights and sounds I had been exposed to in the few weeks I'd been in southern Colorado. What was there about it? Just a great sense of freedom from the confines I had accustomed myself to for more than thirty years. *There's nothing like a vacation to clear one's mind.*

The Commander was riding around in his electric cart when we drove in. How great it was to see him recovering so quickly. He signaled with a big wave of his hand, so I left Juan with my thanks and walked over. My own mobility had improved dramatically, and I felt like I could even break into a run if I had to. It was good to be healing normally.

I saw that he wasn't alone. Carlos was seated next to the big man. It looked like he might have been crying.

"This young man has been looking for you, Van Alan. I told him you were away this morning. He says he had a dream, but he won't tell me about it."

I bent over to look at the boy closer. He wouldn't look me in the eye. "What's the problem, little guy?" I asked.

"I needed to talk to you," he said.

"What about?"

Carlos looked up at the Commander with questioning eyes—and then at me.

"All right, young man," the Commander said. "Why don't you and Mr. Van Alan go for a little walk?" He put his hands around Carlos and helped him out of the seat.

I looked at the Commander, and he gave me a knowing wink. Carlos and I had grown close during the time he had the measles and started writing down his thoughts, and I guessed that's why he wanted to talk to me.

We walked down to the corral, and Carlos actually put his hand in mine on the way. It didn't seem to matter what other boys might think. I was touched, as I had grown fond of him.

We got to the split rail, and he climbed up closer to my height. For a while, we watched the horses being groomed and fed after their morning rides, and a farrier from town was shoeing one or two.

"OK, Carlos, what about this dream?"

He hesitated, and big tears filled his eyes. "It wasn't a dream. I'm scared."

"What do you have to be scared about?"

"I saw it happen, and it was real."

"We all have bad dreams, Carlos. We get used to them. All we have to do is wake up enough to find out things aren't really as bad as we thought."

"It wasn't a dream; it was real."

"OK, let's get it out. Tell me about it."

His body shivered as if he had a chill. "I woke up, and the tent was on fire. I sat up fast to tell everybody. The smoke made me cough, and I couldn't talk. I ran outside, and all the tents were on fire. No one was doing anything. I went back and shook Jay and then Ben, but they wouldn't wake up. Then the burning tent fell down on us."

I waited for him to continue. "Then what?" I asked.

"Everything was burning."

He was right. It *was* an awful thing, but I still knew it was just a bad dream.

After a minute, I asked, "Did it help to tell me about it?"

He protested, "Other things have come true. I'm still scared."

"You really think the camp is going to burn down?"

"Yes. You've got to do something."

And then I realized that this should have been on my list for Saturday. "Let's go back, and I'll call the fire department," I said. "They need to be here. Thank you, Carlos, for reminding me." I had already forgotten about his dream worries.

I lifted him down, and we went up to the phone. Lunch was being served, and I assured Carlos that I would do something, and he went to eat.

When I finally got hold of the chief in town, he told me that they were already on call for the fireworks and would be sending a couple of trucks out. With my prompting, he was also willing to cover the afternoon performance. "As far as having a plan, Mr. Van Alan, we conducted a fire drill out there the first week of summer camp with all the boys and counselors. You must have missed it," he said.

I admitted I was a late arrival and thanked him very much for keeping us prepared. I hoped at least this would help Carlos feel better.

○◉○

Since it was Wednesday night, Tracy asked if I would like to go to the worship service. I wanted to be with her, but I hated to go back to the meeting again.

Carlos met me after lunch and asked me to go with him.

What is this? I thought. *Is everybody trying to convert me?* I finally decided to go but leave if I got uncomfortable.

Tracy was pleased when I told her. "We're going to pray for a successful program Saturday—and for good weather. Does that offend you at all?"

"No, of course it doesn't. I'm sure God will want to bless our prayers. I'm not used to going to God for anything. I usually hope for the best."

It seemed like more boys were there than the last time. I was still mystified why these kids wanted to come to a religious service instead of swimming at the end of the day. I couldn't figure out what the draw was.

Steve started everyone on an upbeat song with his guitar, and as another guitar and a bongo drum joined in, the kids clapped along. We didn't clap in temple either, but there was plenty of it at Jewish weddings. Tonight reminded me of that joy of the marriage feast, and it was easier to get into the spirit as I thought about it.

Tracy was singing along now, and her voice had a beautiful range. The music had taken on a lively tempo. She moved forward and stood at the front to sing with Steve. The two of them sounded so great that I got kind of emotional. They were smiling and so happy that they infected all of us, and some of the boys started dancing around to the music. Even I thought I could have danced a bit if I allowed myself the freedom.

The next song was more subdued. There was no clapping or dancing. Once again, some of the boys started to pace from one spot to another with their heads down in prayer as they sang the words from memory. I just watched and marveled at the change taking place.

Steve then opened the Bible and read something from the New Testament. In the approaching dusk with the campfire blazing, the reading took on a serene quality, with the words of Jesus speaking from across the ages. I was surprised by the authority his words still conveyed. In this part, he wanted the people to know about what he called the "kingdom of heaven," but he cautioned that the road was narrow, and few were going to get there. This disturbed me since I believed everyone went to heaven if they lived a good life. In my view, only the really bad guys didn't get in. Simple as that.

Christians confused me. On the one hand, they were so forgiving, reaching out to love, help, and pray for those in need. On the other, they were narrow-minded and exclusive—with the only way to God being through his Son, Jesus Christ. Not that Jews weren't pretty exclusive too. But hadn't God created us all? Was there only room in heaven for the few who believed in his Son?

Volunteering at what was basically a Christian camp had filled me with more questions than answers. And I didn't want to ask because I was afraid the answers would undermine whatever long-standing, traditional beliefs I came with. Had I realized that my summer was going to be spent among those whose religious persuasion was so at odds with mine, I would never have come. Miss Abrams was Jewish. Why hadn't she warned me?

And then to add to my confusion was this so-called appearance of angels. To my knowledge, no counselors admitted to seeing them. Why just the kids? I had to grant, however, that it was a lot more believable coming from the mouths of babes than from adults who might have been spouting some kind of new belief.

With the music quietly playing in the background again, some of the boys began to moan and cry out. No one came to their assistance. It was as if these young ones needed to lay down some kind of heavy load. I could hear them asking for forgiveness, and I wondered what they might have done to be so broken up. On the other hand, there were others who had reached their hands as high as possible and were asking to be lifted up. They were the ones with great big smiles.

I half expected to see any one of them raise right off the ground any minute, as they went up on their toes.

Carlos was among those dancing with his hands in the air. He was experiencing some kind of ecstasy and was obviously no longer afraid. I would have liked to experience what he was seeing. He believed in angels, and I expected this was what he was seeing now. Then, all at once, he opened his eyes and looked at me. "Did you see him? He is *so* big!" he said.

"No, I'm afraid not, Carlos," I answered. "Tell me about him."

"You've got to see him, Mr. Van. He is so wonderful."

"I'd like to. What did he say?"

"Nothing, but he held my hand."

"Is he fearful?"

"Oh, no. I love him."

I believed Carlos, and at this very moment, I desperately wanted to see what he saw. I wanted to confirm for myself that there really was another world that I couldn't naturally see. It seemed so close that I could almost reach it. It gave Carlos such pleasure, and I wanted some too—but I was being left out, and it was a little disappointing. "How could I see him?" I asked.

"You pray to Jesus."

I couldn't do that. Not Jesus. Why did he have to be between me and the angels of God? I had been taught to reject him, and now he was the very obstacle to seeing what Carlos saw.

At this point, I just backed off and moved to sit down at the edge of the little gathering.

Tracy was still with Steve, and they stood together with their eyes closed, perhaps seeing what Carlos was seeing.

I felt shut out and alone. I didn't feel free to join in without giving up on my own beliefs.

Finally, I slipped away and headed back to my tent. I was out of it, and I wanted to be alone. It was better to sleep and wake up with a fresh tomorrow.

Chapter 28

The fire started sometime after midnight and must have been burning for a while before someone finally woke up and shouted the alarm.

I came out of a deep sleep, trying to make sense of the commotion.

Suddenly, one of the counselors pulled back my tent flap and said, "Get out of here. There's a big fire, and you don't have time to spare!"

I leaped up and grabbed my walking boot in one hand and my pants in the other. When I looked out into the night, there were flames shooting from a cluster of tents over near the laundry building. It looked like they were spreading fast. My heart went racing to my throat.

I saw a group of kids being herded up to the pond, and more were stumbling behind them. I dashed across to the administration building.

The Commander was on the phone. "Where have you been, Van Alan?" he yelled at me. "Grab the big light and direct the fire department trucks across the bridge."

I got into my pants and lunged for the giant battery flashlight at the door.

"Well, git going," he said, showing no patience this morning.

Sirens could be heard in the distance. The Commander had been smart to assign me to direct their way because the little bridge could be dangerous to negotiate in the dark. One slip of a wheel would send the whole truck into the creek.

As I stood waiting for the firemen to arrive, I looked back over the camp and was appalled at the spreading flames. I would have thought these tents were more fire-resistant, but perhaps they were just too old.

The first truck thundered up, and I flashed the light back and forth along the road to show the way. A face appeared, and then I saw the driver waving. The second truck was immediately behind. It slowed and the fireman called out, "Stay there. The ambulance is coming."

They thundered across the bridge. Less than five minutes later, more flashing lights came plowing down the dusty road with a siren that pierced my eardrums as it passed.

I stood in shock where I was, watching the feverish activity throughout the camp. Carlos's dream, or maybe it was a vision, must have been a warning. He had been right after all, and now I could see why he had been so frightened. It was such a fierce fire that it scared me out of my wits too. I didn't know how they could hope to put it out before it licked up every tent in its wake.

I crossed the road and hobbled as fast as I could to join the rescuers. With the powerful light, I was able to go from tent to tent just ahead of the fire, looking for stray kids. I could feel the heat on my back as I searched. Every tent was empty, and I could see that the practice evacuation earlier in the summer had been a success. I just hoped the areas already ablaze had been cleared without fatalities.

Back at the administration building, I stood by, ready to do what I could. A fireman dispatcher had set up a command unit, and we all heard the progress as it was reported. The tanker had begun dousing the worst of the blaze, and it appeared they were already getting a handle on it. Most of the men were speculating about what had set the whole thing off.

Steve, who had taken the boys up to the pond, called the command center. "We haven't accounted for six of our little guys. Has anyone seen them?"

"Let's have their names," the Commander answered, looking at us with wide eyes.

The six included Ben, Jay, and Carlos—and three boys from the next tent.

The news hit me like a fist in the stomach. When I had investigated the empty tents just minutes ago, I was appalled to see that their area was already awash in flames. I expected that they were with all the others.

The Commander had his map spread out. "Start a search of the area for them right now," he told the dispatcher.

I began to pace and wring my hands. There was nothing that I could do but wait. What would I tell Carlos's father? He and the other parents had depended on the camp to take care of their sons. Carlos had a whole lifetime before him.

After only fifteen minutes or so, the captain on the scene reported that the flames were almost contained. Most of the tents were fairly fire-resistant after all, and once the initial inferno was doused, the internal material only smoldered.

Tracy rushed in from the clinic where she had been treating the less serious injuries. Some of the kids had tried to smother the fire with blankets and received some superficial burns. She had just heard the news of the missing boys.

I told her how afraid I was for the six.

She was anxious but somehow more confident. "Let's not jump to conclusions. Until we know exactly what happened, we should believe for God's best. They are in the Lord's hands—no matter what." Along with the Commander, she gathered those of us in the command center for prayer. Her words were absolutely to the point. She asked for the lives of the boys and for swift news of their safety.

The fire workers called in and released us to come down to the fire scene.

The Commander ignored his cart, and I stomped along in my new walking boot. It was still dark, and I used the powerful battery lamp to light the way despite the flashing lights from the emergency vehicles. The sound of the fire truck motors was almost deafening as we came up alongside. Their generators lit up the area in a bright pool of light.

About two-thirds of the four-man tents lay in ashes on top of their charred and smoking platforms. There had been no trees to worry about—only the few bushes and plants and colorfully named street signs. According to plan, every boy had grabbed his sleeping bag or a blanket for protection and warmth on the way out, but the rest of their possessions had been reduced to cinders. Another fifteen or so tents had been saved, but they were either blackened or damaged by smoke.

The captain came up and gave a respectful tip of his helmet to Commander Dougan. He had a very serious expression. "We're going through all the debris in case those six got caught on the way out. Was that their area?" He was pointing into the worst part of the rubble.

"That's right," the Commander said. His face was deathly white against the light from the trucks.

I looked down at Tracy, and huge tears were pouring down her cheeks. I wiped mine too. I was remembering how Carlos had been so scared of the fire he had envisioned less than twelve hours before. He had even seen himself and his tentmates engulfed by the collapsing roof.

"And another thing …" the captain said. He called up to the truck and told them to swing the searchlight over. "Your corral is gone, and if you had any stock, they're gone too. We think that's where the fire may have originated."

The big light illuminated the corral, and absolutely nothing was standing. The barn, stalls, office, hay bales, and fencing were all gone. Firemen were still working the coals with a water hose to get the last of the cinders under control.

"Oh no!" The Commander's hand flew up to his head. "Ten horses and two donkeys!"

I was concerned that he might start having another heart attack.

"What can we do about the boys who are missing?" Tracy asked the captain.

"It won't be light for another three to four hours," he said. "We'll continue searching the rest of the night. You'll be the first to hear the minute we discover something."

On the way back to the administration building, we walked up to the pond. Rows of little sleeping bodies in various positions covered the grassy play area, and a bunch of counselors were watching over them. We moved up to one of Steve's rec teachers and asked how things were going.

"Really good," he said with a nod. "They knew exactly what to do and went right back to sleep up here before you could say boo. A few of them were a pretty scared, but we assured them they'd be OK, and I told them we'd keep watch. You hear anything about the missing kids?"

"Nothing yet," the Commander told him. "You see anything that we should know about?"

"Nope. All I know was someone was yelling 'fire,' and I came out of my bed like a shot. The first thing I could see was that the corral was ablaze, but my concern was for the kids. Did the horses get out?"

"We don't know right now. It's just too dark. Doesn't seem that they could git out," the Commander said with a heavy sigh. "You and the others did a good job of bringing these kids up here and calming them down." He patted him on the back. "Just keep them together, and at breakfast, I'll have an update for everyone."

○◉○

Back at the office, concern for the missing boys was uppermost in our minds, but we briefly discussed the upcoming weekend. Eric Rogers and his entertainers were slated to arrive tomorrow, so I needed to get him on the phone if we were going to cancel.

"Until we can git a reading on how bad things really are and how much damage and what lives are affected, I can't say go or no go right now," Commander Dougan said. "The parking and access areas seem intact. The stage is out of the way. Our primary need is to consider every one of our lads and those who have lost all their possessions. There's a lot of cleanup to do, which I suppose we can leave for later. We're all tired now, and we don't have enough information to make any final decisions."

Daylight brought out the extent of damage more clearly. After sleeping a bit in our chairs at the office, we returned to the ruins for a closer look.

The Commander offered me a ride in his cart.

Only one fire truck remained, and a small group of men was working its way through the debris in their heavy boots. "We've come up with nothing. Those boys are not here or at the corral. As a matter of fact, there are no animal carcasses down there either."

We looked at each other with relief. Yet, if not here, where were they?

We had our answer minutes later. Coming around a cluster of the big sandstone rocks that bordered the area, two of the missing boys plodded along, each with a horse in tow. They looked exhausted, but when they saw us standing with our mouths open, they grinned and jumped up and down and waved their hands.

What a wonderful sight it was. Two of our cherished campers in pajamas and boots were leading the animals we feared were dead. Behind them appeared the other four boys, Carlos included, along with two or three more horses. I'll never forget the sight they made. These were our boys, and I was so proud of them. They had worked themselves into my heart, just as I had also become a part of this wonderful hot, dry, and windy camp. My eyes were filled with tears again as we all ran to meet them.

With hugs and kisses from Tracy for each boy, we couldn't wait to hear their stories.

Ben was the first one to get it all out. "Well, Carlos here had this dream, see? And he told us we were going to have an awful big fire. So us and the guys in the next tent made a plan to save the whole camp. We were going to go around and make sure everyone got up to the pond, like they were supposed to. Well, when someone yelled 'fire,' and we saw the barn was already burning, us guys ran and opened the gates to let the horses out. We chased them, and then they got scattered. We've been trying to find them."

"We're sorry that we didn't get them all back," Carlos said. He was worried that they had done wrong.

"Oh boys." The Commander knelt and took them close. "You are heroes—all of you."

"You scared us all to death," Tracy added. "We didn't know if you had been caught in the fire."

"We wouldn't have died. Carlos knew what to do."

I went over and hugged him and realized he was the only one fully dressed. The great thing was he hugged me back.

chapter 29

The first thing we did was to let the six boys wash up and shower. Tracy brought them fresh clothes from the donation box. Then it was time for breakfast. The mess hall was filled with an assortment of young boys still in their pajamas and blankets. This morning, there was a somber orderliness that I hadn't seen before.

The Commander stood at the head of the room. "Good morning, boys. Before we get some hot food in us, we need to go to our Lord with an extra special word of thanks for bringing us all through safely from the terrible fire last night. While we have a few burns and cuts and scrapes, no one person or animal was lost. For that, we praise God. We can replace the things that burned. Of course, we know that many of you have lost your clothes and personal possessions. We are going to do everything possible to see that you have new things as soon as possible.

"You are all to be commended for the way you conducted yourselves when you woke up in the middle of a raging fire. I am very, very proud of each and every one of you. You kept your cool and did exactly what you were supposed to do.

"Your assigned counselors will be working to help you get back to a normal camp life. I want you to rely on them because they are here for you. Today, all your classes are canceled, and everyone gets a free day of fun and recreation. The fire area is off-limits. We have a limited supply of clothes for you to wear today, so we ask those of you whose tents did not get damaged to share anything you can with those less fortunate. Let's go to the Lord now with our grateful thanks." He bowed his head and offered a fine prayer to start the day.

The boys applauded and headed for the chow line.

Just as I was walking from breakfast, I got a call from Bill Bradford. "What's the story out there? I have a fire department report that says you had a lot of damage and some superficial burns. How serious was it?"

"I'm glad to say everyone is fine. We even had a heroic save of all the livestock by six of our boys. If you want to send a reporter out, we'll be glad to go through it with him."

"Our guy is on the way, as we speak," he said. "OK, now how about Magic Mike and the fireworks display on Saturday? Are we off or on?"

"It's a go, Bill. People will see the charred remains of the tent area and corral, but there's still plenty of space for everything we've planned. As a matter of fact, though, what we could use in your story is a plea for donations of summer clothing, personal sports equipment, swimming and riding gear, and stuff like that. Many of the boys lost things in the fire. We have emergency clothing, but not too much."

"Absolutely. You can count on it."

"Thanks, Bill. We'll be watching for your reporter. He can take all the pictures he wants." I thought how a good story in the newspaper would be very welcome at this point.

After a quick get-together with the Commander and Tracy, and a final OK to go ahead, I placed a call to Eric.

He answered his cell phone almost immediately.

"Hey, guy, where are you right now?" I asked.

"Enjoying the lovely weather on my sister's patio here in Denver, overlooking the swimming pool. I've decided not to come, after all. I'm just about ready to call the gang and tell them they can knock off and join me here for a couple of beers this afternoon."

"You've got to be kidding!"

"Who's kidding, my friend? My brother-in-law knows exactly where you are located, and he's seriously counseled me to stay right where I am—if I know what's good for me. Like, man, who in their right mind wants to get all worked up and build up a sweat on the Fourth of July, no less. And, he did say sweat!"

"I admit it's no Garden of Eden, but there are approximately fifty little boys and several thousand others who will wring my neck if you don't show tomorrow. And then if I live through that, I will personally find you wherever you are and see that you go through a very slow and painful death in front of your next audience of loving admirers. What do you think of that?"

"You scare me to death, Melvin. All right, then. I will finish this drink, have another swim and another beer, and then get in my car and head for your forsaken part of the country. My wife and I will take our time and see the sights along the way, and then if I am still in the mood, I will arrive tomorrow morning sometime before noon and will then inspect everything in sight and let you know if I personally approve of your arrangement for me and my entourage. Do you understand, sir?"

"Thank you, oh great sire. We are forever in your debt. By the way, we had a major fire last night and half the camp is missing, but don't let it worry you. We came through relatively unscathed."

"What? Now get serious, Mel. Your camp had what?"

"We lost over half our tents and our riding area, barn, and corral, but no lives. The performance field, parking, and concession areas are still fine. The place looks kind of scruffy, but we can still handle all the people who want to come."

"Wow! Sounds like you came off pretty lucky."

"It was nothing short of a miracle, Eric."

○◉○

I WAS CALLED TO help the fireworks crew from town that showed up with a truckful of flares and skyrockets and who knows what, so I missed the phone call that came in from Nicole. Tracy took it and later filled me in on their conversation.

"She is *sooo* glad you are safe," Tracy said with an attempt to sound like Nicole. "Bill Bradford told her the bad news first thing, and she was very frightened for you. She wondered if you needed a place to stay. And she hopes you will still be able to meet once a week for *personal instruction*?" Her eyebrows were raised.

I could feel my face turn red.

"I told her you were fine, that you would be pleased to know of her concern, and that you would call her when you got a chance. I am just a little curious about the personal instruction thing, however. Please don't answer if it's something I shouldn't know about."

I tried to keep my voice steady and not trip over my words. "Of course, there's nothing secret at all." I cleared my throat, which I didn't mean to do. "She told me that she wanted to try her wings in the big city. I merely told Nicole that I thought she would be great in my kind of promotional business, and there were a few helpful things that I might pass on to her before she got there. You know, things a client expects, how to get around town, what and who to watch out for … those kinds of things."

"Is she going to work for you?"

"Well, I hadn't thought much about it," I sort of lied. "Perhaps. She's a very clever person, but I've never had anyone work for me before. I would have to think a lot about it."

"Well, fine," she said. "She wants you to call as soon as you can."

○◉○

I WENT LOOKING FOR Carlos. I couldn't get this little guy out of my mind. To me, he was a phenomenal kid and had encounters that were beyond me. At the very least, I wanted to explore what was going on in that fertile brain of his.

When I finally spotted him, he was in line at the pool diving board. I had yet to try out the water, given that I broke my leg the first day I arrived. By now, I was routinely in shorts and had bought some T-shirts in town and was sporting a comfortable sandal on my good foot. I was actually beginning to look the part of a camp counselor by starting a nice tan.

I kicked off my sandal and slipped off my walking boot and hung my legs in the water. The midmorning air was pleasantly cool despite the blazing sun. This would be my last chance to relax before the busy days ahead.

Carlos did a nice somersault into the water and surfaced nearby. He saw me watching him and waved. I motioned for him to come over, and he swam alongside.

"Nice dive, Carlos," I said. "You having fun?"

He only grinned, and then he pointed to my leg. "Where's your cast?"

"It's gone. I'm almost healed."

"I'll draw you a new angel."

"I'd like that," I said. "Come on up here a minute. I'd like to talk to you."

He pulled himself up next to me and sat there with his arms wrapped around each other, the goose pimples popping out on his skin.

"You did a mighty fine job last night saving the horses," I said. "Were you afraid?"

"No. I knew the angels were there."

"You saw them?"

"Yes. Just like at the campfire."

"Oh, did they tell you what was going to happen?"

"A little. I knew it was coming."

"So that's why you slept in your clothes."

"I wanted to help."

"Did they tell you about the horses?"

"Yes, and when we heard the horses banging their stalls, I saw how to help them. The fire opened up, and we ran through it and got them out. The angels showed us."

"Wow," I said. I had to believe him—even though the fire must have been immense with the old wooden siding and bales of hay ablaze. "Have you always been aware of things that might happen?"

"No. Just since the angels came to us. This is the first time they told me what to do."

"Do you worship them? Is that why they talk to you?"

"Oh, no, Mr. Van. We worship only Jesus."

"Do you see Jesus too?"

"No."

"Why not do you suppose? Some people claim to have."

"I don't know, but he's inside me. I don't need to see him."

"Really? Inside you?"

"In my heart, right here." He pointed to his chest. "I know he's here, and I love him."

I was still confused. OK, I always believed God was up in heaven directing the ways of the universe. What I had been learning lately, however, was that he sent Jesus with a personal message to tell us that he loved us. Fine, but if that were true, why did He allow his Son to be killed in such an awful way and not even raise a finger? What kind of father was that? Somehow Carlos believes that Jesus is inside him—even though Jesus was killed long ago, was supposed to have risen from the dead, and then went back to heaven. "Carlos, how can Jesus be in your heart and be in heaven too?"

"Because he sent the Holy Spirit."

I had heard of this Holy Spirit, but it was weird. "Is that what these angels are?"

"They are spirit beings—but not the Holy Spirit. He is part of God and Jesus, but not an angel. You see?"

I could only see that Carlos was itching to get back into the swim and stop trying to educate a very slow learner. This whole belief system was foreign to me, and I needed someone more patient to talk with. Up until now, I hated to let on to others that I wanted to know more, but if I was ever going to learn anything, I was going to have to ask someone who had a little better way of explaining things.

I let Carlos go and tousled his hair. "All right, buddy, thanks for the info. Have a good time."

He slid into the water and swam with quite a good kick to the middle where he turned around and waved again. He was a neat kid, and I sure enjoyed his infectious personality.

chapter 30

Eric Rogers looked like a million dollars when he and his wife drove into the parking lot in his Cadillac Escalade. He had cut his long ponytail, his hair was now short and windblown on top, but he was the same funny, outgoing guy, whom I had worked with back East. "Awesome," he said as he looked up at the imposing cliff behind us. "This is truly God's country."

Eric saw the best in everything. He was wearing white jeans that nicely contrasted with his red cowboy boots and red shirt. He pulled off his wraparound designer dark glasses to see better and stepped over and embraced me in a big bear hug. Then he introduced his lovely wife whom I had not met before. "Lord Almighty, how did you find such a beautiful place?"

I had been making so many excuses for the place since I came that I didn't know just how to respond. "Just lucky, I guess."

"You bet you're lucky, my friend," he said. "I'd trade the peace and quiet of these towering cliffs for a city of skyscrapers any day. Anyway, it's good to see you, Mr. Van Alan."

"Me too, Eric. Do you know how much excitement you've generated by coming here?"

"I hope so. We're looking forward to it."

I turned and introduced some of the crowd that had gathered to see our new arrivals. The Commander was plainly impressed by Eric's wife, who was strikingly gorgeous in shapely denim crops and tight polo top.

Tracy stood back shyly until I brought her forward. "This is

Tracy, our fabulous nurse and overall champion of all the boys here. She's going to see to your welfare and comfort during your stay."

Tracy said, "I've got rooms reserved in town and tent space for your crew. Whatever you need, just ask."

"You are about the sweetest little lady I could hope to meet," Eric said. "Thank you, honey." He took her hand and brought it up for a kiss.

Tracy was totally taken aback with his gallantry. I could see that this had never happened to her, and she wasn't certain whether Eric was serious or making fun.

I also introduced other staff members who were standing close, and then Eric went around talking to some of the curious boys who had come up. He wanted to know how many of them were excited by Magic Mike on TV and got their unanimous vote. That pleased him because it would be needed in just how he would put his program together.

Eric took a few steps from where we were all standing to get a general lookout over the camp and suddenly cried, "Whoa, what did you do to this place? Try to barbecue it?"

A lone fire van was parked down by the old corral, and several men in white suits, boots, and gloves were walking around. What used to be our own unique tent city with its little streets was mostly smoldering ashes. Further off in the opposite field, however, several volunteer crews from Steve's church were busy erecting brand-new tents for the boys.

"We could have lost everything," I told him. "Fortunately, it was put out with the help of a very qualified fire department that responded immediately. They still don't know what started it, but thankfully I didn't need to call and tell you not to come."

Eric was very sympathetic and turned to the group of kids gawking up at him. "Well, we're going to make up for this mess with the best show you ever saw. Tomorrow, Magic Mike will be here to perform for you, and you will laugh until your sides split—and you will be amazed at how he gets everything he wishes for. And you will be able to meet him and get his autograph. So what do you think of that?"

Everyone cheered on cue, and some of them were so excited they grabbed each other and jumped up and down.

"Thank you for your enthusiasm, boys. Now I'm going to get some of your counselors to show us around your wonderful camp." Eric put his arm around his wife's waist and looked expectantly at me.

Commander Dougan said, "You take them around, Van Alan, and then everyone is invited to cool off in my air-conditioned office afterwards with iced tea or whatever."

Tracy had some work to do, so I guided Eric and his wife past the pond that was teeming with a ton of exuberant kids and then along the face of the big rock to the stage that Steve and his church crew had built so well. "Well, what do you think of it?"

"Lord Almighty," he said. "You all have absolutely outdone yourselves. This is beautiful." He walked around it, admiring its southwestern style with its heavy roof timbers, and inspecting the wooden platform with hidden trapdoor. "Yes, this will do just fine. And there are tons of places to install our lights and backdrops. Whoever built this knew exactly what they were doing."

"The builders told me your blueprints were easy; they just followed them."

"Well, they did themselves proud," he said.

"I expect it'll be used for years to come," I added.

Then we walked to the middle of the immense natural bowl that would soon hold our audience. Steve's guys had cut the stray cactus and rolled the ground to flatten some of the sharpest rocks. We stood there transfixed by the grandness of it and the way it rose from front to back so everyone would have a good view.

"We're planning on a whole bunch of people," I said. "We cut off ticket sales at four thousand, but there will be even more later for the free fireworks display."

"That's very good." He smiled. "I want the whole day to be a success for the boys here. Every town we've staged has been a sellout."

We walked the paths to the parking lots. A town road crew was spray-marking the ground with white chalk lines designating lanes for the cars.

Chief Knox was standing with a couple of men, and when he saw us, he came over. "Well, Mr. Van Alan, looks like we're finally going to have our little party here after all."

"Looks that way," I said and introduced my guests to him.

"I thought maybe this was going to be the last straw when I got word of the fire," he said, "but you people keep bouncing back. Somebody's looking out for you."

"You can say that again." I looked around. "Does it seem like you can fit in all the cars we're expecting?"

"Oh, sure. This here's a lot of acreage, as long as people don't get too impatient to get home when the program is over. Fact is, though, after the fire, the chief and his people have already started mapping two or three more temporary exits to connect with the highway. Those little entrance roads would never handle the crowd you're expecting, But this here place has got a lot more room than the town park."

I invited him to join us in the Commander's office, but he declined. "I'll be out here early tomorrow morning, so you look me up if I can help you in any way," he said.

We wandered back to the office where Juan and Tracy had set up some tempting midmorning refreshments.

While the Commander got to know Eric and his wife, I went to see where Tracy had gone and found her redressing some minor burns on one of the boys. I recognized him as Little Joey who had thrown up in the back seat of my car on the way to the hospital, my first day at camp. "Hey Joey, how are you feeling?"

He looked up with a beautiful shy face and said, "I don't know."

"Well aren't you all better now?"

"Yes, but I miss my appennix."

I laughed. "You do? You miss your appendix?"

"I had it since I was very little."

Tracy and I glanced at each other and broke out in laughter. "Of course, but isn't it all right to take it out if it makes you sick, Joey?"

"He's right, Joey," Tracy said. "When our appendix gets infected like yours did, it's got to go."

"I guess," he said.

The night before, Joey had stumbled against one of the fiery tents in his sleepy state and burned his arm, but he was doing well despite some of the pain.

Tracy finished up her work, gave Joey a kiss on his cheek, and told him to stay out of the water.

We watched him leave. He turned back and looked at both of us as he went out the door, with a sweet but slightly lost expression, and then he shut the door and was gone.

"I love that boy so much," Tracy said with a wistful look on her face. "At the orphanage, he's kind of a loner. I just want to hug him every time I see him."

I remembered the feeling I had when I lifted him out of the car at the hospital. He seemed so fragile. "I know. He has a beautiful face, but he looks like he's carrying around some great sorrow."

"Both his parents are dead. I think I know how he feels," she said.

I understood too, even though my parents had been gone a long time, and the hurt was no longer fresh in my mind. "Do you want to go back to the Commander's office with me?"

"No, I'm not feeling social right now," she said.

I was wondering where her perkiness had gone. "What's troubling you? You seem to have been down the last few days."

"I don't know. So much has happened to stir things up for me. I'm used to living a more quiet life with just the mission to take care of. First, it was Dr. Armor—and then the fear of having to lose this place, the Commander's health, the fire, and now this big extravaganza tomorrow."

"I guess I'm more used to a frenzied pace of life than you are," I said. "For me, it's been hard to relax and enjoy what you have here. I'm worried that I may have actually brought some of the outside world into this idyllic place. I'm sorry if I've ruined things for you. I didn't realize what was happening."

"No, no," she said. "You've been wonderful. This camp might not have survived another summer without your creative ideas. You've given the Commander and the other counselors a new burst of excitement. It's just me. I'm a quiet little girl in a quiet little town."

"Well, when this thing is over tomorrow, we can go back to just being Camp Sage and Sand. We'll still be taking care of some energetic boys, and things will be back to normal again," I said with tongue in cheek.

"We'll see," she said. "And who's to say that change is bad? Perhaps I should get used to it. Now, why don't you go see to your guests and let me do some cleaning up before our company comes knocking tomorrow. I want everything to be spotless."

"OK, but in the meantime, I want to see those worry lines replaced by that pretty smile of yours, you promise?" I said.

"Promise."

chapter 31

I lay in my cot, unable to sleep after waking with a start sometime around three in the morning. No sound had roused me. It was just the old panic button that usually hits on the eve of a big undertaking. But this was worse than ever before. I struggled to breathe deep and calm my heart, which was racing in anticipation of the huge day that loomed ahead, but it refused to slow down even a bit.

This thing had grown far bigger than anything I had ever meant to do. With the least effort on my part, the whole plan seemed to have been conceived and executed on its own, and I found myself walking through it, unable to even guess what was going to happen next. I was the one in charge of everything, yet somehow, I wasn't in control. How had this happened?

What worried me now was that we would blow it—or, more specifically, that *I* would blow it—unable to live up to expectations that we had given the public. I could picture them running over each other to fight for the best place to sit, booing the performance, or running out of food. The worries swept over me one after another. And underlying this struggle lay the worst fear that I would always be remembered as "that guy who came out of New York and ruined everything good we had been doing here for twenty-five years."

I sat up in a sweat and started looking around in a panic. I'd never made myself sick like this before. I had also never bought into something so personally as this before. That was it! I had become my own client. The final outcome had never been mine. Not that the camp staff hadn't done a wonderful job. But they had merely done the things I asked them to do. In the end, it all pointed to me. And I didn't want to fail.

Camp Sage and Sand might get over it if things went sour, but I wouldn't. I would never forgive myself. Why had I let myself get so involved in this place out in the desert so far from my natural roots? Why hadn't I taken the first plane out of Cortez the day after I left the hospital? How could I have ever put myself in such a position that everyone was now depending on me?

I jumped out of my cot and took some deep breaths. Then the sweat caused a chill, so I got dressed. I'd never sleep now. I opened up the flaps of the tent and looked out into the quiet night. It was so beautiful out there.

The biggest moon I had ever seen was just coming up over the faraway hills. I swear that it was the most awesome sight I'd ever seen. A glowing orange ball. I could make out every crater and valley. I stepped from my tent and just stood there in awe. I had the feeling that it was watching me as much as I was watching it. Like it was saying, "I see you. I see you, Mel, and I'll be watching over you all day. I'll be here."

That wondrous sight made me forget myself. Something very special was going on, and I was suddenly no longer worried about the coming day. The big moon also shone on the old and the new tents, hovering over a hundred or so sleeping boys whose innocence was in our care. They deserved the very best. I had no kids of my own, but I suddenly knew the desire of a parent to steal into his child's room to watch him sleeping.

There was no need to take a flashlight as I walked the camp. The brilliance of the moon lit the way. I moved past the office and up along the pond, now still after its daily workout. When I got to the massive new stage, I was amazed to see the lights and the loudspeakers all wired and in place. Eric's crew had moved in expertly and set up everything during the afternoon, without a hitch.

I mounted the steps and stood looking out over the silent audience. In just a few hours, this would be full of people eagerly waiting for a good show. I was suddenly overpowered with the desire to kneel. I folded my hands and knew that God was waiting for me to say something, but I was tongue-tied. I wished so bad that Tracy were here now to pray in the lovely way she did. Down in my heart, I just asked him to take care of these good people who personally gave so much to take care of a few boys and to be with all of us in the hours ahead.

When I got back to my tent, I lay down at peace and slept.

○◉○

I was really, really pleased to find Magic Mike at the door of the mess hall at breakfast the next morning—giving every boy a knuckle handshake and a little American flag. I stood and watched this larger-than-life character actor stir up a flurry of excitement among his adoring fans. What a wonderful gesture, I thought, for a pretty famous guy like he was to get out of bed so early and bring such pleasure to our kids.

Magic Mike was a skilled performer, now dressed like a boy of about fifteen years-old, with red freckles scattered across on his nose and cheeks, and a blond mop of hair going in all directions. To the kids, he was their devoted big brother, and to the adults, he was the innocent and amiable teenager next door who was bound to make something of himself.

He wore cutoff jeans and a bright red vest over a white T-shirt. Slightly large tennis shoes gave him a bit of a growing-up-too-fast look. On the stage, "Mike" was funny, but he was not a comic character. He was an extremely intelligent boy who had the ability to get himself out of any trouble he found himself in, with enough magical powers to change himself into anyone and anything he wanted by merely putting his finger in his ear and puffing out his cheeks. To adults, it may have looked silly, but when you saw kids on the street doing it, you knew that they felt it was the secret to facing any difficult situation.

Originally, Eric had animated Magic Mike for television, but like Disney, he had seen the possibility of producing a live show when the demand grew for public appearances. That's when I got involved in the promotional start-up, back in New York City.

Inside the hall, there was a tussle to see which table would get Mike to sit with them. He was having a great time and having fun with the boys and letting them come and hug him, but eventually everyone settled down at their places.

After breakfast, the Commander stood and thanked our special guest for coming out so early, and then he gave the schedule for the day. He noted how proud he was that they all were wearing their new Camp Sage T-shirts, and he invited every boy whose parents or relatives were coming to introduce them to as many of the staff as possible. He also reminded them to be good hosts to the many people from the community who would be visiting. He also surprised us all with the announcement that all the horses and two donkeys had been rounded up and were being kept temporarily at a ranch down the road.

Then, for the next ten minutes, the Commander told the story of the first celebration of the Fourth of July in 1776, when colonists of the brand-new United States stood outside the meeting hall in Philadelphia on a very hot day, waiting expectantly to hear the vote to sever ties from Great Britain. The newly formed Second Continental Congress signed the Declaration of Independence, and thirteen colonies were joined together for the life-or-death struggle that lay ahead against the English monarchy. Then, four days later, the people had a celebration at the official public announcement of the signing. They rang bells, paraded, and shot off fireworks, and this tradition was later made a national holiday by the US Congress.

It was an important lesson in American history, and I, for one, was tremendously grateful that the Commander started the day in such a respectful and educational way. When he had finished, he called for a cheer for our great country, and all the boys stood and whistled and shouted at the top of their lungs, while they waved little American flags.

The Commander and I were able to drag Mike away after several minutes following breakfast to thank him for coming to the camp and to see if there was anything he needed.

When Mike dropped his stage act to become himself, it was so amazing to see how much of a regular guy he was. He had brought his wife, and they were going to tour the Mesa Verde cliff dwellings during the morning with Eric and his wife. He was in a hurry to get back to his motel in order to have plenty of time before he was scheduled to perform. "You have a wonderful bunch of young people, and it's a real pleasure to be here and meet them," he said. "I promise you a super show this afternoon." Then he dashed off with a member of the setup crew who had brought him out in his car.

The Commander turned to me and said, "Well, Van Alan, it looks like the day has officially begun." As he spoke, I was gratified to note that the color was back in his face, and he seemed to be most satisfied with the way things were going. He strode away looking like a proud papa as he gathered "his boys" around him on the way back to his office.

○◉○

The crowds began to arrive at noon, and the staff had just enough time for a quick lunch before we had to get out to help direct the mob.

Tracy had put out a giant wooden box at the parking lot with a sign: "For Fire Relief." Within minutes, it was totally full, and piles of toys and clothes were being placed alongside it.

I rushed to find Steve, and he brought down a huge newly painted trash container from the workshop that we hoped would be big enough.

Two of the first people I recognized were Bill Bradford and Nicole coming from the parking lot.

"We wanted to be the first to arrive," she said. "I couldn't wait to see how you'd fixed up everything after the fire. It was so terrible, but I see some new tents, so I hope you've got everything back the way it was."

"Not quite," I said. "There's still some fire damage."

"Oh, it's so terrible," she said. "How could it have ever started?"

"We don't know yet. And I've been too busy to even ask."

Bill said, "The chief thinks it may have been some boys smoking cigarettes or marijuana in the barn. Perhaps it was even intentionally set. He's found some evidence, but he's not ready to reveal everything. I've got a reporter working on it."

I wasn't surprised to hear it. That could have been where the stash of pot I had seen ended up. A perfect place to hide it.

Nicole took my arm. "Where are we going to sit? I made you fried chicken and a pie."

She looked and smelled beautiful, and I wanted to show her my gratitude and affection, but I couldn't stop what I was doing and sit down. "I plan to join you for the program later, but for now, I'm all over the place." I guided them to the arena and helped them spread their blankets and set out their chairs. It was a beautiful spot in the shade of a big sandstone pillar. "This should be perfect," I said. "The sun's going to move, but not for a while."

Nicole looked disappointed, while Bill seemed to be quite satisfied with the way it worked out. He made no attempt to get me to stay, and for the first time, I began to think he just might be interested in her.

As I walked away, I saw waves of people moving into the surroundings with folding chairs, tables, and big baskets. It looked like many of them were planning to spend the entire afternoon and evening, once they got settled.

I passed Steve's waste container. It was already becoming full of canned goods, toys, clothing, sporting goods, and boxes of model kits. I was gratified to see the generosity from the townspeople. Bill must have added something even more special to the newspaper article on the fire. I was eager to read it.

Over at the office, I greeted several people on their way out the door.

"Look at this, Van Alan," the Commander said, standing at the counter. He held up an envelope. "Another contribution. Folks are actually coming in here and giving us cash donations. There's at least five hundred dollars already. Can you believe that?"

"It's wonderful," I said. "I'm really thrilled for you."

"Not me, boy. This is for all of us—you too."

"Why me?"

"Well, you're the one who got all this started. We wouldn't have had this day except for your ideas. And the fire didn't exactly hurt us either. Just look at how it brought the people's additional attention to our needs."

"I guess it was luck after all—and thankfully no one was hurt," I said.

"No, boy. Not luck."

"Oh, yes," I said. "It was a miracle."

"You bet—and don't you doubt it."

○◉○

Eric and his group showed up. They were already turning red with sunburns from their visit to Mesa Verde. "Lord Almighty," he said. "That is an awesome place. Have you been over there to see the Indian ruins?"

"No," I confessed. "I haven't taken the time."

"Well, you've got to get over there early some morning. It's the most quiet and peaceful place you ever saw, and you can still visualize how the Indians lived in the cliffs. I tell you, it left me emotional. We didn't get to see half of the sites over there, but the big porch was enough to give me a real thrill."

I made a mental note to ask Tracy to go with me someday.

Eric reported that Mike had already slipped back behind the stage to get ready. He said the soundman was relieved he had overcome the echo effect off the mountain. "We have to handle all kinds of challenges on the road," Eric said. "Your stage made it all that much easier for us."

I was glad that things were going so well, but down deep, I still worried that something might happen to ruin everything. I needed to keep from thinking negative thoughts.

Tracy showed up in a white uniform with white shoes, white stockings, and a little Red Cross pin on her blouse.

"Wow," I said. "I've never seen you look so official."

"Forgive me." She blushed. "I had to wear something to let people know I could help them—if they needed it."

"No, no. I think you look great. I just got so used to you in jeans. Only the Commander wears his uniform."

"Well, you won't see me in this getup for quite some time again, I assure you. For one thing, it's hard to keep it clean in these surroundings. Besides, it's much too hot. I'm more comfortable in sandals and shorts."

The temperature had already hit ninety degrees, and it was

still going up. Back in New York, I would have wilted from the combination of temperature and humidity, but the dry air and light breeze helped keep the extreme heat down. We were now less than two hours from stage time, and I was thankful there was no sign of rain. The sky was full of puffy white clouds that shielded the sun on a regular basis, bringing occasional cool shade to the land.

Over at one of the concessions, popcorn was selling at a brisk rate.

Tracy and I were enjoying the way the crowd was moving smoothly toward the performance area.

A stocky man with wavy white hair, looking cool in slacks and knit golf shirt, seemed to be talking to every camper wearing the new Camp Sage logo.

Finally, we walked over, and I said, "Sir, is there anything I can help you with?"

"No, not in particular. Just talking to the boys." He stretched his hand out and said, "I'm Robert Enders."

I thought for a minute. *The name sounds familiar, but I can't quite place it.* And then it hit me. *Robert Enders is the CEO of ENDCO and Camps with Kids!* "Oh my goodness," I said. "General Enders. Welcome to our … your camp. What a pleasant surprise. I'm Melvin Van Alan, and this is Tracy Palmer."

Tracy was staring at me with a questioning look on her face.

I said, "Tracy, this is the General, our boss from Camps with Kids in New York."

She recovered quickly and put out her hand. "It's so nice to finally meet you. My parents and Commander Dougan have told us all how you came to our rescue right when we needed help. If it hadn't been for you, we might not be here today."

"I'm pleased to hear that," he said. "I'm very impressed at what I see going on this afternoon. Our camp director, Miss Abrams, told me about the celebration, and I thought today would be a good one for my first visit."

"Thank you. We're excited by everything that's happened."

"All right now. So when did you have the fire? No one reported this."

"Just two nights ago. We've been so busy that we apologize your office has yet to be contacted. We haven't even had time to assess the damages."

"Our insurance men should handle that anyway. Were there injuries?"

"Thankfully not," I said. "The worst was the loss of some barn structures and those tents." I pointed to the burned area. "We got hold of a bunch of new tents by the next day."

"Good, good," he said. "I like the looks of them. We'll want to replace all the old ones to match."

Tracy said, "Commander Dougan is going to want to see you. I think he's still in his office."

General Enders nodded. "Lead the way."

We headed back to the building.

I said, "What were you asking the boys—if I might inquire?"

"I wanted to know if they were happy campers." He grinned. "They didn't know what I was talking about."

"They're good kids," Tracy said. "I think you'll find that most of them really love being here. And they're getting some good life instruction. I hope you'll be here long enough to tour our workshops and meet the staff."

"I won't be leaving until I see it all," he said. "In the meantime, I want to find out who this Magic Mike is. Do I need a ticket?"

"Not for you," I said. "I hope you'll be our special guest of honor today."

We reached the office, and the Commander was beaming. "We have four thousand dollars in donations now. Some folks just brought in a thousand dollars." Then he saw our guest. "Robert Enders? What a nice surprise!"

Enders and the Commander shook hands heartily. "I was telling Melvin here that I'm very impressed with what I've been seeing today. I don't think any of our camps has ever had anything approaching this."

"Pretty phenomenal. We have Van Alan to thank for it."

Enders looked me over with a little squint to his eyes. "Miss Abrams told me not to get away without meeting you. Seems you are one of our volunteers from New York—is that right?"

"True," I said.

"Well, she thinks you're pretty special."

I looked at Tracy and raised my eyebrows in innocence. "I don't know why she thinks that. I only met her once."

"And talked to her on the phone. You're pretty creative to come up with the money to put on this shindig without our help. Isn't that right?"

The Commander turned to me with a questioning look. "All right then. Why don't we all git us a good place to see the show," he said. "Are you young people going to join us?"

Neither Tracy nor I could. We were both needed in various places.

"I'll watch from the sidelines," I said. "Hopefully I'll catch most of it."

chapter 32

At two o'clock, Commander Dougan mounted the stage and held up his hands. The audio man lowered the background music and brought up the sound from the mic. I had asked the Commander if he would introduce the show, and he gladly accepted.

"Ladies and gentlemen, boys and girls. On this beautiful Fourth of July, Camp Sage welcomes you to an afternoon of fun and fantasy, featuring the exciting adventures of Magic Mike and his partners—and later, the annual evening of music and fireworks sponsored by our very own town of Cortez, Colorado."

Cheers rose from some four thousand people crowded into the natural bowl among the giant red rocks.

"Before I turn the program over to our emcee, Mr. Eric Rogers, I want to thank you all for coming. It's such a pleasure having you here. I'm happy to report the fire that occurred two nights ago did not spread, and we were able to continue our plans for today's show. I want to give a special thanks to the men of the Cortez Fire Department for their effort in putting out the fire in the early hours Thursday morning. And to all of you who have come out today, you have been more than generous with all the items and support you have donated. We are truly grateful.

"I just want to say a word about the camp. For twenty-five years, we have been attempting to provide a shelter for the young boys in our area who need a place to go in the summer to learn a variety of skills, which they will be able to use in their future. Many of our campers come back year after year until they are old enough to take a job and be responsible members of the community. Now that you have visited us, I hope you will get to know our boys while you're here and talk to our counselors—all of whom are wearing Camp Sage T-shirts. We especially want to answer any questions from those of you who might like to enroll your own boys in the future. Again, it's truly a pleasure to have you all here. Now, on with the show!" He turned and handed the mic to Eric.

At this point, I went back to the concession area to observe how things were progressing. A flow of late traffic was still coming in, and I stopped a minute to appreciate the hard work of the volunteers who were directing the cars into the remaining parking spaces. Parents were taking their kids to the portable bathrooms, and others were buying food. Laughter erupted from the audience from something Eric must have said to the crowd. I stood there and marveled at how it seemed like we'd been doing this sort of thing for years.

Out of the corner of my eye, I spotted what I thought must be one of our boys running around the back of the administration building, but he didn't have on a camp T-shirt. I couldn't believe that anyone would purposely miss the show, but this was near where the latrines were located. I hoped he wasn't sick.

I wandered over to where I had seen him disappear, but no one was there or in the bathroom. The only direction he could have taken was back along the performance stage.

I made my way slowly, the loudspeakers became deafening as I got closer. The mystery of where the missing boy went now made me extremely curious. The actors were whooping it up on the stage with an opening song from one of their TV shows. It was familiar to the audience, and they clapped along.

I stopped at the back corner of the platform, completely hidden from the audience by the equipment and several large shipping crates. For a moment, I didn't see anyone, but then I caught a movement under the stage. The sun was so bright that it was difficult to see into the shadows, and the stage was only about four feet above the ground.

I could make out a cluster of kids squatting down together, and then I saw the flicker of a flame. It was obvious that they had been using pot, and now they were trying to start a fire with some cardboard boxes. This was an emergency! My heart started to pound as I realized I was alone in finding them up to no good. But instead of going for added help, I stooped down and went under the stage, catching them completely by surprise. My eyes had begun to adjust to the light so that I could make out their faces. It was Tony and his same little gang of four who had threatened me and Johnny for searching their tent.

"You guys stop what you're doing and come with me," I said, hoping that the authority in my voice would get their swift obedience.

Instead, without any hesitation, Tony said, "Well, if it's not the snoop." He lunged toward me and tried to pull me down onto the dirt.

It caught me totally unexpected, and I was completely unprepared for what came next. The other boys took the hint and piled on top of me, trying to pin my arms and legs. The noise immediately above us was too loud for anyone to hear my yells.

"I'll show you how your note worked." They crowded around me.

I struggled to fight them all off and managed to pull away. Even though I was free for the moment, I had nowhere to go because each guy had taken a position to the outside. I quickly looked around, but the only immediate hope of getting away was the very trapdoor that Magic Mike would soon be using for his quick-change performance.

Just then, the trapdoor slid back, and Mike leaped down right in front of us. Each of us stopped in our combined surprise as we watched him jump into a brown dog suit, zip it up in front, and heave himself back up through the trapdoor as fast as he had come down. He never saw us, and I knew it was too late to escape through the same trapdoor. So I just took off in a crab walk, favoring my bad leg, and headed to the other side under the stage in hopes of finding some way out there.

It seems I was getting somewhere in the chase when I looked back to see how far away I was. Then with a crack that shuddered my whole body, I hit my head square on a heavy beam and saw stars. Oh, how it hurt! I went down, grabbing my head with both hands and groaning in a ball on the ground. The five guys surrounded me, laughing it up and saying something I didn't hear over my own pain.

Then I felt them tying my legs together using pieces of electric wire lying around from the stage construction. They wound them around several times, leaving me totally helpless. The same with my hands and arms, leaving me on my side, attached to one of the foundation pillars.

I started yelling at the top of my lungs again, so Tony took the sweatband from around his head and pulled it around my open mouth, knotting it behind my head. The ugly taste made me gag, but I didn't want to vomit for fear I'd choke.

The gang sat back on their legs and seemed to relish the job they'd done. Now it was very clear to me who was responsible for the fire in the camp. They sat with big grins, mocking me for being a wimp and giving each other high-fives while they picked up where they had left off, smoking the last of their weed. There was obviously no remorse in what they were doing. Finally, they moved out and left me alone.

The music and stage play continued merrily over my head while I lay there struggling against my bonds. Those dirty kids had completely trussed me up, and I couldn't turn on the other side. The ground was hard, and the tight wire was beginning to cut off my circulation. The major thing that ran through my mind was that no one had seen me leave, and I certainly wouldn't be missed—perhaps for the rest of the day, perhaps even after the late fireworks. That could be a very long time, and I vowed I would make those kids pay for what they'd done. In the meantime, I was simply going to have to relax if I didn't want to make my headache worse and bring on a major anxiety attack.

I could clearly hear what was happening on stage. Eric had not changed much of Mike's original routines, and I visualized the play in my mind as it went along. Right now, Mike was getting on with his magical abilities. For most of the time, he was supposed to be the average boy next door who tried to be good, though he got himself in trouble from time to time. He was popular with the guys and becoming a real magnet to the girls. He was boasting to a couple of guys that he could find out exactly what their girlfriends would be saying right now about them at tonight's all-girl sleepover.

They challenged him to do it, so Mike says goodbye and walks away, stopping by a tree. He looks around to see if anyone is watching, and then he puts one finger in his ear and puffs out his cheeks, getting red in the face from the effort. Suddenly, a big cloud of smoke goes off, and he disappears behind the tree. Seconds later, he's a big shaggy dog, walking on all fours.

The crowd goes wild with delight.

Behind the scenes, Eric hits the button.

Mike drops down below the stage, jumps in a big dog suit waiting on a hook, zips up the stomach area, and hops back onto the stage to come out from behind the tree on all fours.

The crowd goes wild with glee as he appears above, looking just like a black shaggy dog.

The act continues as this poor lost dog is found and taken to the girl's house where he sees and hears everything they say. It is a hilarious sequence of events, and it erupts with all kinds of squeals from the audience, especially as the girls start getting ready for bed.

Mike is watching everything.

I lay there and listened to a whole series of magic quick changes that Mike went through during the several acts that followed. Each was cleverly related to the problems that kids encounter from time to time when they desperately wish they could be someone or somewhere else.

My mind wandered back to similar experiences when I was struggling to grow up. It had been a little rough. I could count my friends on one hand, but not one of them was loyal enough to be my best pal. I felt sad and left out if even one went somewhere without me. With no brothers or sisters to share life with, I turned to books and television for solace.

I stopped thinking of myself, and my heart went out to those kids in the crowd. I hoped that the camp was helping them, knowing many were probably dealing with the same problems that I had faced. I needed to dig in now even more to learn what I could about them. I might start with saying, "Are you a happy camper?" It didn't seem such a silly question to me now.

Then, like a recording, my talk with Tracy on the very first day at camp echoed in my mind: "I saw how you carried Little Joey. I want you to be a father to my orphans—and a big brother to the others."

And when I said, "I don't know the first thing about kids, and I don't know what to say to them," she had told me, "You have to start by just being yourself, maybe take their hand, squat down to their level, listen to their ramblings, smile and joke with them, and love them no matter what they do."

My eyes suddenly filled with tears that ran down into my ear. I had wanted to try, I really had, but it was all so foreign, and I had so little experience. And yet, I didn't want to leave this place without making some kind a difference—a difference in my life as well as theirs.

I felt like I could do it too. If I ever got out of these bounds, I was going to follow everything Tracy had told me. She was such a natural, and that's why the kids loved her. I just had to remember that they had the same fears and hang-ups I had at their age.

I planned to make a commotion to get someone's attention at the end of Mike's act, but in all the stress and lack of sleep from the night before, I slept through the final applause. When I woke up, the program was over.

There was a new rustling on the floorboards above me, chairs being placed, things being dropped, and high heels clattering. The band was slowly moving in for the Fourth of July musicale. It must be about six o'clock, and I had been lying there for more than three hours. Things wouldn't be quiet again for several more hours when I hoped I might finally be missed by somebody. I was thirsty and getting hungry, and I got to thinking maybe I'd never be found.

If I had been in the audience, I would have enjoyed the band. They played all the old American tunes and had so much fun that I didn't notice my pain as much, and the time went by fast. The fireworks brought cheers from everyone. I had looked forward to seeing the display fired from a line strung across the big rock high above the heads of the crowd. I know that it must have been spectacular. The booms and crashes hurt my head and seemed to go on forever. I couldn't wait for the whole evening to end—so I would be rescued.

Finally, I could hear the audience leaving and the band packing up. That took a long time, too, and I was suddenly hit with the need to go to the bathroom. It was a terrible experience, knowing that I wasn't going to make it, and then finally relieving myself. I was rather ashamed and very depressed. This had never happened before and was so unlike me. I wasn't certain now I wanted to be found this way, but there was nothing I could have done.

Time continued to tick away, but I found mercy in going back to sleep.

I lost all track of time. When I woke, it was dark. I wondered if I was missed. Were they searching for me—or did everyone go to bed after a very successful day? At first, being under the stage had been unbearably hot, but now it was unbelievably cold. I wore only the official camp T-shirt and shorts. I was shivering, and my body ached in addition to my head from the beating I'd received.

If Tracy were in this predicament, I knew she would be praying. She had turned to God every time we had a crisis such as when the Commander had his heart attack, when we thought we might lose the camp, prayers at the campfire, and for our open house. "Once you give your problems over to the Lord Jesus," she had said, "there's nothing more to do than to sit back and enjoy the ride." It was such a personal relationship that I always thought she might be seeing him as she prayed. I wasn't too sure that He would be willing to help me, but there was nothing else I could think of to do. "Jesus," I said. "Lord Jesus, this is the first time I've prayed to you, so you may be a little surprised. I certainly am. If you can hear me, I need your help. I'm lying here under the stage, and no one knows about it. I truly hope someone knows I'm missing and cares enough to look for me. Tracy told me I could give you my problems. This is a big one. I'm weak, thirsty, and alone, and I need your help. Jesus, I do want to know more about you. I believe now that you spoke to me at the campfire that first night, and every word is still in my mind. You said you wanted to put your arm around me and that you loved me. You said I was one of your lost sheep, and I've been wandering. You wanted to bring me into your fold. Jesus, I want you to pick me up in your arms like the lost sheep that I am. I have so much to learn, and I believe the wonderful people here at the camp can help. Now I want to live more than anything else so that I can find out what you're all about, and why you should care about me. Help me, I pray."

Big tears slid out of my eyes again. For the first time I can remember, I wanted to be totally sincere about something spiritual.

Right now, I was at my lowest, and I needed something far greater than anything I could do on my own, such as positive thinking.

Almost immediately after I prayed, I began to feel a strange warmth seep over my body until I was no longer cold. It was almost as if I had been given a blanket to wrap in. With increased anticipation, I realized that I was going to be able to survive whatever came next. And with a new sense of calm, I was able to give up and forget about the impossible position I was in. It was now up to him, according to Tracy.

○◉○

THE NEXT THING I knew, I was being shaken. I could see that it was light outside.

Carlos was kneeling over me. "Mr. Van, can you hear me? Are you all right?" His tears were splashing in my face.

I groaned and tried to talk through my gag.

He tried pulling it off, but it hurt my swollen mouth. "Uh-uh, uh-uh," I said, meaning "no," and I shook my head. I turned my neck so he could work on the knot that was so tight. He finally loosened it and pulled it off gently. I tried to feel the raw sides of my mouth with my thick tongue.

Then he started on the wires that coiled around my arms and legs. It too hurt so bad that I had to stop him. "Go get Tracy," I whispered through my cracked lips.

He was immediately crouched down on the run.

I lay there savoring the fresh morning air. I was slowly able to get some deep breaths down into my lungs, despite the pain around my mouth.

Within minutes, Tracy had scrambled to my side. Steve was close behind. "Oh, Mel," she said, "we thought you were celebrating at the motel with Eric and all the gang last night. We couldn't find you, and that's the only place we could think where you had gone. Oh, Lord, how could this have happened to you?"

I tried to talk, but I couldn't get my words out.

Steve took over. "OK, guy, let's see what we can do." He started to unwind the wires, and the pain was excruciating as the blood began to flow back into my limbs. I moaned, and he said he would try to be gentle.

Little by little, the wires came off. I knew there would be deep grooves in my arms where it had cut into my skin. No blood, just bruises all the way down.

Tracy touched my forehead with a soft hand. "I'm going to leave for a minute to call the ambulance," she said. "I'll be right back."

Oh brother, I thought. *That ambulance crew is going to think we're jinxed out here. They were out for the Commander and the fire—and now for me.* I hated to think of going back to the hospital. *Aren't I the one who said I wasn't ever going to darken its door again?*

After Steve removed the wires, I tried to move, but it was totally impossible. I was stiff to the point of being locked in place. He tried to help me sit up, but my back wouldn't budge without terrific pain. "OK, just lie there. The EMTs will be here shortly with a board to lift you." He shook his head in disbelief. "I can't understand who would have done this. I didn't know we had anyone here capable of such an evil thing."

"They were kids smoking pot," I croaked. "One guy, Tony, is the leader of at least four. I already had a run-in with him."

"Tony? Yeah, of course. That makes sense. He's one of the older ones who we let come in late with a couple of friends. They're probably running from the law and trying to hide here. We'll find them—rest assured."

Tracy came back and sat beside me. "The Commander is shocked at what's happened, but he wants you to know he's very proud of you and what you did for the camp. The newspaper has some great photos of the celebration this morning. The mayor called and said everyone is talking about the great time they had. Most people didn't realize we even existed. And Nicole keeps calling. Is there anything you want me to tell her?"

"Just tell her I'm sorry I wasn't able to share the picnic she brought."

"I don't mean to gossip, but I saw Bill walking pretty close with his arm around her on the way out."

Despite the pain, I grinned. "It doesn't surprise me. I thought I saw that look in Bill's eyes. Maybe she won't be going to New York after all."

There wasn't much to do while we waited for the ambulance crew. Our small talk had run out, and we were quiet with our thoughts. I could hear the camp coming alive in the distance.

"How did Carlos find me anyway?" I asked.

"He came to my tent and said you were under the big stage. He told me I'd better hurry, that you were very sick. As I ran with him, he said that the angel had 'waked' him up. He told him exactly where you were, and Carlos jumped out of bed to find you."

I was awestruck. "I prayed and asked Jesus to help me," I said. The thought that Carlos was told specifically where to find me brought tears to my eyes again.

Tracy and Steve were equally awed. Almost in unison, they said, "Thank you, Jesus. Praise your name."

Tracy put her hands on me and prayed, "Lord Jesus, we give you our thanks for revealing Mel's location. We ask you to heal him quickly from all injuries he sustained and put him on his feet again soon. We come against those who caused him to be so badly treated last night and pray you swiftly bring them to justice. Amen." Her prayers, always soothing to my inner being, were especially sweet this morning as she sat next to me. She moved her hand to my forehead, and I savored her cool touch again.

The rescue crew suddenly appeared under the stage. One of them immediately took my pulse and strapped on a blood pressure cuff, using a small flashlight he held in his mouth. Once that was done, the other two gently turned me on my back, slipped a board beneath me, and tied me down with a neck brace and band across my head to keep it steady. Then they slid me out from beneath my prison into the light of morning.

Commander Dougan was waiting for them to bring me out. He knelt down and took my hand in his big fist, and I actually saw big tears in his eyes. "We'll find whoever is responsible for this vicious attack," he said. "Now git well."

A delegation of counselors and even some campers followed respectfully along as the EMTs carried me past the administration building and the waiting ambulance.

The Commander shouted, "Let's hear it for Mr. Van Alan." He led them in a series of cheers that left me stunned and humbled.

To say that it helped wash away my immediate pains would be an understatement.

I had never had people pay so much attention to me. In New York, I was one of the millions of faceless people who passed from one building to the next, in and out of taxis, up and down elevators. Here in Desert Country, USA, I had found people who actually knew me, appreciated me for who I was, and personally cared. This wasn't put on or made up. It was real.

Tracy had scrambled into the ambulance as she had done with the Commander and now had my hand in hers. I was so relieved to be released from those awful wires, so cheered by the shouts of goodwill, and now so close to the girl who was in the process of changing my heart that I was unable to speak for fear of crying like a baby. I think it was then that I finally realized that miracles really do happen—and they could even happen to me!

Chapter 33

The doctors found that I was dehydrated and suffering shock due to exposure. The x-rays showed no serious problems and that my broken leg had completely healed. After getting a warm bath and some sleep, I felt almost like a new man, aided by pain medication that dulled the bruises from the blows to my head, ribs, and back.

Tracy stayed close, even as I slept during the rest of the morning, and now she was at my side as we left the hospital and emerged into the late afternoon sun.

Steve had come to bring me a change of clothes and take us back to camp.

Despite the memories of the previous night, I felt an unexplainable exhilaration, and I had to stop a minute outside and take in the richness of the newly mown lawn and bright flowerbeds and the deep shadows that brought out the vibrant colors on the mountains surrounding us. I was overflowing with an inner happiness that I had never experienced before, and for the first time in my life, I had the overwhelming feeling of how great it was to be alive.

I looked at Tracy and Steve as we got in the car, and I realized all of a sudden that they were examples of the most unselfish people I had ever known. In only a few weeks of camp, they had made their way into my heart and become my friends. They honestly cared about me, and their Christian walk had broken through the hard crust that was my defense against the world. They had an inner radiance that they freely passed around.

"I love you guys," I said, surprising myself with such an emotional outburst. "Thank you for doing so much for me."

Steve looked over at me with a smile as he drove out of the parking lot. "Hey, man, we love you too. You've given us all so many blessings that we can't begin to count them."

I was grateful but humbled beyond words. "What now?" I said.

Tracy reached forward from the back seat with a hand on my shoulder. She was giggling like a teenager. "Steve's been busting to tell you, but I wouldn't let him until I was here too."

He had a huge smile. "We made more than seventy thousand dollars in ticket sales, and we received about ten thousand dollars for the fire fund. There are toys and gifts and food goods in a monstrous pile around the donations box. People were so excited about being at the camp and talking to the kids that they wouldn't go home until we had to finally urge them to leave. If you ever, ever think up a better public relations event than this one, I'll eat my ten-gallon hat, which by the way I don't own."

Tracy said, "When General Enders couldn't find you after the show, he told me that he wants to see you the next time you're in New York. He asked me when I thought that would be, and I told him I had no idea." She paused a minute, and added, "Do you?"

"No, I really don't," I said. "No time soon though." I had lost all desire to rush back to my old routine.

The chief of police and the Commander were standing together at the camp office when we pulled up. Like a greeting committee, they came right over and shook my hand as I got out.

Commander Dougan was effusive. "Glad to see you're all right, Mel. You certainly had us worried this morning." This was the first time he'd ever called me by my first name.

The chief was full of new information. "I came out to report that we ran down four boys this morning at a house in town after getting a complaint that they were drinking and fighting. They're part of a larger gang that's been causing a lot of trouble in town, and they have apparently been hiding out here at your camp. We're sure they're the guys who tied you up last night. We're also expecting to charge them with arson for the fire. Marcus Dry Cloud admits he was one of them until they started forcing him to do drugs. He wanted to get away, and that's when you had the car accident. He's agreed to be a witness against these boys."

"I can't believe they fooled me so easily," the Commander said.

Steve said, "They took me in too, acting so young and innocent. They're actually pretty sharp kids. Too bad they couldn't have channeled their efforts in a better direction."

The chief turned to me. "So I understand you actually saw the marijuana they had here."

"Yes, I'm sorry to say the fire and last night's problems might have been avoided if I had just turned them in at first," I said. "I thought I knew what I was doing at the time."

The chief nodded. "There's no doubt that if we'd fingered them a few weeks ago, we wouldn't be standing here, but I think we may actually have a bigger and better case against them now." The chief moved toward his car. "And, hey, I also want you all to know that the entire day yesterday was a great success. I've never seen anything like it. Despite the huge crowd, we had only one missing person, one act of violence, and one injury—and they were all you, Mr. Van Alan."

Everyone laughed, except me. I still had a headache.

○◉○

I OWED NICOLE A call, so I went to the office the moment everyone else was otherwise occupied. "I'm truly sorry that I didn't get to spend time with you yesterday. I missed being with you—and, of course, the fried chicken and pie," I said.

"Mel? Are you all right? I about died when I heard you were assaulted."

"Yeah. I'm going to be fine. I suffered more of a hit to my pride than anything. But I did get to hear most of the program from under the stage. What did you think of it?"

"It was wonderful. Magic Mike is *sooo* clever. No wonder the kids love him. Bill and I stayed all the way through the fireworks, hoping you'd show up. I can't believe that you were right there, all tied up like that."

"The thing that helped me get through it was to realize that everyone was having such a good time, and it seemed to be such a success. We have you and Bill to thank for a good part of it. I don't know what I would have done without your ability to get it all organized like you did. It took a huge burden off me and made all the difference."

"Well, you're welcome, Mel. I'm hoping we can work together in the future."

"Absolutely, I guess we can start with our meetings like we planned."

She paused, seeming to get her thoughts together. "That's something I want to talk with you about, Mel. Forgive me, I'm all aflutter. Bill and I had all that time to talk at the picnic, and he finally shared some things he's been keeping in his heart for quite a while. I was absolutely floored when he told me.

"He knows that I've wanted to go places and see new things, and the last thing he wanted was to keep me from my dreams. He just hadn't gotten up the courage to do something about it. Yesterday, he confessed that he loved me so much he would quit his job and take me anywhere I wanted to go—if I'd marry him. Can you imagine that?"

Now I was the one to be floored. "You're kidding," I said. "How wonderful for you."

"Can you imagine it? I never even realized that Bill thought that way about me and would do something wonderful like that. And do you know why he suddenly up and did such a rash thing?"

"No, why."

"Because he was afraid you were going to take me back to New York with you—and he'd never see me again. Isn't that a scream?"

"Wow. And what did you tell him?"

"I told him it was the most precious thing anyone ever said to me, and I would love to go out with him and get to know him on a personal basis and see what happens. So, you see, that changes our plans about meeting together. Is that all right?"

"Of course," I said. "I want to see things turn out for the best for you and Bill. I couldn't be happier."

"Oh thank you, Mel. I was worried you'd be mad or something. I know how you were beginning to have feelings about me."

That left me speechless. She apparently knew something more than I did. Anyway, I really was happy for her, and Bill was a very nice guy. I hoped that it would work out between them, and if I really had anything to do with bringing them together, I was satisfied. As much as I appreciated Nicole, I was glad to be off the hook with her. She just wasn't my type.

I wished her well and told her I would make sure to see her before I went back to New York. As I hung up, I wondered what kind of girl was my type. The sophisticated, college-trained career girl had never captivated me. Neither had the waitress, hairdresser, or policewoman. There never had been a girl next door. I don't know what that left, but maybe I had been too particular all my life, leaving nothing open for that chance encounter. Too bad I had learned to be so self-sufficient.

I ran into the Commander on the way out of the office. "I've been looking for you, Mel." He had a stern look on his face. "Now let's not play around. Where did the money come from to pay for the advance work and promotion? I know it didn't come from ENDCO, and no one else has that kind of cash around here. So what's the story?"

I reddened. I didn't want to tell him, but he stared me down until I had to talk. "Well, when I got off the phone with Miss Abrams, I knew this was the opportunity of a lifetime, so I decided to use a little money I inherited to get us started. It was my decision, and I don't want you to be questioning me about it."

"I don't care what you think. It's my business to know what's going on around here and who's giving or taking. You continue to amaze me, Mel. I had you down as a liberal do-gooder from the big city who was out here to make yourself feel good for a few weeks. To tell you the truth, I bet Steve you wouldn't last four days.

"You turned out to surprise us all with your determination and good ideas, and then this generous contribution. Look, we won't need it now anyways—not with the gate receipts we received. Consider it an up-front investment, and we'll return it. None of this would have even been possible if you hadn't cared enough to stick with us and use your God-given talents to show us how to impact the community. It's like Tracy just said to me: 'I don't know what I'm going to do when Mel leaves. He's been so wonderful.'"

I wanted to ask, "Did she really say that?" Instead, I waited to see if the Commander had anything more to add. I didn't want to stop him now.

"So, as I say, I want you to let us reimburse you for anything you paid out, and then I want you to let us put on a big banquet tomorrow night to celebrate our success and give you the recognition you deserve for all you did."

"OK, OK, you got me. I'll take the money back if you promise not to mention my name at any such banquet. I want to celebrate what everyone did. Just look at the work that Steve and his buddies put in, and Juan, and Tracy. And even the kids!"

He laughed and smacked me on my back. "All right then. Just know that we appreciate what you've done for the future of Camp Sage and Sand."

"Thank you, Commander," I said. All I really wanted was his approval.

○◉○

Tracy had one of the boys up sitting on the table in the clinic, taking his temperature, when I got there. It was Little Joey again.

I asked him how he liked seeing Magic Mike.

"It was so funny when he turned into a tree and listened to those robbers talk about robbing the bank."

"Mike is very funny—and clever," I said. "Do you ever wish you could turn into something like he did?"

"I'd like to be a fireman and drive a big truck."

That's when I remembered that I had promised to buy him a red fire truck. *Boy, where have the days gone since then?*

Tracy lifted him down and pointed to some books in the corner. "Joey, why don't you take those and sit up on Commander Dougan's bed and read for a while. You can take a nap in there if you get sleepy."

After he got settled, Tracy sat down with me. "He's so cute, don't you think? I'd love to adopt him someday."

I had to agree. He was the kind of kid who needed a mother like Tracy. Someone to give him a good home and lots of love, and help put some meat on his bones.

She turned her eyes on me, the nurse in her starting to come out. "How are you feeling this afternoon? Any carry-over problems from last night?"

"Nothing much." As a matter of fact, I felt absolutely wonderful without the tight wires and suffocating gag.

"How's your leg?"

"It's good too. I won't be needing this boot any day now."

"Did you get something to eat when you got back?"

"Listen, Tracy, I appreciate your concern for my health. I really do. But there's something else I want to talk about."

"What's that?"

"You and me."

Tracy's eyes went wide. "What do you mean?"

"What I mean is that everything I seem to do lately involves asking myself what Tracy would think about this or that. I care what you think of me. Your thoughts have come to influence my thoughts and actions like no one else has."

"I'm sorry," she said. "Forgive me."

"No, no," I said. "It's good. I mean it in the best possible way. You've become such a positive influence on me that I'm humbled in your presence."

She started to protest, and I held up my hand.

"Especially your spiritual beliefs," I said. "I didn't believe in anything much before I came here. You have an amazing way of turning things over to God, and as I watched your approach to various problems, I was awed by how patient and peaceful you were in the very midst of it. For a while, I admit I smiled at what I thought was such sweet naivete, but you've won me over. I prayed to Jesus last night for the first time in my life, and I truly believe that He came to be with me and wrap me in his warmth."

Tears came to Tracy's eyes, and she put her hand on mine. "If that's the kind of influence I've been, then I'm the one who should be humbled. It's only until you experience Jesus for yourself that you understand the Truth," she said. "I'm so happy for you."

"I'm happy for me too. Frankly, this whole morning, I've been walking on air. At first, I thought it was because I was found out there and not left to rot, but more importantly, I know that my prayer was actually heard. It's obvious. Carlos came—because someone told him where to find me. Today, I have a new love in my heart for the world—and, may I add, for you."

I was surprised at her reaction, which wasn't what I'd hoped.

She turned away to look at Joey sitting quietly on the Commander's bed, perhaps to avoid making any comment for the moment. "You doing all right in there?" she called to him.

He looked up and nodded with a sweet smile.

Then Tracy looked at me, and I thought I saw hurt in her eyes. "You know, we talked about this before. You'll be going back East in a few weeks, and I'll be staying here. Let's not make it harder to say our goodbyes when the time comes. I can't get into any kind of serious relationship under those circumstances. Promise me to be a good friend and just leave it at that."

I couldn't promise that. Tracy had become more than a friend. I wanted to take her in my arms and kiss her more than anything. I wanted to feel her heart beating against mine. All of a sudden, I realized that she was more precious than anyone else had ever been to me, and I wanted her to feel the same way. But, right now, I didn't know how we were going to reconcile it.

"I'm sorry I can't be more encouraging," she said. "I think you'd better go now while I shower and see to Joey."

I stood up, feeling rejected, and turned to leave. "OK, I'll meet you at dinner." I quietly shut the door behind me and started walking along the path around to my tent. My mind was numb. She was probably right, of course, but for me, right now, she was all I cared about—not six weeks from now when I'd be leaving. I thought we could at least have the rest of the summer together, sunning at the pool, walking in the evening, maybe even riding horseback. I'd never made any long-term plans with a girl in my life.

The Commander interrupted my thoughts as I passed his office. "Can we talk?" he said.

Chapter 34

He led me to his golf cart and unplugged it from the building while I stood wondering what was so important that we ride rather than talk here.

We went first to the burned-out stables. "The insurance adjuster is due here tomorrow," he said. "The building was so badly in need of repair that the fire was actually a blessing."

We continued on to the old tent area, and he waved at a bunch of boys as we passed.

"Now, this is the good part. General Enders wanted to inspect our housing, and we rode through here this morning. As soon as possible, he wants to replace every tent with the latest features—strong construction and material, screened flaps, retractable vents on top for cooling, and bright tones that we can cluster in colors or scatter. Our old metal bunks and mattresses will be upgraded—along with new platforms made of wood composite material. We'll never have to paint them again." The Commander was excited.

We continued past the classrooms that were well-built but showing wear.

"He liked our layout here," the Commander continued, "but he's going to bring in a contractor to talk with us about our future needs. He wants us on a scheduled update of our facilities. He'd like to see us with a gym next, which I've been aching for."

So far, I hadn't said a word. I was comfortable to sit back and listen to the Commander talk as we rode along.

He came alongside the pond and parked so that we could watch a group of older boys practicing their lifesaving skills. "It does my heart good to sit here and watch these kids," he said. "When I first joined the navy, I barely knew how to swim—and I had to learn mighty fast or drown. That's why I insist on every boy learning at least the fundamentals and then going on to the advanced course, if possible." He turned in his seat to face me. "So what do you think of our little camp now that you've been here long enough to git acquainted with us?"

"I've come to appreciate it a lot," I said without hesitation. "I have to admit it took me a while to settle in, but now I feel right at home."

"That's good, good," he said. "You've been an asset to us."

"Thank you, I appreciate that."

The Commander looked around and stretched out his arm. "General Enders also wants us to expand our facilities to accommodate a hundred or so kids. He thinks we should also consider taking girls in the future. What do you think of that?"

"Girls? Wow," I said. "That's a whole new ball game."

"You bet your bippy," he said. "Personally, I can't see it. Too many potential problems. I'd rather start up another camp elsewhere."

"What does Tracy think?" I asked.

"Didn't ask her yet, but I think she'd agree. However that's not the main thing I wanted to talk to you about, Mel. First, I brought you out here to share the future of our little camp as General Enders sees it, and git your take on it, and then have you ponder a little proposal that me and the General cooked up. As a matter of fact, I just got off the phone with him." He paused for just a moment. "We want you to consider becoming second-in-command at this camp, so to speak, and take on the position that we'd call *administrative director.* We need someone of your caliber to help us git to where we want to go. Now, what do you think of that?"

I was absolutely stunned. Never had I thought that I might be considered as more than just a volunteer. I had no athletic background to bring to this position, no experience with kids. Yet, I was starting to learn the ropes. I had already begun to find myself capable of quite a few things.

"There'd be a good salary and a car for your use. You'll need wheels for the job we have in mind."

While I was processing the thought of becoming more than a mere bump on a log around the place, the uppermost thing was swimming around in my mind: *Could this make a difference with Tracy and me?* "What exactly might this position entail?" I asked.

The Commander turned back again to look directly at me. "Here's the thing: I'm not going to be able to handle all the things that Enders has in mind for the camp. I'm not the fireball that I used to be. I told him that. He expects all of his camp properties to grow and become premier centers of personal development for disadvantaged youth, and it's going to take a younger man to bring it about. He believes in a regular fundraising program where ENDCO will match funds with donors. Of course, you've already taught us a thing or two about such things. I don't know a hoot about how to go about it myself. I'm just an old navy man with a heart for boys.

"Once you hit your stride here the past few weeks, I could see you had all the abilities of being an administrator. All the rest of us took up your ideas and directions, and we sailed along. You have a gift, son, and we want you to use it with us."

"Are you saying you want me to stay at the camp? Work here permanently?"

"Exactly. For the rest of the summer, we have some real basic upgrading to do, but after the kids leave, we want to be raising funds and start building a better place for next year—and the year after that and for the next generation. Can you see it? Isn't it exciting?"

Oh no! I thought. *Such an idea is totally impossible. I wouldn't be going back to New York? How could I handle that? I have my work in the big city. I have an apartment to return to. I have the continuous task of finding clients and keeping them happy. I have the weekends alone without anyone to take out for dinner and a movie. I have the endless noise of the traffic and the surly cab drivers. I'd have to give all of that up.*

On the other hand, I was looking at an offer that would keep me close to the land where the sun shone almost every day of the year, where I was actually starting to become a better person, where I could use my talents to make a difference in people's lives, and where I knew a girl who made my heart beat with a new rhythm that I'd never felt before.

I could see he wanted an immediate answer. Usually I answered such important considerations by saying, "Let me think about it, and I'll get back to you." Today, I surprised myself with a simple, "Yes, I'd like to do it."

"Great, great, my boy." The Commander seemed relieved that he didn't need to talk me into anything. "You won't believe how much I prayed about this since the idea came to me. Thank you for saying yes. I just want you to know that it will be my great pleasure to work with you in the future."

Once again, I was bowled over by his expression of confidence. My soul had been so dry for this kind of affirmation that I had become cynical over the years, never expecting anything nice from anyone and never expecting anything good to happen. I put out my hand for the Commander to shake and said, "No, I need to thank you for believing in me, sir. You don't know how good it feels to be asked to be a permanent part of the family here at Camp Sage and Sand. I just hope that I can live up to your expectations."

"I have no doubt about it. You're perfect for the job. General Enders will be delighted when I tell him the good news."

We glided back to the office in his cart, and while he was plugging it in, he said, "We'll have to keep your office in here with me until we can build you one of your own."

I thought about it. "Let's just keep it this way. I'd rather be in the middle of all the action. To be effective at all, I want to see the boys and make sure they see me."

"Quite right," the Commander agreed.

○◉○

At dinner, with only half the staff present, because it was a Sunday night, Commander Dougan told those around the table that he had asked me to stay on permanently at the camp and become his Second-in-Command. When he said that I had accepted, I looked around to see the reaction of those present. I was seriously worried that they might still consider me an outsider and prone to mistakes. Happily, everyone broke into grins, and hands were thrust forward for me to shake.

Tracy was the quiet one. It really worried me that she wasn't in favor of the idea because she kept her head and eyes down. In a minute, however, she brightened and gave me a big smile. I was so relieved that I almost burst out with a "thank you Lord," like I had heard the others say so many times over the past few weeks.

After we finished, I took her hand and led her back to the clinic door where there was no one to interrupt us. "So what do you think of the announcement?" I asked.

"I think it's perfectly wonderful. I couldn't have been more surprised," she said.

"Why is that?"

"Don't be silly. You were the one all along who led me to believe that you couldn't wait to get out of here and back to New York. I almost expected you to leave right after Magic Mike was over. I thought you were merely putting in your time and would be gone as soon as possible."

"Well, to tell the truth, that was exactly my attitude a while back. But after we won the stay order and essentially stopped Dr. Armor from further action—and even before the Fourth of July celebration—I started getting hooked on everything that happens here. It's become very important to me. And finally, being tied up and alone for the night, I realized that I really wanted to stay after all, but I wasn't sure how I'd be able to afford it—or if I was even wanted."

Tracy took a long look into my eyes, and then she came close and laid her head on my chest. "I thought I was going to lose you," she said.

"I thought I'd lost you too."

A minute later, she pulled her head back, and we kissed. Her hair had the sweetest smell, and her lips were soft and beautiful. After a minute, I said, "At dinner, you worried me when you were so quiet. I thought maybe you were disappointed or something when you had your head down."

"I was thanking God for making it all work out for us," she said, "because after you left the clinic this afternoon, I was really upset about our conversation. I couldn't see how I could become close with you and then have you leave if we got serious. So I asked God to work it out, and he did. It's all so wonderful. I really hope you're happy with your decision."

"You can't believe how happy and excited I am."

"What do you think you're going to do now that you're a full-time staff member?" Tracy asked.

"I want to get to know the counselors well and really learn what they're doing. I want to spend time talking to and getting to know the kids. I want to personally thank and keep working with all the community leaders who did so much to help us this weekend. I want to learn more about Jesus Christ and about the angels at the sunset campfires and join Steve in a Bible study. And, most of all, I want to start dating you."

She laughed. "Did you know the word *dating* is old-fashioned? But I'd like to do it anyway."

"Good. And I want you to start thinking about what you're going to pack in your suitcase now so you'll be all ready to fly back to New York with me at the end of the summer."

"What?" Shock registered in her eyes. "I thought you had agreed to stay here?"

"Don't worry. I'm going to have to go back to close my apartment and decide what to move. In the meantime, I want to show you around the greatest city in the world so you'll know what I'm giving up to be with you here for the rest of my life." I smiled.

"Do you think you'll really miss New York?"

"Probably some. You know it's been my whole existence until a few weeks ago."

"Will you get tired of our way of life then?"

"No. Not if you're by my side. I wouldn't be able to live anywhere else now that I've met you."

"And as long as you have something meaningful to do," she added.

"You're right," I said. "Maybe I could teach writing or something."

Dear Reader:

What do you think? Will Mel attend Steve's Bible study? Do you think he will find the answers to the real questions that are on his mind about Jesus? Here's what Steve is likely to tell him:

- That Jesus wants to have a relationship with him.
- That He died for all Mel's sins.
- That Mel can have eternal life with Him in heaven.
- That to receive this wonderful promise, Mel must confess with his mouth that he believes in Jesus and that God raised Jesus from the dead.

What about you? Do you believe Jesus is the son of God? Do you believe that Jesus came to earth to lay down his life for you? Do you know that He can and will forgive your sins and wrongdoings in life? Have you asked for that forgiveness and are you changing your life to follow the promises of the Bible?

Think about it:
Like Mel, by accepting Jesus you can have the assurance of God's blessings Here on earth—and a future with him in heaven by believing in Him.

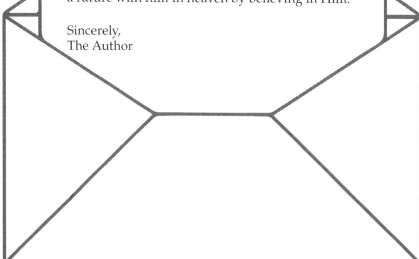

Sincerely,
The Author